NO PLACE TO RUN

Bells! Everywhere! Rockson heard doors slamming and loudspeakers blasting away in Russian. They were on to him. He rushed back toward the fire door through which he had just entered but heard a click just as he reached it. Locked! Rock raced down the long neon lit hall toward the far end some two hundred feet away. He reached it and swung through the door just as a squad of Reds rounded the corner to his right. Another squad suddenly appeared on his left. He was cut off.

The Russians closed in on him from both sides and, as they approached, Rock saw that they all wore the hideous death's-head on their shoulders. They were KGB.

The officer in charged smiled arrogantly at his prey and crowed, "Ted Rockson, I presume? You may as well surrender. We have been expecting you for days. I promise you you cannot escape. The floor is filled with over two hundred of our elite troops. Please—no fuss—yes?"

"Me? Make a fuss?" Rock asked innocently—and then he went for the KGB officer's throat.

It was time to die.

THE SURVIVALIST SERIES
by Jerry Ahern

#3: THE QUEST (851, $2.50)
Not even a deadly game of intrigue within the Soviet High Command, and a highly placed traitor in the U.S. government can deter Rourke from continuing his desperate search for his family.

#4: THE DOOMSAYER (893, $2.50)
The most massive earthquake in history is only hours away, and Communist-Cuban troops, Soviet-Cuban rivalry, and a traitor in the inner circle of U.S. II block Rourke's path.

#5: THE WEB (1145, $2.50)
Blizzards rage around Rourke as he picks up the trail of his family and is forced to take shelter in a strangely quiet Tennessee valley town. But the quiet isn't going to last for long!

#6: THE SAVAGE HORDE (1243, $2.50)
Rourke's search gets sidetracked when he's forced to help a military unit locate a cache of eighty megaton warhead missiles hidden on the New West Coast — and accessible only by submarine!

#7: THE PROPHET (1339, $2.50)
As six nuclear missiles are poised to start the ultimate conflagration, Rourke's constant quest becomes a desperate mission to save both his family and all humanity from being blasted into extinction!

#8: THE END IS COMING (1374, $2.50)
Rourke must smash through Russian patrols and cut to the heart of a KGB plot that could spawn a lasting legacy of evil. And when the sky bursts into flames, consuming every living being on the planet, it will be the ultimate test for THE SURVIVALIST.

Available wherever paperbacks are sold, or order direct from the Publisher. Send cover price plus 50¢ per copy for mailing and handling to Zebra Books, 475 Park Avenue South, New York, N.Y. 10016. DO NOT SEND CASH.

DOOMSDAY WARRIOR #2
RED AMERICA

BY RYDER STACY

ZEBRA BOOKS
KENSINGTON PUBLISHING CORP.

ZEBRA BOOKS

are published by

Kensington Publishing Corp.
475 Park Avenue South
New York, N.Y. 10016

Copyright © 1984 by Ryder Stacy

All rights reserved. No part of this book may be reproduced in any form or by any means without the prior written consent of the Publisher, excepting brief quotes used in reviews.

First printing: August 1984

Printed in the United States of America

Prologue

2089 A.D. Ted Rockson alias "Rock" is the "Doomsday Warrior." He fights back against the Russian invaders who now control post World War III America—a land decimated by nuclear missiles from Russia's first strike.

One hundred years after the massive Soviet surprise nuclear attack much of the United States is still radioactive and impassable. The world now has twenty percent less oxygen, strange and constantly shifting weather patterns, freezing nights and scorching days, purple clouds, storms of black snow. In the USA are regions of land torn by chasms, landslides, and earthquakes. Mutated animals roam the plains and mountains. Killer dogs with dagger sharp teeth and weighing up to two hundred pounds hunt in hungry packs. Blood-drinking rats, two to three feet long, move in masses of thousands across the terrain at night, devouring all that is in their path.

And there are tales of the mysterious "Glowers," who the Russian occupying troops speak of in frightened whispers—radioactive humans who live only in the hottest zones, who glow like a blue flame and whose touch kills instantly. These and even more terrible dangers await Rock as he makes his way across the new America.

Driving stolen Russian vehicles or riding his hybrid horse, shorter and stronger than horses of the past and more resistant to radiation, Rock, armed with his rapid-fire .12 gauge shotgun pistols and the "Liberator" automatic rifle with infrared scope, helps the "freefighters" of the free American towns and villages fight the Russian occupiers. Rockson has two goals—to throw the Soviet murderers out of the U.S., returning America to its great glory and freedom of the past, and to find and kill the squad of Russian KGB officers who murdered his family, torturing them, raping his mother and sisters when he was a child. Hidden beneath a floorboard he had memorized the faces of all ten of the elite Death Squad who committed the blasphemies. One by one he will hunt them down and kill them.

Ted Rockson's trail weaves swiftly across the land, the mountains, the hidden Free Cities, the vast hot zones, as he conquers all that gets in his way in the strange and terrifying world of America 2089 A.D.

* * *

TIME: It is one hundred years in the future. An all-out nuclear war has killed two thirds of the world's population. The Russians, who were able to get off many more of their missiles in a first strike, were victorious over the United States. Now, in control of virtually the entire world except for China, they ruthlessly rule The People's World Socialists Republic.

PLACE: Atomic bombs exploded all over the planet but primarily in the United States. The U.S. lost one hundred million people within one hour of the attack. Another seventy-five million died within a year. The Russians immediately moved in with massive transports of troops and weapons and quickly took control of much of the country. They built forty fortresses in vital parts of the U.S., huge military complexes from which they sent out search and destroy units of tanks and helicopters and radiation-suited troops to extinguish the still burning embers of resistance.

The Russians use the American citizens as slave labor, forcing them to grow crops and work in factories. The Russian high command lives in luxury, the officers have taken the best housing in the remaining cities. The American workers must make do in shabby shanty towns around the fortress complexes. Thirty-five million Americans are directly under the Red rule. Sullen and docile, they carry out their Russian masters' orders, but underneath they hate them. They pray for the day when the legendary Ted Rockson, "The Ultimate American" will come with the freefighters of the hidden cities and release them from their bondage.

ENVIRONMENT: The great number of bombs set off altered the earth's axis. The polar caps began melting and the forested regions turned to desert. The world was slowly warming, the higher amount of CO_2 in the air creating a greenhouse effect. Lakes, rivers, and streams had dried up in many places. Ecology had been almost dealt a deathblow from the war. Ninety percent of the earth's species of plants and animals were now extinct.

The East Coast of the United States is still extremely radioactive. Vast bare plains stretch hundreds of miles in New York, Connecticut, New Jersey, and Pennsylvania on which nothing grows. At the edges of these hot zones are forests of mutated bushes and trees covered with thorns and rock-hard bark. Parts of the Midwest had been spared as the Russians had plans for eventually using the farmland to grow crops for their own clamoring masses back home. But the soil was too radioactive for anything but weeds. American slave labor was taken out by the truckload to work turning the soil in the "medium hot" zones—meaning death within a year from handling the rocks and topsoil still hot enough to send a geiger counter needle off the edge.

The Far West had been hit hard. Colorado was spared mostly because of some bad aiming but further on, in Utah, Nevada, California, there had been heavy damage. The area is now a misty unknown land. Nothing is thought to even live there. Volcanoes and earthquakes have become common, and much of the Northwest had been turned into a nightmare of craters, some miles wide.

The South had been hit in a haphazard fashion as if the Russians hadn't quite known what to strike. Some states, New Mexico, Georgia, were almost untouched, while others, Florida, Texas, had been blasted to bits. Parts of Florida were gone. Where Orlando and Tampa once stood was now a great jagged, hydrogen bomb created canal that stretched hundreds of miles across the interior filled with a red muddy water.

Slowly life tries to force its way back onto the surface of the ripped and ravaged land. Many forests have expanded over the last century in areas that weren't hit. Great parts of the United States are now thick with brush and trees, and resemble the country the way it was in the 1800s. In other places the deserts cover the earth for four, five hundred miles in every direction—unrelenting, broiling, hot snake-filled and cactus-dotted obstacles that stand between other living parts of the country.

THE HIDDEN FREE CITIES: Nearly seventy-five free American hidden towns have sprung up over the last hundred years. Located at the edges of hot zones which the Russian troops are reluctant to enter, these towns, hidden in caves, mountains, and deep-wooded valleys are made up of armed resistance fighters. Each Free City consists of anywhere from a thousand to forty thousand people. They are fiercely democratic, using town meetings to discuss and vote on all issues.

The Free Americans, who have been bred out in the country, away from the Russian dominated "clean" areas, have, through natural selection, become ten times more resistant to radiation than their ancestors. They are bred tough, with weak children placed out in the twenty below zero nights. If the child lives it is allowed to develop. If not, then it is just as well to put it out of its misery now.

Ted Rockson fights out of Century City—one of the more advanced Free Cities, and the manufacturer of the Liberator automatic rifle, used by freefighters everywhere. They attack Russian convoys, blow up bridges. But they plan for the day when they can begin their all-out assault on the enslavers.

THE RUSSIANS: The United Socialists States of America is run by the red-faced, heavy drinking General Zhabnov, headquartered in the White House, Washington, D.C., now called New Lenin. A bureaucrat, careful but not cunning and a libertine, Zhabnov spends days eating and nights in bed with young American girls rounded up by the KGB. Zhabnov has been appointed supreme president of the U.S. for a ten year period, largely because he is the nephew of the Russian premier, Vassily. General Zhabnov rules America as his personal fiefdom. The only rules he must obey: first, no uprisings and second, seventy-five percent of the country's crops grown by the enslaved American workers must be sent to Russia. General Zhabnov believes that the situation in the U.S. is stable. That there are no American resistance forces to speak of other than a few scattered groups that raid convoys from time to time. He sees his stay here as a happy interlude away from the power struggles back in the Kremlin.

Colonel Killov is the head of the KGB in the U.S. headquartered in Aspen, Colorado. He is a ruthlessly ambitious man whose goal it is to someday be premier of the world. Thin, almost gauntly skeletal looking, with a long face, sunken cheekbones, and thin lips that spit words, Killov's operatives are everywhere in the country—in the fortresses, in the Russian officer ranks, and lately he has even managed to infiltrate an American born agent into the highest levels of the American resistance. Colonel Killov believes General Zhabnov to be a fool. Killov knows that the American forces are growing stronger daily and forming a nationwide alliance to fight together. The calm days of the last century are about to end.

From Moscow, Premier Vassily rules the world. Never has one man ruled so much territory. From the bottom of Africa to Siberia, from Paraguay to Canada, Russian armies are everywhere. A constant flow of supplies and medical goods are needed to keep the vast occupying armies alive. Russia herself had not done badly in the war. Only twenty-four American missiles had reached the Soviet Union and ten of these had been pushed off course or exploded by ground to air missiles. The rest of the U.S. strike had been knocked out of the skies by Russian killer satellites that had shot down beams of pure energy and picked them off like clay pigeons.

Vassily is besieged on all sides by problems. His great empire is threatening to break up. Everywhere there are rebel attacks on Russian troops. In Europe, in Africa, in India, especially in America. The forces of the resistance troops were growing larger and more sophisticated in their operations. Vassily is a highly intelligent, well read man. He has devoured history books on other great leaders and the problems they had faced. "Great men have problems that no one but another great man could understand," he lectures his underlings. Advisers tell him to send in more forces and quickly crush the insurgents. But Vassily believes that to be a tremendous waste of manpower. If it goes on like this he may use neutron bombs again. Not a big strike, but perhaps in a single night, yes, in one hour, they could target the fifty main trouble spots in the world and . . . Order must be maintained. For Vassily knew his history. One thing that had been true since the dawn of time—wherever there had been a great empire there had come a time when it began to crumble.

One

It was a storm like no other. Like no other before the Nuke War anyway. It roared across the sky like a lion, shrieking out peals of thunder, ripping the earth with its claws of lightning. Fifty million volt spears of electricity cracked down out of the sky, lighting up the desolate terrain with blinding sheets of white. Immense purple and black thunderheads filled the heavens. Clouds piled atop clouds, huge, hanging in the air like mountains of the purest darkness. The storm, which extended for nearly two hundred miles in every direction, roared across eastern Colorado, smashing away at the Rocky Mountains with an almost malevolent fury. The storm shot down bolts like artillery shells, ripping at the jagged peaks of majesty. Avalanches of rocks and boulders as big as trucks pounded down the sides of the mountains by the thousands of tons. The lightning blasted away again and again as if seeking total annihilation.

It was a megastorm, one of the biggest of the postwar blows with winds up to one hundred and fifty mph, and tornado funnels setting down; swirling winds of absolute blackness into which whole trees and screaming mountain animals were sucked; touch down for seconds, minutes, then disappear back up into the writhing clouds, dark as a sea of death, taking their earthly booty with them into the blackness. The storm took as much life as it gave back with its torrents of rain—rain that would make the earth live again. Rain that would heal the radioactive scars and sores that oozed pus red and brown in wastelands across America.

Beneath this onslaught of wind and rain and fusillades of lightning singeing the very air with their electric heat, beneath the atomic roar of thunder shaking the mountains around them, six American freefighters slipped and slid along a steep mountain trail as they made their way toward their destiny. The destiny of not just their lives but of all Americans. They were going into battle with the Russians and the outcome could well change the course of human history.

Ted Rockson, his chiseled stone face wet with the cold thick drops of rain from the storm, reached around the edge of the mountain trail for a firm handhold. His eyes, one aquamarine blue, the other violet, seemed to almost glow with power. The power of "the Rockson," the man the American slaves called the "ultimate American." The man the Russians had designated as the "most dangerous rebel in America—wanted dead or alive." Rockson found the hold and pulled his feet in close against the narrow ledge of a cliff. The backpack and weapons on his back pulled backwards, trying to pluck him from the ten inch-wide path, two thousand seven hundred and eighty-nine feet up the sheer rock face of one of the eastern Rocky mountains. Rockson looked down for a moment but could see only an impenetrable cloudy blackness as the storm swirled and whipped around him, snapping the loose sleeves of his jacket. He made it around the outcropping and came to a momentary plateau about fifty feet in diameter. Rock stood back and waited while the rest of the Rock team worked around the edge. Detroit Green, Rockson's righthand man, came next, his short bull-like body pressing close against the lichen-covered rock. His black face shone like polished ebony as a crack of lightning blasted into a peak about a thousand feet away. Trickles of rain splattered down his cheeks.

"Damn, this ain't a good night," Detroit said as he joined Rockson on the outcropping. He adjusted his twin bandoliers of hand grenades, making sure that none had loosened or become wet during the ascent. Rock peered anxiously back at the trail he had just been on. The going had been unusually rough—even for freefighters. None of them had ever made this particular crossing of the Rockies and the last two days had been treacherous. Rock didn't want to lose a single one of his men. They had all been through too much together. McCaughlin came next. The huge Scotsman was the size of a barn door but tough as a grizzly in a fight of which he had had many. Next, Chen, the martial arts instructor of Century City, in his black ninja suit that covered him from head to toe in a warm but supple midnight black material. He came easily around the outcrop, his thin face smiling with that ever present self-mocking grin that sat beneath his pencil-thin mustache. Around the Chinese American's waist were his only weapons besides his hands—five-pointed exploding star knives. With these he was an expert, able to nail a man between the eyes from eighty feet. And the explosives, plastic fitted around the razor-sharp weapons, were powerful enough to take out the side of an armored vehicle.

Next came Lang, the kid, the youngest of the group, but as tough as they came. Nearly six and a half feet tall, Lang reminded Rock of himself when he was in his early twenties—arrogant, smart-assed, and tough as nails. The kid even resembled Rock physically—same stone-muscled physique, same chiseled features as if the skin had been worn away by winds and forces beyond imagination to a pure state of impenetrable muscle. He didn't, however, share Rock's white streak of hair running down the center of his scalp nor the different colored eyes. Bringing up the rear came Archer, who despite his seven foot stature and three hundred and twenty pounds, moved with the agility of a cat. His crossbow hung down across his back as the mute mountain man reached around the corner of the cliff and found a hold with his immense hand. Rock breathed a sigh of relief as the last freefighter came onto the outcropping. For his own life he never worried but for his men . . .

"I don't like it Rock," Detroit said, as the six Americans stood in center of the raging storm. At his words a chorus of bolts took off from directly above them and roared down to shattering fiery rendezvous with tall pines and iron rich peaks. "It's a megablow," the black cannonball of a man continued. "Could take us all right the hell off this earth." Detroit looked up at the writhing fists of clouds pounding and punching away at one another. The stocky freefighter was afraid of few things—the megastorm was one of them. He had been in one of the super storms that periodically swept across America and had barely escaped with his life as winds grew to two hundred and fifty mph and tore everything—trees, vegetation, animals screaming out shrill death cries—away. He had made it to a small cave and watched in horrified fascination as the world outside was leveled to a splintered, flooded wasteland.

"We've got to move on, Detroit," Rockson said softly. "The Reds aren't going to wait." He scanned the horizon ahead, trying to penetrate the ocean of a storm and see beyond, see the Russian convoy which he knew lay ahead. "We'll get wet but we're not going to die," Rockson said, looking at the gathered fighters around him, "unless you look up the sky too long and drown. So keep your mouths closed and your feet on the ground and we should be at attack point within several hours." The men glanced nervously ahead, down the side of the mountain where the trail seemed to meander wildly from cliff to cliff. But they all knew Ted Rockson and trusted him with their lives. They would have walked into the fires of hell itself with this man, with Ted Rockson. Perhaps that's just where they were going.

The ground grew blacker as they headed down the steep slope, a sign of a nearby a-blast, in the war of a century ago. Rock took a look at his wrist-geiger, an invention of Dr. Shecter, the head scientist of Century City and surely one of the ten most intelligent men alive in the world today. The man's output of technological innovations and advanced weaponry was prodigious. The needle of the geiger was heading from the blue, safe zone, into the green, radiation-present zone of the watch-sized detecter. But it wasn't even near the beginning of the red—hot zone, totally within acceptable limits for the freefighters. Their genes, as had the genetic structures of all freefighters living out in the more high rad parts of the United States, had mutated so that they were now nearly a hundred times more resistant than their pre-war ancestors had been to the poisonous ravages of radiation.

But though he was safe from the invisible death, the ground they walked on was not. Rock looked around at the black, unproductive, sterile land as they came to the outer edge of a crater nearly a thousand yards wide. He felt a charge of hatred bolt up and down his spine. Hatred for the Reds—the murderers who had done this to America, land of the free, home of the brave, country of the dead. Eighty percent of the U.S. population had died within the first two weeks of the strike, dying either of the bomb blast or of the far more painful and terrifying radiation damage which made the hair fall out like burnt wheat and the teeth fall like rotten black fruit from the bleeding gums of the wounded. The Reds were easily able to fly in their troops and take over the U.S. from citizens in no shape to fight back. For nearly a century the Slavic invaders had occupied America, living off the produce, keeping her surviving population in the chains of slave labor.

But times were changing. Able to mount only small-scale attacks over the decades, the American freefighting forces were at last growing in numbers and strength. The seventy-five Free Cities had only recently organized into the Confederation of United States and plans were under way for a Re-Constitutional Convention at which delegates would be sent from every hidden city to elect a president and congress and prepare plans for an all-out military assault on the Reds. Not that the Americans weren't totally out-gunned by vastly superior Russian armaments, tanks, deathchoppers, and jets, even neutron bombs which the Reds had been using with more and more frequency. Out-gunned until now. But just months before,* Rockson and a small expeditionary force had headed out into uncharted regions of the Far West, "land of the red fog" as the freefighters called it. The expedition had made contact with a strange race of mutated Americans called The Technicians, named after their ancestors, missile technicians who had survived the nuclear exchange in their super-fortified concrete bunkers deep under the western soil. The Technicians had lived there for a century, their eyes growing larger, with almost iridescent pupils as fiery as a cat's, heads as big as pumpkins atop diminutive children's bodies with spindly legs and arms. The Technicians had continued to use their knowledge doing the one thing they knew best—making weapons. Why they produced these weapons they had no idea. For whom? For what purpose? They had been totally shut off from all communication with the rest of the United States for a century and didn't even think anyone was alive out there as the terrain around their bunkers was black as soot, miles of lifeless slag.

Until Rockson showed up. Upon hearing the entire story of what had happened to America after Russia's first strike, The Technicians had gladly

---

*Read *The Doomsday Warrior*

given Rockson five of the particle beam disintegrators they had built. Weapons of such enormous power that a single shot of pure black energy from one of the strangely shaped plastic rifles could bore holes through a mountain. Rock and his men had returned to Century City, their hidden city fortress in the middle of the Colorado Rockies, and proudly presented their black beam weapons to Dr. Shecter, who as Century City's head scientist, immediately took the weapons under his command as too valuable to be used in "just any battle" with the Reds. He had made a careful, controlled scientific testing of the range and power of the particle beam rifles. Results? An unknown energy source with the power of a controlled atomic explosion. As hard as Shecter tried, he was unable to duplicate the weapons. Duplicate, hell, he couldn't even open one up, as The Technicians had made them in a plastic mold, out of an unknown alloy that was impervious even to diamond drills.

At last Shecter had permitted Rock to take two of the weapons to attack a large Russian convoy that ferried supplies from the major Midwest airport of Fort Dobrynin to Denver some two hundred miles away by truck. "We've got to try them out in a real combat situation," Rock had pleaded with Shecter for months. At last the scientist, tight-faced and cryptic as ever, had relented, after attaching a charge of high explosives to the stocks of the weapons which could be detonated by simply pressing a four number combination on a small panel. No Russian would ever get one of these rifles— and live.

A streak of star-hot lightning tore into the trail just

thirty feet head of Rockson, ripping him from his thoughts of Dr. Shecter and home. The arcing lance of pure energy bit into the hard ground and spat out shards of stone shrapnel which flew off in all directions.

"Down!" Rock screamed as all six freefighters hit the deck in a flash. The wave of debris passed overhead or slammed into their thick khaki flak jackets. They rose after a few seconds, wiping themselves off. Drenched, covered in mud they pushed on.

"Even the Goddamned ground is attacking us," McCaughlin sputtered, pulling his big frame from the muddy trail, spitting out black dirt.

"That was our rest stop," Rock said poker-faced to the others and continued down the mountain trail which zigged and zagged as if a madman had carved it, down the side of the mountain. He kept having to readjust his poncho over the particle beam rifle which was slung over his left shoulder. Shecter had sworn the damn thing was impervious to everything he could test on it. But water? All Rockson needed was to aim at a Red chopper coming in at him, fire the particle gun and have a dribble of muddy water come out. He made sure the glass smooth muzzle of the long black-marbled barrel was safely hidden under the plastic coverall he wore.

The storm continued to snap and snarl at the six figures walking along the rock-strewn trail, tearing down at them like a wolf into hot flesh. Bolts cracked everywhere, lighting the night with demonic eyes. The rain let loose in a waterfall from the sky. Within minutes the ground was waterlogged mud, making movement hard as the freefighter's boots made obscene sucking sounds as they slowed to a crawl through this newest obstacle to their destination.

"I thought God was on our side," McCaughlin said to Chen who walked right in front of him.

"Well, there've been many gods in history. It depends on which one you mean," Chen answered with a thin smile. His kung fu shoes floated on the top of the mud easily as the others' boots dug in. "Obviously the rain and the thunder gods don't like us. One of us must have offended one of them in a past life." The Chinese martial arts master looked in a mock accusatory fashion at the big Scotsman lumbering along behind him. But McCaughlin merely grunted, hefting his Liberator automatic rifle on his shoulder. They moved for nearly two hours through the pounding gale, drenched to their bones. Not a man complained. These battle-hardened American freefighters—they had been through it all and more. Anyway, it was in the fifties, thank God. Tonight, when the temperature began dropping down to the twenties and thirties, their soggy clothes could mean death. But in the world of 2089 A.D. you had to take one thing at time.

At last they came to a deep valley which fell off below the peak they stood on, nearly three thousand feet down to a long winding road.

"This is it, men," Rockson said, leaning back against one of a dozen large boulders that dotted the lip of the mountain around them. "Why don't you all rest up, make what cover you can among these boulders, using your ponchos. McCaughlin, how about some coffee?" Rock implored, his breath frosting out in a globe of steam. McCaughlin grumbled as he was fond of doing, but put down his double-sized pack which contained kitchen supplies as well as arms and pulled out a flameless, smokeless tube stove, another of Shecter's inventions, which worked off a chemical inside a pinky-sized tube which, when snapped at one end, gave off an intense heat for about half an hour. The men huddled around the black fire rubbing their hands in the rising waves of heat. The freefighters quickly set up a temporary camp as they waited for the Red convoy to pass below them. Within five minutes they had erected a camouflaged mountain tent and anchored it with twelve inch pegs into the hard surface of the mountain's rocky soil. The moment it was together they all ran inside to dry off and then took out their weapons and inspected them for the impending battle.

Rockson and Detroit would fire the particle beam weapons. The attack on the Red truck convoy was more for testing the black beam weapons in a combat situation than just another ambush on the Russian army. Although it would be highly satisfying if they could destroy a good portion of the diesel fleet. The big tractor trailers would be carrying supplies for three of the Midwest Red fortress cities, enough for six months. The loss of these strategic loads of ammunition, parts, and medical supplies would weaken them drastically.

These are the kind of strikes we need more of, Rock thought, as he checked the long narrow particle beam rifle for dirt or damage. Not the attacks on a few sentry posts, or even the destruction of five or ten tanks. No, the American freefighting forces had to begin turning into a real army and take on whole fortress cities, whole Red armies at a time. Rock could feel that the times were changing. It was in the air, in his blood. An electric tension of things shifting, worlds colliding. And Ted Rockson, the "Ultimate American," the dealer of death to restore life, was in his element.

Rock fingered the particle beam rifle's trigger, checking to make sure nothing had lodged in there. But there was no space for twigs or dirt to find a home. The Technicians had made the weapons with a fluid perfection. He remembered them with fondness, their huge brains and children's bodies, the strange mathematical language they spoke. They had contributed an incalculable advantage to the American forces. For the first time in a hundred years the freefighters could really talk about "winning."

"Looks good, Rock," Detroit said, hefting his black beam rifle and sighting down the three triangular sighting devices along the top. The other men checked their conventional weapons—Liberator automatic rifles. McCaughlin and Lang unpacked a rapid-fire mortar which they manned as a team. The small metalloy shells could blow out the side of a tank or take out a whole hillside swarming with advancing soldiers. Archer loaded a band of ten two foot long razor-sharp arrows onto the side of his crossbow, a device he'd constructed which allowed firing arrows one after another. Arrows which could pierce cleanly through a man's chest or skull, exit, and then slice through another body. Arrows which only whispered death as they flew like hawks unerringly to their target. Rockson had saved the seven foot mute mountainman from certain death in a quicksand pit and since then the incredibly tough mutant giant, whose family had been slaughtered by the Reds, followed Rock everywhere, would not allow him to go on a mission without him.

The wailing sounds of the megastorm seemed to suddenly die down and Chen poked his head inside the tent. "Storm's heading out." The men emerged from the confines of the synthnylon mountain tent and stepped outside into the muddy ground. The last of the coiling snakelike clouds were flying off to the west to wreak further damage. The storm would move all the way to the unknown lands of what had been California and on into the Pacific Ocean where it would finally blow itself out several hundred miles out at sea.

The freefighters let out with a cheer. Their clothes would have a chance to dry off and their targets would be clear and visible for the attack. They watched the clouds roll quickly away to be replaced by rapidly brightening skies. The sun aggressively pushed herself back into prominence, burning away the gray misty fog which pervaded the air. A long arched double rainbow—common after the war due to atmospheric alterations—of pinks and violets and blood red tones hovered shimmeringly in the air across the deep valley. Far down the slopes lined with scraggly black-barked pines, at the far end of the twisting valley, the freefighters suddenly heard the sounds of what could only be one thing. A Red convoy. Smoke from the diesel engines of the tractor trailers sent up a gray haze which followed like a cloud above the truck fleet.

"Better make some sort of camouflage," Rock said to the Rock Squad who stood around him. "With the skies clearing they'll be sending choppers ahead for recon." The men broke down the tent and took off their own brown and gray patterned ponchos, laying them across large rocks at the edge of the plateau. They eased into position as comfortably as was possible in the still soggy dirt and aimed their weapons down onto the road where the convoy would soon pass.

Rock lay flat on his stomach and sighted along the three triangular sights of the black beam weapon. The sights gave off a reddish glow except in the very center of the triangle where the target was. When the target was dead center of the triangles it would brighten considerably, signaling the holder of the rifle to fire. The particle beam weapon contained a memory as well, locking in the coordinates of the target once it had been found. Even if the person firing the weapon slipped or jerked as they pulled the trigger, the weapon itself would compensate as the particle beam shot out.

Rockson could feel his heart beating fast. Normally he was unafraid of battle. He had survived so many. It was part of his history, his destiny to do battle with the enemies of America. But today he felt different. What happened in the next fifteen minutes, half hour, would mean failure or success. A free America or a continuing slave state.

The first of the Red convoy came into view at the far end of the valley. Typical Russian defensive array: swift-moving armored vehicles with machine guns, scouting, darting ahead, followed by ten Soyak-12 tanks nearly fifty feet long and capable of making forty mph on a flat road. Then came the truck convoy itself, nearly a hundred of the big tractor trailers stretched along the muddy road like one of the legendary freight trains of old that Rockson had read about. A rich target. He fingered the long smooth weapon impatiently. Two attack helicopters, black with red stars emblazoned in their sides, flew quickly overhead but missed the Rock Squad, hidden under ponchos, beneath rock overhangs. The Reds couldn't imagine that anything but at least a thousand-man force would attack such a well-armed column. And even then it would be suicidal when the Reds could call in air strikes within minutes. Beside the convoy had never been attacked. Until now. . . .

Two

The road below the freefighters became a solid wall of roaring engines, smoke, and gasoline fumes. The drone of tens of thousands of diesel horsepower echoed off the valley walls and up to the waiting freefighters, their weapons picking choice targets as the column advanced along the dirt highway. Rock waited and waited to signal the attack, making himself hold back until the last possible second when the entire convoy filled the valley road below. He set the particle beam on highest energy output, a beam of about a six inch diameter. This, The Technicians had instructed him was the most powerful of the weapon's settings.

Detroit lay nearly thirty yards away, his elbows resting in mud beneath two man-sized boulders that stood above him leaning toward one another so that they almost touched. He took the safety off and sighted on the lead tank. He looked over at Rockson who lay absolutely still, following the convoy through his sights. The signal. When would he give the damn signal? Sweat oozed through the black skin of Detroit's powerful neck. He moved his finger back and forth on the trigger guard, suddenly craving a cigarette and knowing he couldn't move an inch now to get one.

"Fire!" Rock yelled to the attack squad, his eye trained squarely on the lead tank, broadside. He pulled the trigger. Without a sound the black beam hung in the air bridging the three thousand two hundred and forty-seven feet between Rockson and the tank in a millionth of a second. The tank turned from dark gray to cherry red and then a blinding white in the space of about one second. Then it exploded with a roar, its molecules of steel and magnesium imploding in on themselves. Target destroyed, Rock thought with a grim smile. Where the tank had been was now just glowing pieces of shrapnel littering the swampy road.

Detroit fired a moment after Rockson, sighting the second tank in the convoy. He aimed for the treads, now wanting to disintegrate the tank totally but create a blockage for the rest of the traffic. Then he and Rock could pick off the Reds like tin ducks in a shooting gallery. He pulled the trigger. Again, the beam seemed not so much to move toward its target as just hang in the air, a beam of pure black light, pure energy. The charged particles hit the lower portion of the Soyak, evaporating the section of steel tread along one side. The fifty foot tank lurched sideways, sinking down into the mud as its opposing tread continued to spin frantically, driving the tank around in circles deeper and deeper into the mud until it lay half buried, blocking the highway.

The entire convoy was now halted by the half-melted tank from which Red officers ran screaming, their lungs singed by the super-heated air inside. The other tanks swiveled their turrets, searching desperately for their attackers. They fired impotently up at the surrounding cliffs. The Red troops were panicking, their eyes darting madly around. There is nothing more terrifying than an unseen enemy. Who is it? How many are there? From where? The Red officers screamed out orders to the next two tanks in the convoy to push the wounded giant out of their path. The Soyaks shot forward and began heaving away at their smoking metal comrade.

Rock and Detroit fired again, hitting the heavily armored Soyaks. Two explosions ripped through the valley a hundred times louder than the firing guns of the tanks and armored vehicles. The two freefighters fired again at the next in line. The black tubes of light beelined for their targets. The blackness was darker than any blackness of night or natural color. It seemed to pull light in toward it, appeared to have infinite depth. Around the beams was the almost silent crackling energy of one of the most powerful energy bands in the universe. As Rock and Detroit continued down the column, McCaughlin opened up with the mortar at the troops. Lang handed him the shells and the Scot began sending whistling rounds of death into the confusion. Archer sighted carefully down his crossbow, picking off officers attempting to organize a counterattack. Chen, meanwhile, slid off unnoticed down the side of the mountain toward the valley floor below. He moved like a cat among the rocks and scraggly brush of the slope, a star knife in each hand. If the Reds tried an assault on the peak from which the freefighters were firing, they would be in for a few surprises.

The Reds were growing more terrified by the second. There weren't supposed to be weapons that could just take out their tanks like they were toys. Foot thick, titanium alloy melted away. Not even holes in the sides of the monster tanks or twisted jagged metal—but just steaming melting wreckage. Glowing scraps on the dirt highway sizzling slightly as new bands of clouds began moving in dropping sheets of fine rain.

The colonel in charge of the convoy forces, Colonel Sharynko, screamed through a P.A. on his command car, in sputtering Russian, orders to form defensive formation and fire back on the enemy. One of the tank officers spotted Rockson's black beam as it hit the tank directly ahead of him.

"There! Up there on the western ridge!" The tanks wheeled their guns around preparing to fire, but were not given the chance. Seeing that the particle beam rifles were working perfectly, Rockson and Detroit opened up on the scampering Red forces below. They aimed and fired, not even waiting for the explosive implosion to occur. For just a second the beam would hang in the air and then they would move onto the next target. Within minutes nearly all the tanks and armored vehicles had been destroyed. McCaughlin and Lang continued to fire the mortar, sending out rounds every twenty seconds. The mortars landed among the troops trying to find cover among the rocks and blew them into piles of bloody flesh. Smoke and a ghastly odor of death, of burning bone and metal, of boiling blood, filled the air. Some of the trucks at the far end of the valley road began trying to back up, but Detroit and Rock fired nearly a mile and a half down the road and took out the two rearmost tractor trailers. The trucks erupted into fire and toppled over, completely blocking any exit from the trap into which the convoy had driven.

Chen lay hidden in a grove of red-barked dwarf pines halfway up the mountainside from the Red column. Beams, bullets, and shells from the Red tanks flew past him looking for something to destroy. Suddenly he heard rocks sliding just below him. He peered around the edge of the grove and saw six Red soldiers with submachine guns coming up the slope to outflank the American attack force. With a star knife in each hand Chen jumped from his hiding place and whipped them through the air at the soviets. One of the five-pointed blades ripped into a Red chest, the other into the shoulder blade. Both exploded on contact, turning the upper half of the two men into a spray of red mist. The legs with no body stood for a second and then crumpled to the ground, suddenly realizing they were dead. The four remaining commando force aimed their subs at Chen and fired but found only air. The martial arts master had flipped backwards behind the pines. As he hit the ground, landing on both feet, Chen whipped out two more of the star knives and, without stopping his motion, turned and came running out the other side of the grove so that he caught the Reds by surprise from their right flank. He spun the two razor-sharp star knives which whirled silently through the smoky hillside. Again both made contact with flesh. The remaining two Reds stared in horror as two more of their force were turned into oozing mounds of hamburger. This time Chen came at the two Reds who were left. They tried to lift their smg guns and fired but missed the leaping, spinning Chinese freefighter. He reached the closer of the Reds, a big red-faced bruiser who sneered and ripped out a foot and a half long bayonet from his pack. Chen feinted to the right and the soldier lunged forward. As the big man came Chen stepped to the left and kicked up with right foot. The leg swung up with lightning speed, catching the Red under the chin, snapping his head back with a loud crack. He fell to the mountainside dead, his spine cracked neatly in two.

Chen spun as he felt a bead being drawn on him. His years of training, nearly twenty-five of them, had given him extra senses, super fine-tuned perceptions so that he could sense another man's intention to strike as the attacker himself felt it. He dove forward, rolling down the hill in a ball. He came alongside the firing Russian and knocked him to the ground like a bowling pin. The Russian soldier struggled to right himself, as he reached for his service revolver. But Chen was upon him as the pistol left the holster. He slammed three quick strikes to the man's stubbly throat, cracking the larnyx, crushing the windpipe. The man threw his hands over his throat, gasping like a fish out of water. He fell face forward, his brain already dead from lack of oxygen. It would take his heart minutes to stop. But already the would-be killer was motionless. Chen surveyed the slope down to the valley road but saw no others.

Back up on the ledge of the mountain the freefighters didn't let up their fire for a moment. They swept through the convoy like the tornado of a megastorm. Six men trapping a thousand. Six men destroying over a hundred armed vehicles. Something for the history books.

Rockson and Detroit fired down the single file line

of huge diesels, firing twice at each one. Once into the forward, driver's cab, then sweeping the beam of purest black across the truck's side to make sure that all the military supplies were destroyed. To the Red troops it was as if the hand of God had come down to deliver punishment to the Russian occupiers of the once free America. Their eyes grew wide in horror as the black beams made their way towards them. Most of them, even the bravest of the Red troops, screamed in mortal terror in the few seconds before they were evaporated into madly spinning atoms of imploding energy. The line of trucks turned into a row of bonfires, bonfires of flesh and rubber, burning with a flame so hot that it fed on the metal rubble of the trucks. The supplies inside erupted in secondary explosions as bullets, tank .50mm cannon shells, grenades, and other Red ammunition joined in the conflagration.

The last of the big diesels went up with a roar as both Rock and Detroit sighted it. With the energy of both of the particle beams hitting it at once, not an atom remained untouched. The shower of glowing particles that had been the truck floated like little seeds of shrapnel back down to the blood-splattered muddy ground.

The two freefighters stopped firing the weapons and, seeing they had ceased, McCaughlin as well stopped sending down mortars. The freefighters looked slowly along the valley road at a scene of total destruction. A trail of melted, twisted, smoking wreckage fused into the very mud itself; into impossible shapes and configurations that death takes on when it dances among the armies of man. Nothing was left. Just piles of bubbling metal and glowing rubble lighting the smoke above the road as if lighting the way for the souls of the dead to leave this valley of death.

At the far end of the roadway, just beyond the last of the destroyed trucks, two armored vehicles that had been taking up the rear tore off. Detroit raised his particle beam rifle but Rock yelled over to him, "No! Let them go! Let them tell the others what happened here. I want the whole damn Russian army to understand that the ballgame has changed. We'll strike at their morale just as we've struck at their supply route." The roadway looked like the bowels of hell itself, smoking metal and human corpses, piles of grotesquely melted Russian bodies, their flesh running into one another, bones sticking from out of red mud.

The freefighters looked at what they had done and at each other. They felt no guilt, no shame. Nor happiness. They had accomplished what they set out to do. Had done it beyond their wildest dreams. Now at last they had the weapon they needed. A weapon as powerful and awesome as the atomic bomb itself, the twentieth century's gift of extinction. But now the twenty-first century as well had its weapon of superdeath.

Rockson felt the moment. Let it sink into him. The death, the power of the weapon. It was an historic moment. There was no turning back for man now. Yet another weapon of incalculable destructive power had been unleashed upon the world. Deep in his rock-hard gut Rockson prayed that someday there would be no more new ways to kill men and that the old way would be buried beneath ashes as final as those of the convoy below. But it was necessary for the liberation of America. The Reds would be hopping mad now. Killov in his Denver monolith, ruling the KGB Death Squads across America, Zhabnov in his ridiculous guise as "president" of the United States, in his luxurious quarters in the White House in Washington, even Premier Vassily back in the Kremlin. Yeah, they'd be mad as hell. And scared to death, too.

Three

The White House was festooned with large red silk flags. Across the front gate of the Capitol swung a banner with four profile pictures in gold of Lenin, Drabkin, (who had conquered the world through nuclear war a century before), Premier Vassily and President Zhabnov. It waved lightly in the cool November breeze as if welcoming the visiting dignitaries from the global Soviets who walked below. The speeches had already begun though delegates were still arriving at Chekov Airport in monstrous Ilyushin-9 and Tupelov-180 long range jets. They walked as unobtrusively as possible into the halls of Congress, into the Senate chambers where rows of guests, mid and upper-level bureaucrats from the Soviet provinces throughout the world, sat and listened to boring plodding speeches about the greatness of the Russian Empire.

Where once Democrats and Republicans had debated the issues of a free society, now Red speakers made a mockery of the slogans carved in stone around them. Slogans such as THE WILL OF THE

PEOPLE and ONE NATION UNDER GOD. The Soviet delegates approved of everything that was said with thunderous applause, knowing full well that any speeches given were already policy, approved on high. The main speaker of the illustrious gathering, president of the U.S.S.A., General Zhabnov, would speak last. To walk in late on his words was treading on dangerous ground. But the preliminary speakers going on endlessly about improvements in transport and food production, here in the U.S. and the like, were already into their second day of nonstop talking.

The lower level functionaries who had to listen attentively to these dry messages daydreamed of their soon-to-be fulfilled desires: a Washington D.C. party. The delegates who had attended the bashes in earlier years came back with tales that were unrivaled anywhere in the world for their sumptuous debauchery. The delegates to the 2089 A.D. convention squirmed in their seats, waiting, listening to the plaudits and audits, the pundits and digits, droned out by Pushkins and Drubkovs. They yearned to hear the last words of President Zhabnov's speech and be off to the parties. Parties supposedly to celebrate the one hundredth anniversary of the Red occupation of America.

A cold wind began blowing outside and a few desultory snowflakes fell to the ground with a swirling grace. But the delegates felt suddenly cheered as word passed around that the speeches were to be curtailed as Zhabnov was anxious to begin his speech, a speech the drab brown and gray-suited red-faced commissars from around the globe would listen to attentively. Something was up. Something big. Although two huge banners with pictures of Colonel Killov, the head of

KGB in America, stood on both sides of the dilapidated Sanitation Building on the outskirts of the capital, barely visible on the ride in from the airport, there was not another KGB emblem or picture in all of the assembly halls and chambers—an unprecedented snub. Moreover, stiff-collared, blackshirted KGB officers were in a distinct minority among the delegates. Something was going on and it had to do with a power struggle between the two most powerful men in America, Killov and Zhabnov.

Everyone knew that the Grandfather, Premier Vassily, who ruled the entire world from the Kremlin, was dying. The power struggle of succession had begun already. And both Killov and Zhabnov were vying for the top post. The two were at each other's throats. Assassination attempts had been tried on both and failed over the past year. But still the two had pretended to have amicable relations, if only to keep Vassily from becoming involved. But here, for the first time, it was out in the open. Would Zhabnov not just remove the banners of the KGB but actually come out and attack Killov in his speech—a speech ostensibly a State of the Union speech—a tradition since pre-war days, devoted in the past to praise of food production under Zhabnov and his benign ability to keep the peace?

The nearly two thousand delegates rose slamming their hands together in thunderous applause as Zhabnov, sporting a neatly trimmed goatee, appeared at the edge of the stage in full dress uniform, his chest covered with gold and silver medals. He strode jauntily to the podium and stared down at the assembled dignitaries with a beneficent smile. The applause didn't die for several minutes as none of the delegates wanted to be noticed as being the first one who stopped clapping. Consequently, though the Speaker of the House, General Durgov, banged the gavel several times, everyone remained on their feet, churning out waves of applause until Zhabnov motioned to them to stop with a wave of his hands.

"Friends, comrades." Zhabnov smiled out from under the enormous red banner containing his likeness, hand-stitched with silk thread. "You are all good friends to come all this way to my little soiree here in the frontier capital of Washington." Slight snickers quickly choked off could be heard among the delegates.

"Friends, how good it is to see you all," Zhabnov continued. "Each and every one at this momentous occasion. But before I begin let us bow our heads and give thanks for the continued leadership of our great leader, our benefactor, the premier of all the Soviets, may he live for centuries, Premier Vassily." The assemblage bowed their heads for a few seconds and then caught Zhabnov looking up, unclasping his hands and smiling down at them again. He took a drink of water as each delegate edged forward in their seat—here it comes they thought.

"Now," Zhabnov began, "there is the question of food production in America and how it has matched up with the last five year plan. I am pleased to tell you all that we have not only achieved our goals but surpassed them with nearly two million bushels of surplus wheat, which has been stockpiled in emergency warehouses outside Moscow. Furthermore . . ." He droned on and on, citing statistic after vital statistic as the delegates withdrew into themselves in pained boredom. So, there was to be no overt official speech condemning Killov after all. Zhabnov was just telegraphing his feelings through symbols such as the numbers of KGBers present and the removal of banners. He was not yet strong enough to come out and say what everyone already knew: that the war of succession between himself and Killov had begun. Still, it showed he was perhaps cannier than many gave him credit for. And assuredly there would be plays made to all who attended the wild parties—endowed complete with music, women, vodka—to be loyal to Zhabnov's faction.

The speech lasted for nearly three hours and seventeen minutes—sixteen minutes longer than the previous year's pronouncements. President Zhabnov was interrupted seventy-two times by applause. At last he walked off to more applause and shouts of support. The ordeal was over. Now the delegates would revel indoors as the snow began falling more heavily. Revel and parlay votes for favors.

It was at the biggest bash that Zhabnov honored the participants by appearing in casual clothes—a cardigan sweater with just one medal, and blue pants. The KGBers were long gone from Washington, walking out immediately after the long applause at the end of Zhabnov's speech and boarding one of their own heavily guarded skylifters and heading west to Denver to report back to Colonel Killov himself. They had seen the insults and listened for clues of strength and intention in the speech. Their narrow eyes had polled the audience faces to see who might not be smiling too broadly, who hesitated ever so slightly to applaud. All would be reported back to Killov. Secretly even these icy officers longed for the revelry they would miss. Everyone knew of the drugs, the women, the entertainment that would be proffered upon the delegates—the real reason, after all, that so many attended. The delegates always left the three day festivities in America more committed to Zhabnov than before. And this could well be the last such convention before the death of the Grandfather. The delegates prayed that he would hang in there for a few more days at least so they could have their fun.

Zhabnov walked around the ballroom shaking hands. Already many of the Red representatives were ensconced in side rooms and upstairs chambers, taking advantage of the seemingly endless supply of young and willing women whom Zhabnov had provided. The rest of the delegates indulged in opium-filled rooms in the subbasement, watching erotic dancers gyrate before them, or passed the time gambling in a fully equipped game room that Zhabnov had provided. The wiliest of them, however, had remained on the main ballroom floor to greet and shake hands with Zhabnov personally or share a toast.

"To the Soviets. To the World Soviets and all the wonderful things they've done for humanity," Zhabnov shouted, raising his champagne glass. All shouted *nazdarovya* and drank down the bubbling elixir. They then joined Zhabnov in throwing the crystal glasses into the wide roaring fireplace—in this former vice president's mansion in Georgetown. Zhabnov pointed to the big oil painting of George Bush over the fireplace. He took another glass from the Negro waiter's tray and raised it high in the air. "To George Bush—to all the American forefathers of our great socialist republic." There were a few gasps but everyone knew that Zhabnov was a joker. They all shouted *nazdarovya* and drank again, smashing their glasses into the fireplace which was now filled with a thousand glistening shards of glass. Indeed the drinking to their ancient enemy's picture loosened them up a bit. Anything goes here in Washington they thought, both nervous and excited.

Zhabnov mingled with his guests, walking around the large ballroom, shaking hands, laughing louder than anyone else. He came to Sikorsky, second in command of the Armenian Republic and took him aside.

"Vlad, how goes it in Armenia? Are the gypsies still stirring up trouble?" Zhabnov asked, putting his hands on the shorter, portly man's shoulder.

"Very well, Mr. President," Sikorsky answered somewhat nervously. With his thick bifocals and hesitant, almost trembling demeanor, the man had a certain comic air about him. "The gypsies are being put into new pacification centers. It's going very well. Food of course is . . . well . . . scarce. As you know, our region took some heavy losses in the last harvest storm."

"I understand that you are sympathetic to our . . . cause," Zhabnov said, looking reassuringly at Sikorsky. "And not so friendly to the maniac—you know who."

"Yes Mr. President," Vladimar said, looking around nervously to see if anyone was listening. "But how did you know?"

"Ah, I have my ways." Zhabnov smiled broadly. "By the way, I'll speak to some of your production staff about getting some grain out your way. There's been a surplus for two years now. I don't think Moscow would mind a little channeling. Do you?"

"Ah yes, that would be wonderful." Sikorsky smiled for the first time since he had set foot in Washington. "And of course you can count on me voting the right way in the . . ." he hesitated for a moment before continuing, "in the Post-Vassily era which will soon be upon us."

"Good, Vlad, good. In fact excellent." The president slapped the smaller man heartily on the back, nearly knocking the martini from his hands. "And do feel free to go to the top floor. There is something extra, extra special—for your tastes."

Sikorsky flushed. He tugged at his tight collar. "My tastes? I—"

"Ah, enjoy, Vlad, enjoy. This life is too short." Zhabnov faded away into the crowd. Sikorsky ascended the stairs. How did he know?

A guard let him in while stopping others from entering the purple-curtained chamber. He was directed through a white door with the vice-presidential seal on it. It was dim inside. His eyes caught the motion of whips swinging through flickering candlelight. Two six foot tall, very robust women in black leather suits, slapped their whips impatiently across their thighs as they sat on a large bed. In the center of the room, on a plush white pile carpet, snakes slithered across the hog-tied struggling bodies of three naked young girls.

"Welcome," the taller blond women said. "Your wishes have been already taken into account here."

She walked quickly over to him and held her long cigarette holder with a lit cigarette in it against his hand. He winced as tears came to his eyes and the tiniest flicker of a smile to his mouth. "Welcome to Washington," she continued, grinding the glowing ashes into his open palm. The other woman was fooling with one of the snakes, guiding it up the leg of the youngest and prettiest of the girls. She guided it to the light fluff between the girls' thighs. The prisoner screamed but the room was triple soundproofed. The tall woman handcuffed the delegate and led him to the bed. The representative from Armenia would get his fantasies fulfilled tonight, courtesy of his benefactor—Zhabnov.

The main entertainment—for the less important personages to the D.C. festivities—was in the Senate theater. There seven women dressed in southern belle costumes flirted with dashing actors portraying dashing Russian soldiers of the Occupation. They giggled and drawled and they were each, in turn, musically and slowly disrobed—to reveal that each was a different kind of mutant—much to the guffaws of the bald delegates who watched. Women with four breasts, extra sex organs, hair covering their bodies . . . they danced and got nastier and nastier as the night went on.

In other sections of D.C. other entertainments abounded. For the highbrows the finest opera company in the world, The Washington Company, performed at Wolf Trap Auditorium to a packed house. Puccini's arias swept out into the cold air. In the Negro section to the east of the Potomac, where only the most daring of the Red delegates trod—and then only with beefy bodyguards—dingy barrooms filled with voluptuous femmes fatales who sang the blues from Bessie Smith to Reena Hoarness. Heroin was sniffed and shot up in the wooden booths. In the nearby basement of an abandoned machine warehouse, normally used for cock and pit bull fighting, two terrified black teenage girls ran hysterically around inside a fenced-in enclosure, trying to fend off sex with several large and well trained dogs. An appreciative crow watched them lose.

In the All Soviets Embassy on the other side of the airport, drunken delegates linked arms and did impromptu dances, spraining several backs as they tried to mimic the Mazurski dancers of Minsk who had performed earlier, flown in especially for the occasion. Vodka flowed like the Volga through the assembly of notables. Three giant roast pigs with apples adorning their orifices were paraded in to toasts and a mad rush at the juice-dripping treat.

In the New Southern Hemisphere Pavillion atop the former Smithsonian Museum, a stunned group of the most minor delegates watched in horror and amazement as lions devoured mutant men and women, captured freefighters, given only small knives with which to defend themselves. And so on throughout the city of Washington, D.C. where every nook and cranny contained some perversion, some act of violence or degradation took place for the satisfaction of the bureaucrats who ruled the Soviet Empire.

President Zhabnov sat wearily at his desk looking at the confidential analysis of swayed delegates drawn up by his intelligence staff. He had gotten at least another thirty delegates firmly in his grasp and the possibility of picking up ten or fifteen more. He would need only another twenty to have the premiership sewn up. Twenty men between him and world dominion. He looked up at the unfinished Stuart portrait of Washington across the blue room, where he pondered the affairs of state. He hated the damn thing but Vassily had forbade the removal or destruction of any of the White House's furnishings, saying that the preservation of history demanded that it be left untouched. But the Grandfather's days were nearly over. Perhaps Zhabnov would dispense with the hall of past president's pictures altogether—move a collection of his favorite American painter in instead. He adored those Keane's with their big eyes and untainted innocent mouths. Yes that would be nice. . . .

Zhabnov walked over to the laced windows and peered down into the snow covered rosebushes of the White House garden. The weathered bronze statue of a very heroic looking Premier Drubkin was ordering the launching of the First Strike that had decimated America. His hand was held up, frozen forever in time, giving the command to fire, the hand caked in glistening icicles as the temperature slowly dropped. It was now minus twenty degrees Fahrenheit. The premier's war had not affected the weather in a kindly way, but at least the capital of the Soviet Union wasn't radioactive, having been spared any close hits by high-rad nukes, so it was able to continue as the seat of power for the entire world.

Zhabnov wondered for the thousandth time what it was like to hear on the radio that you had only a few more minutes to live. Were the Americans resigned? Scared? Were they told? History tapes said the air raid sirens had gone off and broadcasts were made over radio and television about what was happening. But the history tapes were unreliable, having been rewritten a dozen times according to party ideologues, new lines of propaganda since the war. There was no denying that the Drubkin plan to destroy America while Russia escaped unscathed had gone at least partly awry. About twenty submarine-launched ballistic missiles and several cruise missiles had gotten through the killer satellite defensive network of the motherland. Because their trajectories were so low, the anti-missile systems had not detected them. Minsk, Odessa, Leningrad, Volgograd . . . all destroyed.

But we had won the war, and that was what mattered, Zhabnov thought, clearing his head of any doubts. Besides, if the intelligence analysis was correct, the history tapes said that the U.S.A. had been about to regain technical superiority and launch their own strike. Then the premier had done the right thing. Otherwise Americans would be sitting in Moscow today. Wouldn't they? Having power struggles and telling their Red slaves where to live and work. No, what is inevitable is inevitable.

It was inevitable as well that Zhabnov should rule the world once the Grandfather was gone. He would make a much better premier than that Killov, who was without question a madman and growing more psychotic by the moment. But Zhabnov had no illusions about the looming battle between the two of them. Killov was terribly powerful and clever. More clever than Zhabnov, even the president knew that. But Zhabnov now had a secret weapon that Killov had no idea of—the mindbreaker, a device that his own scientists had invented just months before. At first, the globe which covered a prisoner's entire head and slowly lowered laser probes into the brain cavity, burning away memory, causing pain more intense than could be borne by the strongest man, was used primarily for torture and trying to extract information from captured freefighters. And it had worked well, forcing several prisoners to reveal their hidden cities location, able to break through the hypnotic blocks that the freefighter's psychologists and hypnotists had been able to implant in them. But now his researchers had discovered another aspect of the machine: it could be used to change men's minds, rearrange them, alter the memory patterns and even the loyalties of anyone. Of course, many prisoners' brains were irreparably destroyed by the device, but then Zhabnov had more than enough workers to play with. They were, after all, his subjects, his toys, his to do with what he wished.

Thus came Plan Lincoln into being—without question, Zhabnov's peak of intellectual inventiveness. They would take American workers from a number of Red fortress cities and brainwash them, change their very brain patterns so that they thought they were Russian troops. Then they could be armed and sent out against their fellow citizens—the freefighters hidden in the mountains and valleys of the vast wastelands. It was ingenious. Zhabnov still smiled whenever he realized that *he* had thought of it. He had immediately diverted funds meant for the building of several new fortresses into the construction of Pavlov City—a hastily erected center that would be devoted entirely to transforming docile and submissive American workers into a new army for Zhabnov. An army that would give him a whole new power base that could be used against the rebels—and against Killov himself if it came down to that.

The city was now nearly complete and had been filled with over ten thousand of the mindbreakers. Already, thirty thousand men had been processed. Twenty five thousand of them had either died or been brain damaged beyond repair. But new projects always had a few bugs to iron out, all his scientists agreed. Soon Pavlov City would be turning out fighters for his new army by the thousands. Things were going well for him, very well.

Zhabnov whistled from between his ruddy jowls as he headed out of the Oval Office and down the hall to his sleeping chambers. He was glad that he was president of the United Soviet States and that he had two pink-faced young virgins drugged and ready in his huge presidential bed.

Four

It took nearly nine days of cautious riding, almost entirely at night along mountain trails thought impassable by the Reds, for the freefighters led by Rockson to reach Century City. They had gone down from the mountainside attack point to check out the damage they had caused the Russian truck convoy and had managed to capture five soldiers who had somehow survived the hellfire, one of them the second ranking officer of the fleet. The Rock Squad had then retreated back into deep wooded valleys and mountains toward the west where they had tethered their hybrids: large sturdy mutated horses that freefighters throughout America used as transportation. With the Russian prisoners tied up, they had made their way back to Century City, one of the most powerful of the seventy-three hidden rebel cities.

Three pine trees next to three aspens was the only sign of the main entrance into the underground fortress, home of Ted Rockson, Doomsday Warrior. The squad rode silently past the trees and into what appeared to be nothing but dense underbrush. But the brush parted easily and the party headed through a tunnel of vegetation and camouflage netting. A bluejay screeched just ahead of them.

"That's the signal this month," Detroit said to Rockson who rode lead. Detroit, who was the birdcall expert of the Rock Squad, put his hands over his mouth and gave out rapid renderings of a hoot owl. The jay screeched two times rapidly—and the owl responded with a long drawn-out hoot. The Russian prisoners marching behind the hybrids looked on curiously. They were short of breath at these heights.

Suddenly there was a grating noise. The huge granite boulder in front of them slid sideways and there appeared a quickly sloping concrete ramp lit by faint green phosphorescent overhead lights. Ted Rockson, the attack squad, and the Red prisoners headed down the tunnel entrance into Century City, home of over fifty thousand souls, comprised of twenty levels, with thirty thousand miles of electrical and water systems. As the hybrids' stone-hard hooves beat out symphonies of clatter in the long smooth-walled tunnel, Rock saw a glint of brightness ahead. The second doorway to the Debriefing Center—a large chamber where medical doctors and intelligence aides were seated. Rock and his men handed over their 'brids to members of the debriefing staff and walked through the wide door where Intel Chief Rath, his familiar gaunt face and hooked nose bobbing up and down, greeted them excitedly. He was anxious. So much depended on the success of the mission.

"Did it go well?" he asked, unable to contain his questions.

"Scratch one Red convoy," Rock said laconically. "And I mean scratch. We could hardly find any wreckage to look at when we went down to check damage."

"Wonderful, wonderful," Rath said, rubbing his hands together and beaming as if he'd just received his longed for Christmas present.

"The particle beams perform miracles," Rock continued. "Even knocked out their heavy metal tanks—the Soyaks—though it took a second to melt through their thick skins. That's one shipment of supplies that the Reds will never see again. I'd say it took us a total of ten minutes from commencement of attack to complete destruction of the fleet. It was something to see, Rath. Almost frightening. I felt as if I were seeing a new energy source being unleashed on the earth." Rock looked down, a strange expression on his face.

"You were, you were," Rath piped in. "A weapon that will drive the Reds from America. Oh Rock, this is a great moment. Perhaps one of the greatest in my life." Rath looked positively glowing. Unlike Rock he was not one to hide his feelings.

"Destruction, Rath, so much destruction," Rock said softly. "All my life I've spent fighting the Reds. Yet suddenly when I was holding that particle beam weapon in my hands and firing down I realized I had the power of God at my fingertips. The power of lightning, of earthquakes. I just wonder if man was meant to ever possess these kinds of weapons. For the first time in my life I actually felt unsure about what I was doing."

"But Rock, for God's sake, man. We're not killers. If the Reds would leave, we wouldn't follow them back to the Kremlin. We're not bent on world domination.

This is our land for Christ's sake, and these weapons will be used to get it back." Rath was almost shouting.

"And if the Reds should get their hands on these or discover the energy source? Then what?" Rock stared at the intel chief with glowing eyes, purple and aquamarine. Almost too intense to look into. "Can you imagine if the Reds had them?"

"They won't. You can be damn sure of that," Rath said firmly. "That's exactly why Dr. Shecter built in the explosive charges. The weapons can be blown up within seconds."

"Someday there's got to be an end to war, Rath," Rock said. "I'll fight. I'll fight until the day I die to free this land. But someday, someday," he was whispering, with a look in his eyes that Rath had never seen before. "Someday there must be peace. We can never forget that that is what we're fighting for. Never!" He looked sternly at the head of intelligence who shrank beneath the stare. "Anyway, the things work. That's for damned sure."

The phone rang on the wall and Rath reached over, picking the cordless receiver up. "Hello? Dr. Shecter! When are we expecting them?" He smiled at Rockson who let his own features soften. Rath certainly wasn't his enemy. Rock let a slow grin fill his face as Rath handed him the receiver.

The other end was a nonstop series of questions asked so fast that Rock could barely understand "Yes, things went well, sir. No, no casualties. Yes, the camera we brought to film the attack functioned perfectly." Rock waited a few seconds for the voice to stop and catch a breath. "Sir, instead of going over all this on the phone, why don't I come up and talk to you in person . . . good." Rockson put the phone back down on its mount. "I'll see you later after you get a look at the Red prisoners we brought in, including a top brass."

"All right Rock. And listen, I know—know what you mean. We do lose track sometimes of just what we're fighting for and why. But don't think that means we have forgotten—we haven't. Not a man in this city or I'll wager any other city. That's what defines us, Rock. Makes us different from the Reds. We fight in the name of life. They fight in the name of death."

"Thanks Rath," Rock said simply and headed toward the elevators and Dr. Shecter many levels below, in the bowels of Century City, built entirely beneath a mountain. He pressed his thumb into a lit glass square and the stainless steel elevator doors opened and shut the moment he entered. Rock descended the eighteen levels rapidly, the bottom dropping out of his stomach. He stepped out into the main level of the science section of Century City, and, as he strode down the antiseptically clean white floors, (Shecter was a stickler for cleanliness), he realized that he hadn't bathed for nearly three weeks and probably smelled like hibernating bear. Ah well, Shecter would have to put up with the earthy odors to assuage his curiosity.

Far down the curved hall, Rockson suddenly saw Shecter, his tall lean frame half stooped over in his omnipresent neck-to-ankle white smock, sliderule and calculator in his breast pocket ready for service at a moment's notice. Funny, the man has no title except scientist, Rockson thought, and yet everyone snaps to it, even he, Ted Rockson, when the doctor called for them. But after all, everything in the Free City had been made by the man: the power sources, the hydroponics, the weapons. The man was still churning out his technological innovations daily even at the age of seventy-eight and appeared to have no intentions of slowing down.

Dr. Shecter firmly shook Rockson's hand. "Good to see you back safe and sound. I had a funny feeling about this mission. But I'm glad to see that I was wrong." His fierce brown eyes stared straight into Rockson's own multi-hued eyes. He was one of the few who could or dared try. "Well?"

"You should have seen the attack. Those beams—they're beyond weaponry. I can only think of the word punishment," Rock said, "to describe the damage created by those black beams." The two men walked about a hundred feet back down the hall to Shecter's office where the scientist sat down behind his immense mahogany desk with as many drawers as he had ideas and every one of them neatly expounded, coded, and filed for future investigation. Rock collapsed in one of Shecter's overstuffed armchairs, resting his six foot three inch, two hundred twenty-five pound frame of steel-sinewed muscle for the first time in weeks. He glanced around at the doc's collection of scientific gadgetry that adorned the walls of the office. Models of the Liberator automatic rifle now in use by freefighters throughout America and Century City's main export to the other hidden cities. Miniature versions of his thermal engine which channeled steam and heat rising up from beneath the bedrock of Century City and turned it into enough energy to power Century City's living needs and industry. And oddities as well. Things in jars, floating in murky liquid that gave Rock the creeps. He'd seen some strange mutations in his day, but Shecter seemed to have gathered the most hideous ones and kept them on perpetual display. Embryos with scales and puckered little faces out of a nightmare, snakes with feathers and nearly human features, a bird the size of an eagle, black as midnight and covered with icepick sharp spikes. Things half hidden behind the clouds of liquid in which they were encased. Rock pulled his eyes away with a shudder.

"You like my collection?" Shecter asked, stoking and lighting his pipe. The sweet smell of cherry tobacco wafted across the room like a perfume. One of the few privileges of power that Shecter had taken—to take one of the hydroponic tanks for the growing of tobacco—a product he swore he needed in order to think. Nobody had dared object.

"*Like* isn't the word," Rock said, leaning back in the chair and letting his whole body just relax into the plush softness. It was only when he let his defensive systems down for a moment, his radar, that Rockson realized just how wound up he was. "I'm horrified and fascinated at the same time. I don't know if I'd want the damn things staring down at me all the time." Rock grimaced, looking up again at beady black eyes peering out of countless containers.

"These are my friends, Rockson. These are the inhabitants of our new world. Many of them will die out there. But some will survive. Oh yes, of that you can be sure. The world is changing, perhaps faster than any of us realize. The radiation that was laid down around the globe a hundred years ago is just now beginning its second stage of 'mutation-evolution' as I like to call it."

"Mutation-evolution?" Rock looked across the

wide folder-covered desk at the brilliant scientist whose head was nearly enshrouded in a halo of smoke. "I've never heard you use that expression before."

"It's something I've been musing over for the last several years Rock, and only just now am I starting to formulate a theory as to just what's happening out there. You see, there are two distinct stages in the mutation process from radiation. First, comes the immediate mutations caused by radiation. The next generation that is born—human, lion, plant life, whatever—will produce many disfigured and usually unviable creatures. Most of these will die out. These generations, those that survive that is, will also produce mutations similar to themselves, and most of these will die. But after about three or four generations, roughly a hundred years, the survival quotient starts evening out. Those mutations that remain have not just survived—they have become a new species adapted to life in this post-nuclear world. Those are not monstrosities," Shecter said, sweeping his hand toward the shelves containing the creatures. "Those are the new inhabitants of the earth, Rock." He looked at the Doomsday Warrior with an intense expression. "The old days are gone forever. The old species are extinct. People still think in terms of returning to the old days. Recreating things as they were. This is all a pipe dream. I don't talk about it too much. People need their illusions. But that's not how it's going to be. We're heading into a new phase in the history of the earth. For the first time, every creature on this planet will have evolved not from the hand of God, but from the hand of man. The atomic hands. We have repopulated the earth with our own 'monstrosities,' as you call them. But now they *are* the animals of our world. Just as you, Rockson, with your blue and violet eyes, your white streak of hair down your scalp, your strength and almost extrasensory perceptions. You are an adaptation of the human species as well—to deal with this strange new world. My people are dying out." Shecter looked down at his own skin and pinched it. "This flesh is not made for the world of today. There are two distinct species alive at this moment, Rock. Two human species. Just as Neanderthal and Cro-Magnon man competed for survival a hundred thousand years ago and the more equipped and intelligent survived. So today there are two species: Homo sapiens and homo mutations. The first is dying out; the second will take its place. I am extinct," the scientist said with stinging sarcasm. "Your people will live and rule the earth. The Russians don't even realize it but their days are numbered. Their bodies which are protected from the radiation have not evolved as the freefighters have out in the hotter zones of America. The Reds need elaborate survival gear to operate: masks, anti-radiation pills, decontamination. You can't go on like that forever. It's all just a holding action. In another hundred years, mark my words, there won't be a Homo sapiens alive on this planet. You, the homo mutations, will rule."

Rockson didn't know if he liked the sound of all this but he knew and respected Dr. Shecter as the most intelligent man he had ever met. The man was not in the habit of shooting off with half-baked ideas.

"Ah, but enough of all this endless speculation. Speculation is for old men like myself who have time to sit around and ponder the imponderables. It is men like you who act, make things happen. How did it go, Rock?" He leaned forward, putting his knobby elbows on the shiny desk and waited. "You said successful—how successful?"

"The mission was one hundred percent successful," Rock said simply. "I've never witnessed anything like it. It wasn't a battle—more like a shooting gallery. The Reds must have thought the Christian Gods were rising from the grave and extracting vengeance. We let a few get away so they could scare the shit out of Zhabnov and Killov. Let those two fine gentlemen stew in their own juices for a while."

"Effective—good. I trust the cameras were mounted before the attack and you filmed the whole thing so we can perform a computer analysis of every shot—any problems—"

"I think we got most of it. One camera about halfway through took a piece of shrapnel from a nearby Red tank shell and got blasted. But we got enough to provide some entertainment for you and your science staff," Rock said drily. "Hollywood style."

"Hollywood—what's—oh, of course. You and your history studies. Hollywood was where the ancients made movies for the masses. Right?"

"Yes. That whole part of the country—California, where the Hollywood studios were all located, was, as you know, hit so heavily with nukes that the San Andreas fault opened up and the whole damn thing sank. A second Atlantis. Why I've—"

"We'll have to discuss it some time, Rock," Shecter said abruptly, cutting Rockson off. "Did you have the film sent to processing? I'm dying to see the damn weapons in action, after puttering around with them here in the lab for months."

"McCaughlin was going to take them to the Audio Visual Section immediately. Give them a call." Shecter made a quick buzz to the film lab and was told the prints were ready and had come out clear as a bell.

"Reserve Screening Room two for me," Shecter said over the phone. "And chairs for twenty and—let's see, a big pot of coffee. I and my staff will be going over these films all night, I'm sure." He hung up with a smile. "It's looking good, Rock, very good." Shecter was beaming. He felt personal pride when the machines and labs of Century City were all functioning at one hundred percent. Woe to the lab worker or technician who stripped gears on a valuable piece of machinery or overexposed some important film or let a petri culture accidentally become contaminated with bacteria-ridden air. Then the science staff of Century City quaked in their proverbial boots, as Shecter was notorious for outbursts of temper when everything was not "just so."

The two most important men of Century City, possibly in all of America, walked side by side back down the slowly curving corridor to the elevators. Though nearly the same height they were contrasts: the man of science, stiff, stooped over with a slow deliberate gait of one always deep in thought; and of the man of action, the warrior, straight as an arrow, every step purposeful, every sense on alert. Rockson felt slightly strange as he walked alongside the great scientist. "Not human!" The words had a strange ring to them. So he and the rest of the "mutants" were an entirely new race. What did that mean? All his life Rock had thought of himself as a member of Homo sapiens, the human race—the sentient life form on the earth for fifty thousand years. Now, in a few sentences from Shecter, he had found out he was not, after all, who he thought he was. It felt strange. As if he were suddenly from another planet. But as he let the words sink into his bones he knew Shecter was right. He hardly ever saw normal wildlife in his treks anymore. Even when he was younger there had been the occasional deer, moose, bear that resembled the pictures of the creatures from before the war. But now. Now, one out of a hundred was a normal. The rest were all mutants: horned, tusked, spiked, multi-headed. It was the normals who were the odd ones now. And somehow that made Rockson closer to those murderous beasts out on the plains and wastelands of America than to Shecter and the other "normal" humans. He was one of the atomic freaks of nature who would inherit the world.

They walked to elevator bank five and took the ride up twelve levels. Shecter at his age didn't like the gut-wrenching speed the elevators moved at. In case of attack or emergency the closely packed underground city had to be able to react quickly, and instant accessibility to every section of Century City was vital. As they passed the floors, three to a level, in a whiz of motion, Rock thought about the origins of Century City: how the vast underground fortress of fifty thousand had started as two thousand rush-hour commuters, driving through a mountain tunnel of Interstate 70 about four hundred miles southeast of Denver, Colorado, had been sealed inside by atomic explosions that collapsed the entrances at both ends of the two mile structure; how they had organized and survived; how they had dug out after several weeks to see Red troop planes overhead dropping its occupation army; how the commuters had hidden and expanded the tunnel, using the machinery from their cars and their knowledge—and by the grace of God there had been knowledge aplenty in the tunnel: engineers, doctors, scientists, even a hydroponics expert. Nearly half the original inhabitants of the tunnel had died from radiation poisoning, from fear, from unknown causes. But the strong survived and reproduced and even, after a time, prospered. The name Century City was given to the tunnel as it slowly grew and reached out into the mountain above it to create more living and work room for the survivors. Century City—for it would take one hundred years for America to be free again and the inhabitants would make sure that that day came. And after one hundred years it still survived and was the greatest threat to Red hegemony in the world.

They arrived at their level and headed quickly to the screening room where Shecter's staff was already seated, note pads on laps, sharpened pencils in hand. They stiffened slightly as their mentor arrived and took his seat at the front of the oval-shaped film auditorium. The lights dimmed and Rock began narrating the film, explaining the action that was occurring. Shecter heard Rock's explanation of each maneuver but was more interested in later shaky hand-held close-ups of the damage to the tanks and trucks.

"Ah, just as I thought, Rock—some metals are more easily cut through. Look, there's still pieces left of some of the armored vehicles, the most modern of the Red mobile units—magnalloy. It appears to be slightly more resistant to the total destructive force of the particle than the other metals." His staff were madly scribbling in their lined notebooks every word from Shecter's mouth. "If the Reds find out that magnalloy is less damaged by the beams, they'll put every scientist from Red Square to the Crimea on double duty to come up with a defense. We'll be one step ahead of them and find out how to neutralize their neutralization." The science staff chuckled appreciatively, though Rock failed to see the humor.

The lights came on. Shecter shook Rockson's hand. "Good show. Now, it's up to us to go over these films with a fine-tooth comb." Rock exited the theater as Shecter's strong voice demanded "Show them from the beginning, gentlemen. . . ."

Five

Colonel Killov popped another Benzedrine pill into his narrow hawklike mouth. He had been up for days now taking the little yellow pills every three or four hours, sitting alone in his eightieth floor suite of offices at the top of the monolith—the center of all KGB operation in America, located dead center of Denver, Colorado. He was obsessed. Obsessed with one man—Ted Rockson—the so-called Ultimate American, as the peasantry called him. Rockson had dared attack him, had dared to hurt him. But even more, had dared to challenge the power of the man who saw himself as the most powerful and ruthless man in the world. And like Captain Ahab, he could think of only one thing—revenge. He looked even thinner and tenser than usual, his ramrod-straight body nothing now but bone and gristle, his black eyes wide and cold as the vacuum of space. He had been taking more and more of the pills lately, ever since his run-in with Ted Rockson several months earlier. His body trembled with an almost invisible shaking as he stared out the dark windows at the Rocky Mountains off in the distance, their black peaks silhouetted against the purple sky, writhing with pink and orange waves of atmospheric electricity.

Killov slammed his fist down on the black-marbled plastisynth table that curved around in a semicircle facing the ten foot high polarized picture windows, his gaunt face skull-like in the growing dawn.

"No one must know. No one must ever speak of what happened that night out on the Utah Plains," Colonel Killov, the supreme commander of all KGB forces in America muttered half madly to himself, not even realizing he was speaking. "No one must ever know of this defeat of mine out in the desert by a band of brigands." His mind couldn't stop returning to the scene of the battle. It had to be Ted Rockson and his men who had attacked Killov's squadron of attack helicopters, destroying all the gunships save his alone. He remembered the carnage and the black beams that the small band of freefighters had shot up at the choppers just when it seemed their fate was inevitably sealed by death. Killov had had many nightmares about those few moments.

"If I hadn't had that last second urge, that slightest caution to hang back as the fleet of black death's-head helicopters went in for the kill, I'd—" The rest of the thought remained in his mind, unspoken. He would be dead. Burned into a pile of smoldering, glowing metal like the others. The freefighters had come up with a fantastic new weapon, the likes of which Killov had never seen. How could they have made it? Their hidden cities couldn't be that advanced—could they? Capable of producing technologically advanced weaponry far ahead of the Russians? It didn't seem possible. And yet he had seen the evidence for himself. Had barely escaped with his life. Vassily and Zhabnov, the fools, believed that the freefighters were just ragtag groups of unshaven mountain men, but Killov knew. Perhaps he was the only one who truly understood that, for the first time in a century, the Red rule was threatened here in America.

It was growing lighter outside, the blood-red rays of the morning sun biting their way through the black purple skies of night. Surrounding his black steel and glass skyscraper were the towering snow-covered Rocky Mountains—and somewhere in those vast peaks of ice and pines lay Ted Rockson's hidden city. Killov glared out at the mountains angrily as if it were their fault that Rockson managed to escape capture by his elite KGB Death Squads again and again. As the red waves of morning light washed down over the blue slopes like blood dripping from the guts of some immense corpse, Killov popped several more pills. He had been taking so many of the things lately that he had to keep counterbalancing the effects of first one then the other; taking ups for hours and then feeling as if his head might explode through the ceiling, taking tranquilizers to force his enraged body to relax slightly. He had bottles of the drugs on a shelf behind his desk—pink ones, yellow ones, ovals, and squares. He could hardly remember what did what anymore and it hardly mattered anyway. Nothing could take his rage, his hate away from him, and that was what really powered Colonel Killov; the hatred for Ted Rockson—the only man who had ever outfoxed, outmaneuvered and out-willpowered him. Killov was not used to such games. Men had died instantly for much less. Red soldiers through the years had learned not to cross this hawk-faced, power-mad ruler. He was one of the three or four most powerful men in the world. And within months, if things went according to plan, he would become *the* most powerful man in the world.

The sun crept up slowly, inching its way above the pointed peaks that surrounded Denver like spears pointing the way to the stars. They were starkly beautiful now, turning red, purple, and orange as the sky grudgingly lost its panoply of stars. Silently he stared out at them. How could he defeat Rockson? How? And how could he wrest the empire from the dying Grandfather back in Mother Russia before Zhabnov took its reins. He had been pondering this for months and he had been toying with an elusive thought all night—slipping from his grasp as he was groggy from the pills. He'd have to cut back a little. There was a limit to everything, even for those who could get anything they desired. But he had an idea. A glimmer that burned stronger with each moment. What was that archaic American expression—kill two birds with one stone? Yes—that was it. Smash Rockson and use the captured deathray weapons he possessed against Zhabnov and the regular Red Army forces—quickly accomplish this before—

The phone rang with the force of a bomb blast in the quiet solitude of his eightieth floor office, jarring Killov from his murderous musings.

"Yes?" Killov said curtly. "What the hell is it?"

"Colonel, we have a report on the super weapons that were used on the convoy to President Zhabnov's Pavlov City, wiping the entire fleet out. The damage is the same as the sample wreckage you gave us to analyze. If I might ask where did those samples of burnt helicopter metal com—"

"None of your damn business," Killov retorted sharply. "What is the nature of the weapon that was used?"

"Sir, that's what's puzzling us. It's definitely not an explosive device. Although some mortar fragments were found, they did not contribute to the complete destruction of the armored vehicles and trucks of the convoy. Frankly sir, we've never seen anything like this. I've arranged to send some samples to the Central Metallurgic Institute in Moscow for ana—"

"You what? You fool!" Killov exploded into the phone. "What is your name and rank, idiot?"

"Petrin, sir. Lieutenant Petrin," the voice on the other end replied meekly.

"Listen Petrin," Killov said with ice in his voice. "Get those samples back or you're a dead man. You understand?"

"Yes sir," the voice gulped almost inaudibly. "They haven't been shipped out yet, sir. I'm sure I—"

"And call me as soon as they're retrieved. And in the future, idiot, if you have a future, don't send anything anywhere without asking me first. Is that clear?"

"Clear, sir."

Killov slammed the phone down so hard that it bounced up in the air several inches before settling back down into its cradle.

Why did he always have to deal with idiots? Here, he had the facilities, the armaments to destroy half the world and he couldn't capture one stinking American bandit. Meanwhile his own men didn't seem to know their ass from their elbows. This Petrin would have to be eliminated. The man was too much of a fool to work for him any longer. Besides he knew too much. Killov wrote the lieutenant's name down in a small notebook and popped another pill.

By now Rockson would have found out about Zhabnov's new brainchild of Pavlov City. The man always seemed to know what the Reds were up to almost as soon as they did. And since Pavlov City had been going up for nearly three months now and had begun bringing in workers from surrounding Russian fortress cities for brainwashing, Rockson would undoubtedly plan some kind of attack. Rescue the poor downtrodden workers whom Zhabnov wanted to turn into brainwashed soldiers to send out against their own countrymen—the freefighters. But this time Killov was one step ahead of Rockson. The best place to lay a trap for this "Ultimate American" would be Zhabnov's Pavlov City. Its ten thousand mindbreakers running twenty-four hours a day in attempts at converting vast numbers of workers into fighters would draw the rebel leader.

"And I'll be there when he does attack," Killov mumbled aloud. My KGB has the right to know what the hell Zhabnov is up to anyway. It could affect my chances to ascent to the premiership. For I and only I have the vision—a total empire—total subjugation of all the world. And the complete eradication of all resistance. Vassily was too softhearted to do what was necessary and Zhabnov too stupid. No, it is up to me. It's my destiny to create the first total world empire that the earth has ever known.

Yes, he would lay a trap and get hold of the super weapons that Rockson now possessed. They would attack—he knew it. He would lay a trap with elite troops. He had to be damn sure that Zhabnov didn't get hold of the super weapons. Whoever had them would win the fight of succession that was already increasing in intensity in the Presidium and would soon spread to worldwide confrontations as supporters of the different factions began battling it out. His men had been able to sway ten more pro-Zhabnov delegates to the hastily assembled party summit in Moscow, and tonight a plane carrying nearly fifty pro-Zhabnovs back to Russia from the president's sex parties would be blown up over Siberia. But still it wasn't enough. Once Vassily kicked off, and that would be any day now, since Killov had his men feeding poison to the premier in his sickbed in the Kremlin, the struggle for succession would come to a head.

It would all be decided within the next few weeks. He would win or face execution. He had thought the rotund Zhabnov a total fool—until Captain Yablonski had tried to assassinate Killov two months earlier by lunging at him with a hypodermic filled with cyanide. Mindbreaker probes had failed to reveal who had given the command to him. Yablonski had been under some sort of powerful mind block that literally destroyed his brain when the mindbreaker went to work. But there was no doubt that the order had come from Zhabnov—to eradicate Killov before the ailing premier died.

The Grandfather was more concerned with the life of some trees than with the survival of the empire—trying to block the use of any more nukes. The man was a throwback—good thing he was near death. And when he finally passes away I will help carry the casket in Moscow as it parades through Red Square as will Zhabnov and the others who are vying for power, and we will all weep crocodile tears. And then the battle of succession.

He stared out at the snow-covered peaks of the Rockies which now blazed as if aflame from the brilliantly clear rays of the sun. I will rule everywhere. The world—the whole world. But he must have those super weapons. Everything depended on it. There was no need for advice on this matter. He would order Gernik and the other KGB generals to assemble a joint force of elite fighters with 3-4-5 gas to take over Pavlov City. According to conventions still in effect—three hundred KGB members must be permitted within any army fort without advance clearance or special permission. This would be the battle that would win the world. Like the trojan horse of the ancient Greeks he would get his men in and then . . .

The rest of the morning and afternoon he made plans for the takeover. Detailed maps and plans of the huge Pavlov City complex were brought into his office. At three o'clock he assembled his top staff and told them of the attack. He himself would lead it. This was too important to leave to underlings. The generals were eager to at last display their power. At last they would be allowed to fight their rivals—the regular Soviet Army. Russian against Russian—it had to happen.

The meeting had just ended, the last few officers getting final instructions from Killov when the red scramble phone from Moscow rang.

"It's Menzies, sir. Dr. Menzies of the Kremlin Medical Institute," a voice said nervously thousands of miles away.

"Ah yes, doctor," Killov said with as friendly a tone as the KGB chief ever got in his cold voice. "How is *it* going?"

"I'm afraid I have bad news, sir," the doctor said quickly. "The Premier is as tough as a steppes' rat. He's just not succumbing to our treatments."

"But you're still injecting him with the poison?"

"Yes, Your Excellency—but—"

"Increase the dosage. Double it—triple it."

"But, sir, an autopsy would immediately detect that amount of poison. We—"

"I'll worry about the autopsy, doctor, you worry about getting the premier into the next life, or you may see it yourself much quicker than you had ever thought possible. Vassily must die within the next two weeks. You hear me—MUST!" Killov slammed the phone down. Damn—was he the only one who knew how to get things done? It seemed like every job he had given to an underling recently had been botched. If those fool doctors didn't get cracking, allowed Vassily to linger on, even get stronger, Killov's situation could deteriorate drastically. If the premier died today he could swing the votes necessary to take control. But a few more weeks and . . .

The three conspiring doctors, Sverdlov, Minkin, and Menzies were in their meeting place, an old inn ten miles outside of Moscow where they could be assured that the premier's ever-present microphones were absent. They had each come by a roundabout route to insure they weren't being followed, and they sat huddled over bowls of borscht which none of them ate but merely stirred the thick muck with their forks. They sat next to one another, discussing what had gone wrong with their poison plot. They spoke in whispers, turning every minute or so to see who was near them—only a few old peasants soaking up gravy from their greasy bowls with big crusts of bread.

"He's healthier than ever," Minkin said nervously, running his hands through his long white beard. "It doesn't make sense. The poison was supposed to accumulate in his system."

"Do you think that servant of his, that nigger, might have had something to do with it? It's rumored that he has Rasputin-like powers. The premier trusts him totally. He is the only one the Grandfather lets come near him," Sverdlov said bitterly.

"No, that's ridiculous," Menzies said, sweeping his hand across his face as if sweeping the thought away. "The nigger, Rahallah is his name, is just a slave. The premier cannot be that senile that he lets a slave tell him what to do."

"But the Grandfather won't even let us get near him anymore to give him the injections for the cancer we told him he has," Minkin said angrily. "The closest we can get is to that damned nigger who swears he gives the premier the doses. But how do we know? How the hell do we know? If he was getting the doses he would be dead by now."

"Killov is asking what's going on," Menzies said, his eyes darting around nervously. "He said if something doesn't happen soon to our dear premier, we may take his place in the ground. What am I to tell him?"

"Tell him we can't get access to the premier anymore, that the plot has failed," Sverdlov, the youngest of the conspirators, said.

"No! No!" the other two doctors both croaked out at once. "He'll have our hides if we say that," Minkin said, his eyes opened wide in horror at the younger man's suggestion. The fool!

"No, we must tell him that suspicions have been raised at the Kremlin and that it is more difficult but that we are working on it and shall soon succeed," Menzies said firmly. "That the premier is sinking fast—maybe a miracle will kill him and save us. Because, gentlemen, in case you don't realize it, it has come down to that—either the premier or we shall soon be dead."

"Do you know what I think?" said Sverdlov, the youngest, stroking his cherubic red cheeks, his face eerily cast in the overhead shaded light that hung just above them, twisting ever so slightly in the breeze that leaked in under the doors and windows from the freezing Moscow night. "I think the black man is a wizard—that he's part of a world conspiracy of niggers to take over when the premier dies." The others laughed for a moment. Then all the breath seemed to go out of their laughter as they stared at the youngest's milky eyes.

"Seriously?" asked Menzies. "You believe that?"

"I do. Even as a scientifically trained physician I do believe in magic—witchcraft. These blacks, they should have all been killed right after the war. Why we let the darker, inferior races survive is beyond me. The world should have been totally cleaned when we had the chance. The dark races have the power to steal a white man's soul. My grandfather told me many tales of—"

"Enough! Enough tales of terror in the night," Menzies snapped. "I'm returning to Moscow. We must all insist we treat the premier personally. Put every bit of pressure we can on his senior staff. Perhaps even tell them we think the nigger is poisoning the premier's mind. When we gain access to the Grandfather—a triple dose. Do it right once and for all."

"But what of an autopsy?" Minkin asked, his voice trembling.

"Bah! Once the premier is dead, Killov will take power and we will be protected. And then we will be rewarded handsomely for our risks."

They agreed to use every connection they had in the Kremlin to directly administer the poison. They set up a meeting for the following week and walked out to their separate limos parked outside. The drivers were roaring the engines to keep warm as snowflakes began falling. It was minus twenty degrees and dropping fast. They'd have to get back to Moscow quickly or the roads might well become impassable. That was all they needed now. To be stuck in some twenty foot high snowdrift and not be found until the following spring.

Six

Morning began peacefully enough in Fort Nijinski. Or as peacefully as it ever did for the American slave laborers of the Russians. Every Red military fortress was built next to a large concentration of factories where American workers were forced to labor six days a week in return for half rotten food, drab clothing, and what were called "worker's housing units" which the Russians had put up when they first came in with their occupying armies nearly a century before. Shantytowns in fact was what they were. Pitiful hovels made of rusted tin, disintegrating cardboard—whatever the Americans could get their hands on to create some sort of shelter. The original two-story concrete housing units had long ago crumbled into dust, and the Russians had henceforth not paid much attention to their American worker's needs. That was their problem.

The world of the American workers of Fort Nijinski was dog eat dog at best. There were nearly ninety thousand of them crowded into a twenty block area of ruins, hovels, subterranean lairs. Dirty, disease ridden, the American workers were expected to put in twelve hours a day in the Red factories working at grueling labor: making clothes, operating canning machines which packed agricultural produce into cans by the ton, simple machine manufacturing, and the dyeing of animal hides. Virtually all the goods would never be used by those that made them—Americans, that it. The production was destined for Russia—the all consuming, mother empire. The center of the world that sucked in goods from its slave states around the globe, leaving little behind for those who produced them. Nearly five hundred million people working to feed the Russian bureaucracy of seventy-five million which ruled the earth. What little that remained after the shipments back to Russia and after the Red occupying armies had been fed and clothed the Americans were allowed to have.

The workers put in their sweaty, back-breaking hours and then returned to their filthy lairs each night. Rats as big as cats ran through the tortured, twisted alleyways of the American sector. Gaunt dogs fought with one another for the few grim scraps that filtered down onto the dirt streets. And the American workers, always hungry, always on the verge of illness, their eyes long devoid of color or hope, struggled to live. Yet somehow they survived. They had no choice but to keep going even in these horrible circumstances. The instinct to survive is maddeningly powerful, even when the mind wishes to end it all. Only one thing gave them hope—the freefighting Americans. Even in their downtrodden condition they swapped stories of the freefighters; how they had blown up another Red convoy, how they had committed daring acts of sabotage inside the Red fortresses around the country. Too terrified and beaten to actually stand up to the Reds themselves, still they cheered their warrior brothers and sisters on, daring somewhere deep inside themselves to hope that perhaps someday . . . Occasionally one of the workers, slapped around too much, fed up with such a life of nothingness, would escape from the Red forts and make his way through the high-rad wilderness. A few survived and eventually made contact with freefighting forces where they were interrogated thoroughly to make sure they weren't Red plants. Then they were welcomed with open arms.

But more often those who tried to flee their living hell were consumed by the harsh world of 2089: eaten by one of the many carnivores that roamed the nukelands or destroyed by the broiling sun, the freezing nights. Their lives as dumb servants for the Reds had hardly prepared them for the dangerous life of the outer world. Their lack of decent food for so long made them weak, unable to sustain more than simple actions for very long.

Thus were the workers of America condemned to lives of suffering, lives that usually ended before the old age of forty-five or fifty. Born into poverty and slavery, living out their lives in the dank factories and then dying, skinny, starving, often alone, in the back of some Godforsaken alley.

Yet even within this framework of suffering the Reds were no longer content to let things proceed as usual. According to President Zhabnov's directives sent out to all the midwest fortress cities Plan Lincoln was now in full effect. Each fort was responsible for shipping half of their workers to Pavlov City for processing in the mindbreakers. They would be turned into zombie soldiers and sent out to fight their own freefighting American brothers. Their Red masters, pulling the puppet's strings, would stay safely behind the walls of their impenetrable military enclaves.

On the morning of Nov. 15, 2089 A.D., a morning like a thousand others—gray-pink sky cracked with spiderwebs of glowing green from low flying strontium clouds, still highly radioactive after a century, Smith-14 woke with a start on his small sweat-stained cot. Where was he? He had to shake his head to try to remember. In bed! He had been drinking last night. Drinking alcohol from stolen medical supplies from the Reds. He looked around the filthy gray basement dwelling where other sleeping workers lay on blankets, towels, pieces of cardboard, or just the hard-packed cold dirt floor. They lay strewn like the dead, arms stretched out, legs twisted weirdly behind them in impossible positions. The living dead. Smith-14 shared this subterranean "home" with twenty-five others, all of them men who worked in his factory—the Norsky Uniform Plant—where they produced uniforms for Russian Army troops.

In the distance factory whistles began their shrill screams signaling wake-up time—six o'clock in the morning. The workers had to be at their jobs by six forty-five or face punishment: fewer food coupons or after several offenses a visit to the dreaded KGB Worker Regulation and Control Section. The laborers around the basement room slowly roused themselves moaning and grumbling. Unwashed feet kicked stubbly faces. Lice crawled from scalp to flaking scalp.

Matted hair hung down in the musty moist air. The stone walls of the basement were cold and sweated with the ooze of the night's frigidity meeting the heat of the sun's first rays which looked hesitantly through a single foot wide window at the upper edge of one of the walls. The ray was like a golden blade of hope in the middle of the morning darkness.

The workers were depressed, lethargic. It was hard to rouse themselves for yet another day of meaningless grinding toil, especially after their one day off, the day before, on Sunday. Even the Reds had to acknowledge they needed one day to rest. They were, after all, human. They had spent the day consuming gallons of gut-wrenching alcohol trying to drink themselves into oblivion. They had drunk and drunk and then fought with one another, punching each other's faces until they were black and blue. When one is unable to attack one's true enemy one turns to those closest. Now they awoke, puking their guts out, aching as if every nerve and muscle in their bodies were on fire. But the penalties for not showing up at their jobs was something they didn't wish to think about. They had all visited the KGB Punishment Sector and once was usually enough.

So they rose slowly, pulling on their ragged garments, splashing dirty water from a large wooden barrel onto their faces. They made feeble attempts at combing their hair into place in front of a large mirror that had been cracked into a jigsaw puzzle of shiny fragments held in place with tape. Smith-14 looked at himself in the mirror. An unrecognizable face stared back. Who was this? Big bloodshot eyes bulged from a chalky sunken face. Once he had been handsome, somewhere back in the distant past. There had been a girl, a young girl with blond hair. He couldn't remember her name. The KGB had taken her away one day for their personal use. He had never seen her again. The past—so painful, razor blades piercing layers of repressed rage and desire.

The rest of the inhabitants of the basement fixed their matted hair into place in the mirror, the prize possession of the basement dwellers. They headed, stumbling, eyes blank and dull, up a wooden flight of stairs and out a door half off its hinges to the dirt-paved street outside. There, other workers were already walking in long lines, few talking or moving with any vigor. They placed one foot down after another, plodding toward their fate.

Smith-14 joined the migrating throngs. He felt strange today. He had had the dreams again. Weird, disturbing dreams with much blood and screaming. He knew he was more than what he was. That inside this mind and body of a scrawny drone was an intelligent man. A man who had been imprisoned all of his thirty-two years of life within the walls of the Russian enclave of Fort Nijinski. Attacked from without by the Red guards for the slightest infraction, attacked from within by his own mind, his own unconscious. The dreams were getting worse everyday now. Dreams of bloody teeth opening and closing around his head and body. Of radioactive creatures from far out in the glowing wastelands pursuing him, catching him and ripping him to shreds with razor claws. Nowhere was he free. No place to run, no place to hide. He felt sick inside as if a disease that had long laid dormant had suddenly sprung to life. A chill coursed through his bones, his heart. He had had enough. Enough of this life. Life? Ha, it was a joke. The others tried to pretend that there was something to live for—their next drink, getting a few extra food coupons once in a while, screwing some grimy hooker every month or two, and spending a full week's worth of food coupons to do it, too. They all pretended that this living hell was something worth living for. But he knew. Smith-14 knew the truth. It had lain hidden, too. That was it. The disease he felt erupting inside him was the truth. He had caught the incurable malady of seeing clearly, and the pain of his situation was unbearable.

He walked with the other workers down the straight gridlock of dirty streets. Lines of them, streams, then brooks, then a river of the gray and black-garbed slaves heading toward the looming concrete structures that housed the factories. Aimless, windowless—the Reds treated the cattle better.

Suddenly there was noise, yelling just ahead. A checkpoint. The Reds had set up a large wooden barricade blocking the entire main street of the American sector that led into the Russian factory area. Squads of Russian elite troops lined the sides of the intersection, their rifles aimed at the crowds. A captain, beefy, nose as red as an apple, crisscrossed with bursting veins from too many years of too much vodka, shouted out orders over a megaphone.

"All those with even numbers to the right. Those with odd numbers to the left." The river of workers was being cut in two. One half of the work force was sent on to their factory jobs, the other half to . . .

Some of the workers who were being siphoned off grew alarmed. Large trucks awaited them just the other side of the electrified barbwire fence that separated the two sectors of the fortress. The Red troops herded them onto the trucks which stood parked in long rows, nearly fifty of them. They loaded truck after truck which, once filled, immediately tore off out of the fort, the American workers packed inside like sardines with only holes drilled in the side to provide air. Some of the workers began resisting, more out of fear than bravery, but were instantly met with officers holding electric cattle prods who quickly shocked the resisters on their way.

Smith-14 was even numbered and therefore destined for the trucks. He tried to walk past the gate but a guard asked to see his identity number tattooed on his upper arm. Smith-14 rolled up his sleeve and the guard looked at the identification mark which had been burned on years before but was still red and ugly as the day he had been marked. The guard whipped the butt of his Kalashnikov up in a sudden arc, smashing Smith-14 in the side of the face, ripping open his cheek to the bone. Smith-14 fell to the damp ground, pain resounding through his brain like the echoes of a scream.

"Get the fuck over there, scum!" the guard snarled. But Smith-14 had had enough. Something inside of him snapped. Some little thread that had held him down all these years, that had made him obey all the rules, that had pretended that everything was somehow all right, was gone. He knew that he must die. Now! He would not go into the trucks to God knows where to suffer more pain, more torture. He would die today, now. But he would take as many of the Red animals as he could.

As he lay on the ground trying to focus his eyes, trying to make the excruciating pain in his head go away, he thought of all the times the Russians had abused him in his dismal life—had commanded him, had screamed at him, hit him, kicked him, beat him. He thought of the shame, the humiliation, and the pain. And he reached in his back pocket where he had it stashed—his weapon wrapped in a greasy rag. He took it out behind his back as the guard turned his head for a second as another worker made a break for it. Several Reds fired and the fleeing man fell to the ground skewered with 7.2mm slugs. Smith-14 took the jagged piece of glass from his pocket and held it firmly in his hand. It was long and narrow, shaped almost like a knife and sharp, terribly sharp. Smith-14 had killed twice with it already. Holding the rag around the bottom, wider edge of the fifteen inch weapon, Smith-14 leaped to his feet and ran toward the distracted guard.

"What the—" the guard stuttered, sensing the motion. He turned and saw a flashing object in the worker's hand coming toward him. Smith-14 ripped the glass across the Russian's throat. It sliced the white flesh open. A curtain of bright red blood splashed out of the throat cut from ear to ear. The guard fell to his knees gurgling madly as he gasped for air but found only blood. Smith-14 ran toward the next guard who also had his back turned and his rifle aimed at yet another dashing worker. He stabbed the glass knife forward with all his might through the soldier's upper back. The shiny tool of death went in deeply, cutting into the Russian's heart from the back. He threw his arms in the air and fell forward, blood pulsing out of his gashed back from the severed but still pumping heart.

Several of the other Red troops saw what was happening. They whipped their rifles around, trying to get a bead on the mad American killer. But Smith-14 began running, dodging, twisting. He dove on another Russian, stabbing up from below into the man's groin which exploded in a shower of red. Then another. He was a killing machine powered with the accumulated rage of a lifetime of submission. He cut and sliced, charging through the troops. Bullets began making contact. His arm, then his calf were hit. But he felt no pain. He killed and killed again. Three, four, five—and as he killed he screamed out. "Join me! Die like me! They'll kill you anyway."

The Russians trained their rifles on the yelling mob. Some of the workers began moving in on them, their faces weird, contorted, their mouths moving, issuing forth unintelligible cries of anger. The panic-stricken troops began firing. The first row of workers closest the fence fell but the next group behind them charged and then the next. The Reds opened up with everything they had, firing down from two concrete towers on each side of the entrance with machine guns. They fired even into their own troops trying to stop the rebellion before it exploded. Bodies lay everywhere, writhing, crawling along the blood-soaked ground, leaving trails of their torn flesh.

Still Smith-14 surged forward, now inside the Red ranks slashing away. An officer came at him, his pistol drawn. He got a bead and fired, catching the mad American on the right side of the stomach. Smith-14 lurched forward, slicing at the officer's face. The glass made contact just below the temple and ripped the top of the Russian's skull open. The glass knife slid across the eyeballs of the soldier, cutting them in half like boiled eggs. Bubbles of white liquid followed by a gush of blood oozed out of the eyeless sockets as the Red screamed, his hands covering what had been his eyes. He fell to the dirt, letting out a cry that sent shivers up the spines of the other Russian troops.

The endless lines of workers charged. The unrest turned into a riot and then a pitched battle. The workers knew the trucks meant something horrible, more horrible than anything they had ever experienced in their already miserable lives. The hysteria of the mob took over. They had no fear of dying, only a desire to kill. To strike back at their Russian tormentors. They charged the lines of Russian troops who fired as they retreated. Four hundred Russians against ten thousand and more all the time as the crowds behind the forward workers kept coming from their basement lairs, their alleyways, their hidden sleeping holes.

The Americans fell to their deaths by the hundreds but continued to sweep forward, an avalanche of anger, punching, kicking, trampling the Russian troops to death. They grabbed whatever weapons they could find and fired back. The Red troops continued to fall back as many were torn to pieces by the insane mob. Nearly a hundred of them lay on the dirt roadways which converged at the gate separating the Russian and American sectors of the fortress. The rest of the Red troops fled back behind the metal fence under the cover fire of the machine gun posts. Reinforcements were frantically called in over the tower radio. The workers charged the fence, recoiling at the highly charged metal. They fired with their captured weapons up and across at the Russian gun emplacements. The huge square where the Reds had been totally in control just minutes before was now filled with howling Americans. Screaming in happiness, feeling power for the first time in their lives. It felt wonderful.

"We are free!" screamed Josephson-28.

"They are scared. They are cowards!" yelled out Perkins-209.

"See them run from us," the crowd yelled in glee. They fired their captured weapons at every Russian uniform they could see and ran in circles, grabbing at each other, their eyes bright with the excitement of the newly powerful. All their lives they had lived in fear and trembling of every Russian soldier. Never had they been able to strike back. And now, together, by the thousands, they had killed hundreds of their hated enemy. The streets were theirs.

"We are free! Free! We won the streets!" Everywhere the voices rang out in a chorus of gleeful rage. Smith-14 lay dying in the blood-stained dirt, the still twitching eyeless corpse of the dead Russian officer lying across his legs. He was doomed but he smiled as he saw his brothers yelling in victory, dancing with the frenzy only the newly liberated can ever feel. They *were* free, he thought. All of them. It would only last minutes, at most. Smith-14 knew that. They all knew that. They had existed in misery too long to have any illusions about their reality. The Reds would call in their death machines, their helicopters bristling with firepower and they would fill the square with gas and riddle the workers with white-hot slugs that would rip them into so much red meat on the ground.

But for now. For these few moments. For the first time in his life, Smith-14 was a free man. It felt so good. His eyes slowly closed to remain shut forever. But the smile on his slowly cooling gaunt face stayed firm and sure.

Seven

Ted Rockson sat back on the bed in his private living chamber and breathed out a deep sigh of tiredness. Sometimes it seemed that every moment of his life since he had been eight years old, and had fled from the Russian soldiers who had massacred his family, had been filled with fighting and death. He should feel wonderful that the particle beam weapons had performed so successfully, yet he couldn't get the images of so much destruction out of his mind. Never in his thirty-four years of life had he ever doubted himself or his mission to rid America of her enslavers. And it wasn't that he questioned the need to chase the Reds all the way home to Moscow. It was just that he held the power of the gods in his hands for a few moments and it scared him.

He wasn't a god—just a man. Perhaps the toughest man on earth but still, a man, mortal, imperfect. He wasn't used to self-doubt, or self-analysis, and it felt peculiar, not particularly pleasant. He punched out a code on the computer panel next to the body-contoured plastibed and a small bar slid out from a wall enclosure. Rock poured himself a double scotch, another of Shecter's miracles. All the drinks in Century City were based on purified alcohol distilled from potatoes grown in tanks—hydroponics, but Shecter and his crew had come up with flavorings that gave the flat-tasting alcohol the tongue-tingling flavor of all of America's old liquors—from gin to scotch to bourbon. No one really knew if this was just how it had been in the old days, but no one cared either, not after a few sips of the fiery brews.

He drank slowly. He wasn't a drinker, but he needed this one. He was changing, maturing, growing a little older, seeing too much—who could say for sure. He had felt it first after returning from the trip to the Far West. Little lines were etched around his eyes, the white streak down the center of his midnight black hair was tinged with silver. But his rock-hard muscles were still as strong as ever, and his senses, his eyes, his ability to react instantaneously to any attack, were if anything, even sharper.

The visiphone on the white alumisynth table next to his bed beeped and Rona Wallenda's face appeared on the small screen.

"Rock, it's me. I—I want to see you. Why didn't you call, I've been—"

"Rona, I was going to beep you in a minute," Rockson said, switching on his end of the circuit so she could see him. He raised his glass to her image. "I swear!" He grinned the perpetual lopsided smirk that she knew and loved so well.

"I bet, mister," she said sarcastically. "Why I bet you've got some girl hidden under the bed right now. I know your type." Her beautiful green eyes flashed with half real indignation.

"Not one, three, Rona," Rock answered sardonically, taking another sip of the delicious pseudo scotch. "You know a man like me needs more than one."

"Well, this woman is equal to any three wenches you could ever dig up," Rona snapped back, tossing her mane of shimmering red hair behind her alabaster shoulders. She softened suddenly, realizing that her coy barbs were not quite taking the conversation in the direction she wanted. "When will I see you?" she said, her voice now seductively soft. "I've missed you terribly."

"I've missed you, Rona," Rock said softly. "Let me just let these muscles uncoil. Give me half an hour, baby."

"Sure Rock. I'll be in the gymnasium." She smiled, revealing perfect pearly teeth and then clicked off. The image slowly died on the screen.

Rock sipped the drink through his teeth, letting the scotch sift down through his tongue and throat, and thought of the woman who had just beckoned him. Half the men in Century City would have given their right arm to spend a night with Rona. Her beauty was breathtaking. A descendant of the Wallenda gymnastic and tight-rope walking family of the mid-twentieth century, she had been trained as a child in all the circus skills. She had traveled around the country with her father, giving performances with a small circus, but secretly gathering information as they entertained Russian troops inside their fortress cities and passing it on the freefighting forces. Until her father was caught with the plans of one of the largest munitions dumps in the country. He had been summarily shot without benefit of trial, jury, or any of the other trappings that the Reds had dispensed with since their takeover. Rona had barely escaped with her life, being sneaked out of the fort underneath a stack of hay in a mule-drawn wagon. She had joined the free forces of Century City where she had lived ever since. She kept up her gymnastic training and under the tutelage of Ed Chen, the Chinese-American martial arts expert of the hidden city, had become an expert in karate and jiujitsu. Her body was as strong and firm in its feminine form as was Rockson's in its male solidity.

Rona, beautiful Rona, Rock mused. The woman who was always waiting for him—to make love with him once again before another dangerous mission took him away. Their relationship played second fiddle to the realities of the war against the Reds. A hit-and-run relationship, warm, sexual but never a romance in the sense that people who expect to live past tomorrow have—with dreams of the future, with sweetness and sentiment. So Rona had to be content with living for each day with Rockson. Savoring the moment, enduring stoically each leaving of the man she loved. Such was love in 2089 A.D.

She sat waiting for him in the meditation chamber where the fighters and workers of Century City went to restore their psychic strength, strength of mind, of health, of will to live, for life could often be hard, terribly hard. She stared at the symbols on the walls—cultural remnants of the once great American civilization: a cross, a wheel, a six-pointed star, a crescent moon and star, a circle with a black and white snake down the middle—the religions of long ago merged now in meditative understanding that all is one—the cosmic mind and the individual mind all inexplicably one.

Rock came in silently as Rona sat yoga style on the floor lost in the subtle state of transcendence as Chen had taught—the peace of the void—luminous, empty, friendly, indifferent. He walked over to her and kissed her softly on the forehead. It was like the stars falling from the firmament above into her expanded mind, a mind that at that moment was all things and nothing. Without further words Rock sat about five feet away from her and they both were soon riding in that celestial realm of near death, their pulses slowed, their agitations halted as all men and women need from time to time to restore themselves to the basic thought of life—it is good. The creation, the essence of life . . . good.

The session, which she was already a half hour into when Rock arrived, lasted until the automatic meditation gong's sonorous chime pierced the air softly but insistently, demanding that the meditators return to the real world. Slowly they came round and stood up, shaking out the stiffness of their joints. They embraced softly, tenderly and then they walked arm in arm silently towards Rona's living quarters on C level. Still without words, only smiles and the glow of each other's aroused eyes they undressed one another as soft music—a composition of Rona's (formed after a deeper than usual meditation a year earlier), streamed out from speakers mounted high on the walls. Strange yet soothing sounds from a synthesizer, sounds of nature—of whales singing, of stars spinning with a sizzling symmetry across the skies, of grass growing, of opposites joining together.

They lay down on her bed and pressed one another close, flesh against flesh and descended onto the cool purple sheets of bliss. Rona's long supple pale body, her flaming red hair strewn across the pillow, her large firm upturned breasts crowned with the cream-colored white aureoles so prevalent among mutant women, pushing up, demanding Rock's lips and tongue. He caressed and sucked the hard nipples and slid his powerful hands down along her spine, sending shivers through her body. His violet, aquamarine eyes met her bright clear green eyes as she pressed her full strawberry lips to his. The passion swept over them and her hand searched for and found his manhood now swollen to its full size. She groaned the groan of the female about to be entered, reveling in the feeling. He moved his lips over her face, her neck gently perfumed with the scent of her moist sex. He moved her thighs apart with his dark veined hand and opened her with his fingers, sliding the fleshy lips apart. Then he rolled on top of her and drove home.

He woke with a start, the insistent beep of his belt beeper still attached to his pants which lay thrown on the floor. The beeps came every second, demanding his attention.

"Damn! Won't they ever leave me alone," Rock snarled as he detached himself from the warm Rona, her eyes still closed, her arms trying to hold onto the man who seemed to always be leaving her.

"Rockson here," he snapped into the mike on the small square beeper. "What the hell do you want?"

"Rock? This is Rath," the voice on the other end said somewhat surprised at the vehemence of the Doomsday Warrior. "I'm sorry to have to disturb you. I know you haven't even had a chance to rest up but—but I think you better get down here. We're using the mindbreaker device we captured from the Reds on that Red officer you took prisoner and—"

"All right, all right, I'll be there in ten," Rock said and snapped the off button down. He turned back to Rona who was sitting up now, looking angry.

"Oh Rock let them screw off. Stay with me." She sat up, the sheet only covering her legs. Her large breasts stood straight out, bright red hair draping down over them as if coyly hiding them.

"I've got to go, Rona. This officer is the highest ranking Red we've ever captured. The information he reveals could be incredibly important. You know we must come second, Rona. Our desires, our needs, must be subjugated to the needs of our country. Someday, perhaps someday—"

"Oh fuck off then," Rona said, her eyes filling with tears. She dove under the sheets, hiding her pain from the man she loved. She hated to show any weakness to men, especially Rockson. He dressed quickly, confused, angry himself, but knowing he had to go. He kissed the shape beneath the sheet and said, "Sorry baby." Then he headed out the door without looking back.

Rockson made the trip to the interrogation area within five minutes of receiving the call from Rath. He walked into the brightly lit room, antiseptically clean, where the captured Russian officer was now strapped into one of the Red mindbreakers that had been taken from a convoy several months before. It was the newest addition to the Russian armory of torture devices capable of producing exquisite pain in the brain of anyone strapped into the wretched machine. It had already been used successfully by the Reds to break through the hypnotic mindblocks of several captured freefighters from other cities, forcing them to reveal the locations of their hidden headquarters. And as soon as the Reds had found out, they had sent out bombers with neutron bombs and blown the populaces back into the dust from which they had been born. So there was a touch of ironic revenge which all the Americans in the room felt while watching the Red officer strapped into the large globe.

Rock sat down next to Rath who stared intently at the officer, the mindbreaker covering the top of his head as the once strong Russian captain screamed in mortal terror as the laser probes dug deep into his smoking brain tissue. Two white-smocked assistants slowly adjusted the knobs on the control panel several feet from the strapped Russian soldier, making the probes dig into the memory cells of the man's brain.

Rock winced as he watched. Though he had killed countless Russians, he was not one who believed or liked torture. That was for the Reds, yet, they had no choice. This man knew too much. He could imagine what the officer was going through. He had seen what the full force of the mindbreaker had done to some captured Americans.

The officer, Ivan Smolineck, was dreaming. He was on a boat on the Odessa with Karenina, but the boat was crashing into rocks and she was going under the waves. He dove down, down into the darkness. He couldn't rise, the light above him seemed to disappear. he was being sucked into a whirlpool of pain, spinning, agonizing. His worst fears began emerging as the technician adjusted the knobs several feet away. Rats were gnawing at his hands, then his face. Razor teeth were ripping at his eyes, then moved down to his genitals. They tore away, ripping his manhood from his body, running across a nightmare red floor with the bloody organ, tearing at it, biting it into pieces. He tried to move, to punch, to kick, but his body was tightly bound in the chair.

Suddenly he heard a voice. "What was in the convoy? Where were you bound? Answer and the pain will cease."

"Stop the pain, yes, I will talk." He didn't even know where the voice was or what was happening. Perhaps it was the God the Russians said didn't exist. "We were carrying mindbreakers to Pavlov City under direct orders from President Zhabnov himself."

"How many?" the disembodied voice demanded.

"Two thousand," Smolineck screamed out. "Stop the pain! I beg you."

"What for? What were the mindbreakers for?" the voice asked.

"For Plan Lincoln," the Red officer cried out. "For the Plan Lincoln that is being carried out in Pavlov City." Shecter and Rock looked at each other. They had never heard of the city or the plan. What were the Reds dreaming up now?

"What were the mindbreakers for? What is happening in this Pavlov City?"

"I don't know, I swear," Smolineck moaned as the rats came at him again. "It is some huge plan directed by the president himself using thousands of mindbreakers. Workers are being brought in from around the country for some sort of brain modification—but I don't know what—I swear. Oh please God, if you are God, free me from this pain."

"For what? Just tell us for what and your pain will stop."

"I don't knooooow, I swear. Please, please bring back the Odessa, the boat, my Karenina in my arms."

The technician at the control looked over at Rath for orders. The intel chief nodded and turned his hand to the right. The assistant turned the dial on the panel up one more notch, forcing the probes deeper into the officer's brain. Everyone in the room could now smell the highly unpleasant odor of burnt brain tissue as a small stream of smoke drifted up above the man's skull.

"Ahhhhh. Oh God, God, God. I don't know any more."

Rath made the off sign with his hand and the technician abruptly switched the torture machine off. The Russian's head slumped down onto his chest. It wasn't a pretty sight what one of these blasted devices did to a man, every American in the room thought to himself, looking at the Red officer. Thin trickles of blood ran from his eyes and ears. Small veins broken during the interrogation covered his face and arms, swollen, bright red as if the very flesh of the man were about to explode. His mouth hung open limply. The man's mind would never be the same, that was for sure. God knew what they would do with this shell of a creature. Rath vowed never to use the mindbreaker on anybody but KGB in the future. They had earned it. Two of Rath's assistants dragged the stumbling Russian away back to his cell.

But at least the freefighters knew that something was up. Something big! The Reds were bringing large numbers of workers into this Pavlov City, a city that hadn't even existed until several months ago. And all under President Zhabnov's personal direction.

"What the hell are they up to?" the intel chief turned to Rockson who sat next to him, a concerned look on his rough-hewn face.

"Something new, that's for sure. Some damned trick and I don't like the sound of it at all," Rockson replied. "I didn't think that fool Zhabnov had it in him to do any independent thinking. It may well have something to do with the power struggle we know is going on between him and Killov. But what sort of information would he be trying to get from factory workers? All they know is how to survive with nothing. It doesn't make sense."

"No, it doesn't Rock. At least with the information we have. And I think we got all that officer knew. No one is capable of lying with one of those damned devices strapped to their heads. But look at the numbers—thousands of mindbreakers—tens of thousands of workers being shipped in. What did Lincoln do again, Rockson? You're the historian."

Rock's semi-photographic memory went into action. "Abraham . . . Lincoln, sixteenth president of the United States. His election on an anti-slavery platform divided the nation, leading to the Civil War, which was finally won by the Northern States in a four year war with the Southern States or the Confederacy. After the war he was shot by a mad actor. One of our country's greatest presidents, an inspiration to read about."

"What do you make of the name? A coincidence?" Rath asked, stroking his bony adam's apple absentmindedly.

Rock thought for a moment. "I don't think so. The Reds usually use functional names for their projects. There's definitely a clue. Let's see, the American workers are slaves—and that's puzzling—somehow the Reds are going to free them? Doesn't make sense."

"Maybe something else about Lincoln—" Rath said as he motioned for his assistants to tidy up the area around the chair that the Red officer had sat in, which was now dotted with specks of blood. But Rockson was thinking about burned down Atlanta, Sherman's march through Georgia in the war to save the Union. The freed black men and women following the Union soldiers en masse, many of them trying to help the bluecoats fight.

"That's it—fight!" Rock yelled out, startling the intel chief.

"What?" Rath stuttered.

"The Reds want to use the enslaved Americans against us. Who are the secessionists from the Red hegemony—us!"

"Rock are you serious—the mindbreaker has no such ability to control men's minds, just to destroy them. You've seen it all for yourself."

"Couldn't it be modified?" Rock asked grimly. "Somehow altered so as to change the memory patterns of a man's brain, even affect his loyalties?"

"Anything is possible, Rock. I'd be the first to admit that, but it sure as hell would be a hit and miss situation. They'd have to use thousands of workers to get hundreds who could successfully be controlled. And those would most likely be zombies more than real fighting men. This is all guesswork, of course, But, I can't believe the Reds could have advanced the technology of the mindbreaker that quickly. I know how their science staffs work and frankly, they're not the brightest or most innovative of minds around."

"But they don't care how many lives they waste. Thousands of workers dead means nothing to them. that could be why so many are being shipped in. We've got to find out what's going on in this Pavlov City and find out fast."

"I'll call an emergency meeting of the council for tonight, Rock," Rath said. "I agree with you—this situation calls for some sort of immediate response—before things get out of hand. Good God, we could be seeing American fighting American—another Civil War orchestrated by the Reds."

Eight

The Council of Century City came to order slowly. The democratic process that was adhered to religiously was often loud and boisterous—yet somehow the work got done. The freedom to argue, to disagree were the freefighters greatest legacy from the past glories of America. Something the Reds could never know or even imagine—the taste of liberty. Council President Willis, the head speaker of the council, walked slowly to the front of the meeting hall. Bart Willis, tall, eloquent, the most respected member of the council and at seventy-five, the oldest. He was the son of one of the original founders of Century City—George Willis, an executive with a computer company who had been trapped along with hundreds of other cars and trucks in the tunnel when the bombs hit. Willis often told stories of the early days of Century City to spellbound audiences of children and adults. How it was before they had had all the conveniences of the last twenty-five years—since Dr. Shecter had performed his miracles of science and transformed the underground city into the technologically most advanced of the Free Cities in America.

Willis banged the gavel on the wooden slab of the speaker's lectern and coughed loudly several times. The many voices talking and arguing around the nearly hemispheric chamber slowly quieted down as the one hundred elected representatives from all the sectors of Century City came to order.

The gray-haired Willis looked down over the now attentive assemblage. "I'm glad to see we're all so energized tonight." He smiled wanly. "It will serve as well in the discussion we're about to engage in. The first item of the evening is Rockson's report on the mission to test the particle beam weapons. Rock . . ." Willis stepped away from the wooden speaker's platform as Rockson bounded up the steps at the side of the raised platform three at a time and walked quickly across the stage to the center.

"Good day," Rock said softly with a slightly cynical expression as he looked out over the upturned faces of the assembly. He and the council members knew each other—friends, adversaries—they fought for the same goals with different intensities and philosophies. Rockson believed that the way to fight back against the Reds was with force—the only message they understood, while many of the council members thought that perhaps some sort of accommodation could eventually be reached with the Russians. That America could be shared by both American and Russian occupying forces. That it was unrealistic to really believe they could kick the Red armies out lock, stock and barrel. Not with such overwhelming forces.

Rockson knew they were wrong. But he treated

them with respect—always. They were, after all, all free Americans and their beliefs and the fact that they *could* disagree and think differently was literally at the heart of what separated them from the Red automatons. Tonight, Rock knew that the tide was changing. With the power of particle beam weapon positively demonstrated, the council members could no longer believe that the freefighters did not have the power to effectively fight the Red forces. They did! So today Rockson had a narrow smile and a deep feeling of confidence as he began speaking to them.

"I am here tonight to tell you that the times are changing. What was yesterday is no longer. Many of you have in the past stated that the Russian occupation forces were just too powerful to take on. That we would only invite complete destruction of our Free Cities with nuclear attack if we tried to take on the Reds in full scale battle. Today, ladies and gentlemen of the council, I say to you that we can not only take on the Russian armies—all three million of their troops—from regular army to airforce to KGB Death Squads—that we can not only take them on but that we can win! And we will win!" He banged his fist down hard on the podium stand. Murmurs of approval and disapproval swept through the assembly like waves on a pond. Rock waited a few seconds and then coolly continued.

"We have tested the particle beam weapons. Two of them. Myself and a team of only five men attacked a Russian convoy of nearly one hundred and twenty vehicles including ten tanks, armored cars, support ground troops numbering at least five hundred men, and nearly one hundred of the K-R 7 transport trucks. We attacked, gentlemen, with two weapons, two black beam rifles of the type Dr. Shecter has already spoken to you about. And when we finished nine minutes later, not a vehicle was left standing. And I don't mean a tire missing or an axle snapped in half by an exploding shell. I tell you, representatives of the people of Century City, that nothing remained. Just smoke and shreds of metal."

The council members listened in fascination, trying to think already of how to deal with this changed political situation. For things definitely were changed. The entire alignment of doves and hawks on the council would be unalterably shifted. The delegates began plotting how to best alter their beliefs to the reality of the new weapons.

"With just a hundred of these black beam weapons," Rock continued, "we could literally take on the armies of Russia. And win! The power of these beams is almost inconceivable until you see it for yourself. It is a step beyond atomic weapons, perhaps makes them obsolete. Why, one of these rifles could—could—melt an atomic missile in the air. Not only can we attack against the Reds but we can now neutralize their most powerful armaments—their n-bombs with which they've been destroying free American cities at an alarming rate—four in the last two months. We need many more of these particle beam guns. We must find a way somehow to arm all the Free Cities with them. Why just two or three particle beam rifles in each city could give them unlimited power—squads could go out and attack whole convoys, take on entire Red search-and-destroy squadrons. If we could just make more, could just—"

"Impossible, Rock," a deep voice boomed out from

the side of the council chamber. The entire room of representatives turned their heads to the left. "It can't be done," Dr. Shecter said, rising from the rear seat on the left, the place he always liked to sit, far in the back, invisible to all while he took in the proceedings. Shecter walked unsteadily, his long thin legs having another of their arthritis attacks. He grimaced slightly as one of his knees nearly went out but his two assistant/bodyguards who always accompanied him reached forward and steadied the scientist. Shecter hobbled up the stairs and made his way to the podium. Rock and he exchanged quick glances. They fought for the same goal, of that Rock was sure.

"My people and I," Shecter said, addressing the gathering, "have tested these damned weapons every which way. And damn it, we can't make head nor tail of how the things are constructed. We can't pry them open without risking complete destruction of the weapon and we can't figure out the energy operation. It just doesn't compute," he said looking down at the representatives. "For the first time in my life I must confess that I'm totally stymied. According to all our calculations the weapon is impossible—it can't exist." A few snickers could be heard in the audience. "It must be using some energy source that we haven't even discovered yet. But as for making them—forget it. I'm sorry Rock, but the only way we're going to have more of these things is for someone to go back and pay a visit to the people who made them—The Technicians."

Shecter returned to his seat and Willis took the podium again. Rockson sat down in his front row seat as Willis called Rath, chief of Intelligence, to the fore. Rath seemed nervous, breathless as he took the stand.

He was not used to speaking in front of the entire assembly, but these were unusually dangerous times.

"I've got some information to reveal that I fear calls for some sort of immediate action. We've finished interrogating a captured Russian officer that Rock and his team brought back with them from the attack on the convoy and—under the influence of a mindbreaker that we were able to get our hands on—we've found out that workers from numerous Russian fortresses are being rounded up and shipped to Fort Pavlov, a newly erected extremely well-protected Red center some five hundred miles to the east. The officer revealed that there is a plan—Plan Lincoln involving these large masses of workers and thousands of mindbreakers which are also being shipped to Pavlov City by the ton. Something big is going on. Exactly what I don't know: the officer apparently was not privy to the exact purpose of the operation but I can assure you of one thing—it's bad. Very bad." He paused for a moment to see what sort of effect his words were having on the council. Every eye was riveted on him.

"Rock and I talked briefly before the meeting and had a few ideas. Since the plan is termed Plan Lincoln we thought that since the Reds tend us use ironic names for their plans that this might actually have to do with brainwashing and then arming these wretched American pawns to go out and fight the Free Cities—brother against brother—for those of you who know your history—just like our own Civil War of two centuries ago." The Intel chief paused for a moment, gathering his thoughts and his breath.

"Something must be done! I feel that we must use the particle beam weapons and mount an all-out attack on Pavlov City. Stop this horrendous plan, whatever its exact nature, in the bud before—"

"No! No! Absolutely not!" a voice boomed out, reverberating through the chamber. This time it was Rockson. He stood up, all six foot, three inches, two hundred and twenty-five pounds of chiseled mutant muscle and addressed Rath. "You know me, Rath. If anything I'm the man who's always saying let's get in there and kick ass. But this time I think it would be a terrible mistake to attack, risking the particle beam weapons of which we have only five, possibly even their capture by the Reds. We don't even know for sure just what the hell is happening inside this Pavlov City. That theory is a good guess but we both know it's just bull unless it's confirmed by hard facts. We've got to have some real intelligence on the situation inside those walls before we can even think about mounting any sort of attack. We have to know!"

"Rock's right," Shecter piped in from his back seat. "We can't risk these weapons. They're too important. If the Reds should get hold of even one at this stage of the game, they might be able to somehow neutralize the beam. For Christ's sake man, this is the first time in a century that we've been handed the possibility of really hurting the Russian machine."

"And from the sound of it," Rock added, "this Pavlov fortress is armed to the teeth. The officer said, under the mindbreaker, that this was his second trip there and that they had the place absolutely porcupined with heavy artillery and a full fifty unit helicopter, twenty MIG air force squadron ready for just such an assault. No! Zhabnov or Killov or whoever the hell is hatching this plot is shipping rubles in by the ton and they're protecting the place with everything they've got."

"Exactly," Shecter said. "That's why we can't risk the particle beams. It would be madness."

"Or a big strike force," Rock added. "They'd make mincemeat of anything we could throw at them with that kind of firepower. But someone's got to go in. One man might just be able to do it. Get inside and find out what the hell is happening, just what their defenses are, and get that information back."

There was silence in the chamber as all eyes focused on the Doomsday Warrior. "Yeah me," he said coolly. "I'm volunteering." Numerous voices spoke out at once in protest, insisting Rockson was too valuable, too important a catch for the Reds.

"I'm the only one who can," Rockson responded. "I know the way through that section of the country better than any man in this city. I can get in, find out what the story is and get out again."

"What of an expedition to get more of the black beam weapons from The Technicians?" Shecter asked, somewhat irritated.

"Have Erickson mount a second expedition," Rock replied. "He knows the way and The Technicians know him. Only this time he can take twenty men and teams of hybrids. They've got to bring back as many of the damned weapons as they can. The Technicians had them piled to the rafters in their laboratory."

The council discussed the proposition to mount a second expedition and agreed to bring it to a vote in a remarkably short time, considering their usual habits of debate. The motion carried. As for Rock's volunteering to go to Pavlov City—that was a military decision. Although the council members had numerous objections and both Rath and Shecter seemed disturbed about it. As the highest ranking military officer of Century City Rockson himself had the final say. With much trepidation they wished him well. But Rockson didn't wait around to hear the eulogies; he was already off to Supplies to prepare for the long trek to the brainwashing fortress of Pavlov City. Though he had volunteered for the mission, it wasn't something he would enjoy. Of that he was sure.

Nine

There were four huge gates to the walled fortress city of Pavlov—one facing each of the four points of the compass. At dawn on October 27, 2089 A.D. in the driving snow, nearly five hundred KGB elite troops under the direct command of Colonel Killov arrived at the East Gate without notice, in their desert halftrack carriers, all coming from scattered directions and converging only within sight of the sixty foot high concrete walls—a maneuver to avoid any attack on the convoy by American freefighters. They found the puzzled fortress guards, high in their machinegun posts atop looming towers, looking down with confused expressions. But all recognized the death's-head emblem of the KGB on the armored vehicles and especially the crossed falcon escutcheon of the commander himself, Colonel Killov.

Word was sent immediately to the post commander when Killov and personnel alighted and demanded entrance citing Section Six of the Bilateral Agreement between Soviet Army and KGB forces (1999). None of the commander's staff had heard of such a law but they could indeed find it in the thick Occupation Regulations Manual. "My God, we have to let him in," the commander, Peshtro, said to his staff. He made a quick call to Washington D.C. where Zhabnov's personal secretary awakened the president.

"What the hell is it?" he snarled sleepily, pushing the drugged body of a young blonde to the side of the bed as he grabbed the phone.

"Is the Grandfather dead?" Zhabnov asked hopefully, thinking that would be the only reason they would dare wake him before the sun was even up.

"No, no, this is Commander Peshtro at Pavlov City, Mr. President. I'm calling because Colonel Killov and some five hundred men are here at the city walls demanding entrance—"

"What? What the hell are you talking about?" Zhabnov yelled, sitting bolt upright in the silk-sheeted bed. The young girl beside him groaned from out of her drug stupor and then settled back into a relatively blissful unconsciousness.

"They're demanding entrance, sir," Peshtro repeated, somewhat nervous at speaking to Zhabnov. "Colonel Killov is citing the Section Six of the Occupation Regulations or something—"

"Section Six, Section Six," Zhabnov ruminated. "I vaguely remember something about that." He pushed a button by his bed and a servant came running in. "Quick," Zhabnov said, "get me my legal advisers right away. I want them here in my room within ten minutes or heads will roll." The servant ran out white-faced. He could see that Mr. President was heading into one of his ornery moods.

"Stall them, commander," Zhabnov blurted into the phone. "Say anything. I'll get back to you within half an hour."

"But—" the phone clicked dead.

Back at the walled fortress of Pavlov, Killov was growing impatient.

"Are you going to let us in?" he screamed up at the tower guards through his halftrack P.A., "or must we blow the gates apart?"

"Forgive us, colonel—our orders are not clear," shouted down the nervous young Red Army lieutenant.

"Then I am giving the order—let us in!"

"Commander Peshtro is on the phone to Washington sir, he—"

"I will give you thirty minutes. Then my men will begin firing. Under Occupation Regulations the KGB has the right, as protector of the Soviet doctrine and enforcer of ideology, to inspect any army fortress at any time. Tell your commander, that fool," Killov said, his voice icy cold, "that I'm not the type of man who plays games." He slammed his hand down on the P.A. switch, nearly breaking it. Killov settled back in the relative warmth and comfort of the sixty foot black monstrosity of a halftrack as the snow began falling heavier outside. It was multi-colored flakes, common in the Midwest—purple, green, orange, spinning, dropping like flecks of a rainbow. The head of the KGB watched the gate through a periscope. Zhabnov had undoubtedly been awakened by now, he thought, and was calling in all his advisers. They'll tell him he doesn't have a leg to stand on—he'll have to let me in.

In the power politics of America, Killov was about to humiliate the president. His thin white lips, narrow as a pencil line, stretched out into as much of a smile as the KGB commander's face ever allowed itself.

In Washington D.C. the Oval Office was filled with half-dressed groggy-eyed legal advisers. President Zhabnov, still in his nightshirt, had squeezed himself into JFK's antique rocker and was tapping on the arms with his fingers, drumming out an impatient beat.

"What you're telling me, all of you, is that I'm bound by this ridiculous article—nearly ninety years old—to let my mortal enemy—I mean of course, our distinguished leader of the KGB—into my most important fortress of Pavlov City." Zhabnov looked around at his advisers who wouldn't meet his angry eyes. "Does this mean he has the right to know everything about Plan Lincoln as well?"

"No, Your Excellency," hastened Swerdlov, the youngest and brightest of the sorry lot. "He has the right only to enter, station troops, check for possible cells of subversion, which comes down to talking with senior officers, receive adequate food and lodging and care of their vehicles, and in seventy-two hours, depart. He is not required to have access to any classified army documents."

"What the hell is he up to?" Zhabnov asked aloud. "To destroy Plan Lincoln, or to spy? That's it. He plans to find out what I'm up to. But he won't. We'll let him into the city, but keep an eye on him and all his damn Blackshirts. I'll have my men trail every one of them, keep on their heels like Goddamned dogs." Zhabnov got the commander of Pavlov City on the phone and gave him explicit orders about keeping the

KGB men on a tight string and to report back to him the moment they left. With that he returned to his bedroom and the girl who was just starting to stir.

The huge East Gate was opened at last and Killov and his men rolled in in their vehicles, sending up waves of smoke from the diesel-powered engines. These damned outland fortress cities aren't even paved, Killov thought with disgust, contrasting the shoddy look of the place with his own immaculate Denver headquarters. He stared out the periscope of the lead halftrack. When I am Supreme ruler, much more attention will be paid to modernization of all Russian fortresses in America. If something wasn't done, the entire Red Army would collapse into dirt and barbarism within a few more years. All of Killov's men were spit and polished like mirrors, their black collars starched as flat as paper. The colonel demanded nothing less than perfection in everything and everyone around him.

They exited their vehicles once parked inside the fortress and were given quarters, from hovels for the lowest ranks to luxurious suites for Killov and his top brass. Killov was escorted by the commander of the fort and his right-hand men who greeted the KGB leader with huge phony smiles and plastic warmth. Killov smirked at the gestures and the slovenly appearance of the army personnel. No wonder he would win—if these were the fat fools who were his only obstacles to ultimate power. The moment he was inside the suite with the fort's commanding staff around him, he ordered his own Plan Pavlov into effect.

"Seize them," he ordered his elite bodyguards, who immediately pulled out their Pushkin 7.2mm service revolvers and lined the six top ranking officers of the fortress and the commander against the wall, disarming them.

"What the hell do you think you're doing?" Commander Peshtro asked, turning his head toward Killov who stood about ten feet away. One of Killov's guards swatted the commander in the face with the butt of his pistol, snapping the man's face back around toward the wall.

"I'm taking over the fortress," Killov said coolly. "Isn't it obvious? My, you army types are slow. Tie them up," he commanded his men. The ranking officers of Fort Pavlov were trussed and bound like so many pigs to be slaughtered and set in the center of the V.I.P. suite. Around the fortress, squads of Killov's KGB commandos were carrying out their operation with clockwork perfection. The Communications Section were taken at gunpoint, the radio and telephone operators imprisoned, and Killov's own men took over control of all incoming and outgoing communications. Nerve gas cannisters were hurled into the officers' sleeping quarters, knocking out all eight hundred and fifty men as they slept. Within fifteen minutes the elite forces had managed to completely take control of one of the most heavily protected fortresses in America.

Killov sat down in the velveteen armchair of the luxury suite as the phone rang. "Yes?" he said, picking up the gold French antique phone.

"The entire city is ours, Excellency," reported Antonovich, the head of the commando units.

"Excellent, excellent," Killov replied, popping a pill in his mouth from an ample supply in his inner pocket. He sipped some cold water from a crystal goblet on the phone stand. "Casualties?"

"Sixteen of our men—about a hundred of theirs. Most wounded, perhaps twenty dead," the commando leader replied.

"Good. Kill the wounded. Round up all the officers who are on duty and imprison them. Once the fortress is completely secure I want you to take a hundred men and take control of the mindbreaking facilities. Do not interfere with the operation, just control it. I will be there shortly to see just what our friend Zhabnov had been up to."

"Yes, Excellency, immediately," Antonovich snapped. Killov hung up the phone and turned to the commander of the fort who held the side of his face which dripped blood from a long gash opened by the gunbutt hit.

"So," Killov said to the man, who this time kept facing the wall so as not to receive another smash in the face, "You see we are already in control. Now, just tell me where the records are being stored of this Lincoln operation and perhaps I will let you live."

"Never," Commander Peshtro said loudly, trying to sound brave to himself as much as to Killov.

"Never?" Killov laughed. "Please do not bore me with a dramatic scene of bravery. I will find the records anyway. My men are already searching for them. Your life means nothing to me, but I would imagine it holds some sort of meaning for you." Peshtro's face twitched with indecision. If he told Killov anything, Zhabnov would have his testicles torn out. If he didn't . . . Somehow he feared Killov more. "I'll tell you, I'll tell you," he blurted out, avoiding the accusing looks of his senior officers.

"Good, wonderful, in fact. Please have a seat," Killov said, pointing to the chair next to him. Peshtro, still holding his hand to his cheek as blood oozed through the pale fingers, sat down several feet away from the skull-like visage of Killov.

"You'll find the computer tapes of progress to date in Sector Seven-B. The file reports are in the Central Storage Warehouse behind the main brainwashing building." Killov snapped his fingers and two of his aides ran from the room to find the records.

"Now tell me, Commander," Killov said, smiling a fearsome thin grin at the trembling Peshtro, "Just what are you all up to here in Pavlov City anyway?" He poured the man a drink, a crystal glass filled with golden brandy from a decanter and handed it to him. Peshtro drained the glass in a second and, gasping for breath, told Killov just what Zhabnov's plans were for the creation of an American worker army to fight the freefighters. Killov listened intently.

"How ingenious," the KGB commander said when Peshtro had finished. "I really didn't think that the fat man had so much imagination. I've underestimated him. But tell me one further thing. Did not Zhabnov also have plans to use this American army against my own KGB forces, knowing that his regular Red Army troops would be loathe to fight me?" He looked at Peshtro who seemed to wince at the question.

"I—I—" he stuttered, too nervous to answer.

"You needn't go on, my dear commander. Your stuttering speaks volumes." Killov turned to his officers. "Take him out and dispose of him." Peshtro began sobbing.

"You said—I'd—"

"I said nothing," Killov replied, taking a sip from the goblet. "Let's see, how high are the walls of the city?"

"Sixty feet, Your Excellency," an aide said instantly.

"Throw him off the wall!" Killov said, looking away.

"No! No!" Peshtro screamed as guards dragged him away. Killov's eyes were narrow as razors. It was sand below, he thought. Maybe all the Commander's bones wouldn't be broken. Maybe he could crawl the two thousand or so radioactive miles to Washington and get a medal for bravery from Zhabnov. Their conflict had, with this action, moved for the first time into the open. If the doctors did their work in Moscow there would be no repercussions. If not, all traces of the operation could be eliminated with explosives and blamed on Ted Rockson and the freefighters. He went to the window of the suite and looked out. He could see across the vast plains over the small fires of the poverty camps. Yes out there the commander might find some water, maybe in a hundred miles or so. He laughed and popped another "alert" pill and instantly felt the tingling exhilaration fill his bloodstream. He was hooked now but he didn't care. Power, he wanted more and more power. The phone rang.

"Yes!" Killov answered.

"We have total control of the fort now, Excellency. Anti-air defense is in place."

"Good, permit only the brainwashing of the American prisoners to continue. I will come shortly to visit the operation." He hung up. There was nothing like a good disciplined force of even a few hundred men against anybody. Discipline was what counted, and

Killov's Death Squads were the most disciplined forces in the world for they knew the penalty for failure. Fear! Fear was the best teacher, and of that emotion the colonel was an expert. He would rule because he deserved to rule—the world.

Within the Kremlin's grim walls Premier Vassily lay dying—a victim of the spreading tumorous cancers that blotched his frail face and gaunt body. Near him sat his faithful servant Rahallah, a black man whose ancestors had been servants of the Russian elite for as long as any of them could remember. Rahallah would bring hot water bottles to place on the painful areas of the premier's diseased body and speak softly to the Grandfather-of-all-the-world, telling him that—*yes* he was loved, and *yes* he was a great and beneficent leader. Rahallah, the premier's only confidant, the only man he dared trust, kept news of the power struggle unfolding in the U.S. from his master as much as possible. The old man lay almost motionless for days at a time, coughing up bits of bloody sputum onto the white satin pillows beneath his head, just waiting for the moment when the icy hand of the reaper would grab hold of his throat and squeeze for the last time. Then Rahallah would kill himself, the black servant had already decided, rather than serve his master's enemies.

Rahallah believed that his master was basically good. It was after all, a relative judgment—these concepts of good and evil. But certainly compared to the truly evil Killov or the banally evil Zhabnov, the Grandfather was a benign character on the stage of the post-war world. Vassily demanded that the Soviet Empire be careful with the balance of nature—what was left of it. He resisted the calls for massive atomic destruction of the empire's enemies by many of his advisers and particularly Colonel Killov, who seemed to have quite a taste for the neutron bomb, which he constantly requested permission to use. Vassily was, in the cast of characters of 2089 A.D., a moderate and scholarly man who despised only the rulers in the Kremlin who, one hundred years before, had pressed the buttons that spelled atomic cataclysm for most of the peoples of the world. The Grandfather had spoken many times of how the premier responsible for the holocaust, Drubkin, shouldn't be lying in Lenin's Tomb beside the founder of the nation; how he should be in a garbage heap, reviled, not worshipped. But now the Grandfather, destined by fate to rule the world, was dying, and in place of this canny old goat would come wolves like Killov.

Vassily pulled Rahallah's head closer and whispered to him.

"Do not let those doctors near me, my faithful friend. I know they mean me ill. You—you are my only friend. The only man on this planet I can trust."

Then the black servant of the ruler of the world felt the hand go limp, sag like a doll's hand in his. He ran and called in the doctors with their stethoscopes and hypodermics. The medical men rushed in, their black bags in their hands. The head physician, Menzies, opened his bag on the night table and extracted a vial with a rubber stopper. He pulled out a needle and punctured the stopper, filling the hypo with a clear liquid. His colleagues pulled up the frail premier's night robe to reveal his blotched sunken chest. Rahallah felt something strange—the way the doctors looked at one another, the way they smiled too broadly at him.

"Wait!" the black servant yelled out. "I'll give it to him when he feels better. Not now!"

"But—" Menzies began to protest. "He must get these drugs right now—or the prognosis is not at all good. I'm—I'm afraid he doesn't have long without receiving these treatments."

"Rahallah! Rahallah! Where are you?" the premier whispered feebly, holding his thin veiny hands up in the air.

"Here! I am right here, Grandfather," the black servant said, reaching out and grabbing hold of the trembling hands of the leader of the world.

"How long?" sighed the servant.

"Two weeks—a month. Who can say?" Menzies nervous eyes stared into the blackness of Rahallah's impenetrable eyes, trying to read the man's reaction. He couldn't. The doctors left Rahallah with the serums, telling him to inject the premier every eight hours. They would return the next day, they promised, and departed.

As soon as they were out the door Rahallah went downstairs, determined to do something. Something he had been taught as a boy by his grandfather who wished to pass on the secrets of the medicine men of the Imbagi tribe of East Africa from which Rahallah's people originally came. He still kept the knowledge buried in his memory—all the strange incantations, herbal cures that he had been shown—before his training to become a servant, before his training in Russian, mathematics, in forgetting his tribal knowledge. He gathered herbs from the kitchen staff. Although just a servant he had somehow become a powerful figure to the Kremlin staff over the years. They almost forgot his stature, so natural had it become for Rahallah to command; first carrying out the premier's orders, transmitting them to others, even generals; then without even realizing it, beginning to think for the premier—giving out orders that he knew the premier would have wanted.

Rahallah went to his private quarters, a large room a floor below the premier's with all the luxuries of the very rich. His window looked out over Red Square, the constant crowds passing by, staring up at the home of the most powerful man in the history of the planet. The black servant reached under the bed and pulled out an old leather satchel that he hadn't touched for nearly fifteen years. It was filled with the potions, fetishes, secret teachings that his own grandfather had passed on to him. Rahallah prepared a concoction of various foul-smelling powders and liquids and placed them in a plastic bag, tying it securely closed. A poultice that the doctors, if they ever saw it, would abhor: a poultice to remove the bad things in the body. To remove as his mentor had told him, the demons from within. The demons that made the red blotches, for they had red cancer sores even in his tribe. The mutated form of skin cancer was now worldwide due to radiation. He would remove the evil within Vassily and restore his vital energy. He would slip it under the premier's nightshirt and remove it whenever the doctors came and he would not give Vassily the pills. The Red medicines had failed, or worse, were poison. Rahallah would reach back into pre-civilization to save the Grandfather. The past and the present would do battle within the body of the failing premier.

Ten

Ted Rockson set out on his long trek to Pavlov City at about three in the morning after saying a farewell to a tearful Rona. She always mentally cursed herself for falling in a deeper love with Rockson every time he came back to Century City from one of his many perilous encounters with the outside world. And this, perhaps the most dangerous mission of all. She stood at the eastern exit of Century City, staring silently at the shadowy figure as he rode off. She watched until the dark shape atop a hybrid was swallowed up by the night. Then she turned and reentered the subterranean caverns of Century City, the steel door covered with leaves closing quickly behind her.

Rockson rode down the steep mountain trail, the cold night air refreshing as it blew sharply against his skin. The moon hung low in the western sky, a curved scimitar colored deep violet by the poisoned atmosphere. It was theorized by Dr. Shecter that the atmosphere had at least four layers of radioactive material circling above it, covering it with a shroud of death.

Strontium, krypton, hydrogen, and plutonium—still as radioactive as the day they were released into the sky in writhing red-hot mushroom clouds. Shecter believed that as the radioactive atoms slowly fell back to earth they would be destroyed by the planet's own natural cleansing processes—of rain and gravitational grinding until they were slowly dispersed over the entire planet, still deadly but reduced to single molecules incapable of much damage. But first, there would be centuries more of even worse climactic conditions as the radioactive blankets blacked out more and more of the atmosphere, condensing in lower and lower orbits into a single great revolving ring of death.

Great! Rockson thought, musing over the doctor's hypotheses as he stared up at the orbiting moon looking oddly wounded as if bleeding from her dark craters. The half ball of purple-white ducked ever deeper behind the high pine trees that knotted the trail ahead. Rock turned around but already couldn't see the mountain beneath which Century City was built. He was alone again, in the vastness of the night sky, where he had been a thousand times before. He and the unfiltered forces of life and death. Rock was in his element: the solitary facing of all challenges. The stars overhead twinkled by the trillions, burning through the dark clouds that hung over the planet. Burning with promise and hope. Hope for America. Hope for those who fought to live free.

The Doomsday Warrior rode through the night atop the sturdy hybrid, Snorter, whose keen big eyes and senses were perfectly attuned to the night. The palomino who was named after its habit of snorting and looking back around at Rock whenever given a command, as if not quite wanting to obey Rockson, or at any rate showing Rock that another creature existed who served at its own will—not his. Yet, it always obeyed this man, the hybrid that stood a shoulder taller than any other in Century City, the hybrid that could run like the wind itself as Rock had found several times when pursued by enemy forces.

They rode through the night and had almost reached the edge of the eastern range of the Rockies by morning. Just ahead lay long flat plains stretching off to the horizon, dotted only by an occasional odd hill composed mostly of wreckage from the war. Rock rested just at the edge of the green mountain woods, waiting for the day to pass. He napped the light sleep of the warrior as the hybrid stood nearby, its eyes closed in sleep. The Red spy drones had been plentiful in this area lately. He prayed that they weren't zeroing in on Century City. So far they had been lucky. But the war would be stepped up now that the freefighters were conducting such bold and successful attacks on the Russian convoys. Things would get a lot hotter in the next few weeks and months.

The sun set quickly that evening, dropping like a stone. Bulbous clouds covered the evening sky, sickly, orange looking. Rock hoped he wasn't in for an acid rain or a tornado. The damn clouds had the most eerie color, like the inside of a corpse. He headed the hybrid out onto the wastelands and rode him at a good pace once the land really flattened out. The 'brid positively flew along the red and green-tinged hard-packed ground. It reveled in its power and speed, letting its muscular legs pump away with full power. Rock bent forward in the saddle, pulling his head close to the 'brid's thick neck to cut wind resistance. The steed moved at a gallop as the thick orange clouds dropped lower and the air became bitterly cold.

Ahead were several bodies of water. Rockson had seen them before. He had passed several times through this area: the Five Lakes region. Five immense lakes almost side by side where five 2-megaton h-bombs had gone off errantly. Probably a multiple warhead aimed for some entirely different target that had ended up blowing up the middle of nowhere, Rockson mused. Maybe got winged by one of our defensive missiles. There had probably just been a few ranchers and farms to begin with in this area, then nothing. Rock pulled the reins lightly and the hybrid skirted the first of the large black lakes almost perfectly circular in shape and a good two miles across. No trees, bushes, not a blade of grass grew around them. What should have been fertile soil was, in fact, poisoned by the still radioactive lakes flat as sheets of glass on this cloudy day.

They came to the second, then the third of the lakes, passing by them in just minutes as Snorter tore along the rocky ground with Rockson crouched full forward in his black leather saddle. As they were passing the fifth and largest of the man-made lakes Rock saw a shadow in the middle. A large head broke the surface, something with an impossibly long neck and scales. "What the—" Rock muttered out loud. He stopped the 'brid by the bank of the lake, pulling sharply on the reins which the Palomino responded to instantly. Rock pulled out his field glasses and sighted out to the center. Nothing! Just ripples where the thing had been a second before. He moved the binoculars around, searching. The hybrid suddenly reared back and, moving like lightning, ran about forty feet away from the water's edge. Rock nearly fell off but threw his hands forward and grabbed the 'brid's thick mane. He was about to berate the disobedient steed when he heard a loud sound as of a waterfall behind him and turned around in the saddle. There—a large head was breaking the surface of the lake only a few feet from shore. The hideous head was reptilian on a neck a good twenty-five feet long. Scaly flippers flapped madly as the creature tried to edge onto the shore in search of its meal. Its five foot wide jaws filled with row after row of bayonet-sized teeth snapped at the air, toward Rockson. Rock saw why Snorter had fled. Smart creature. Smarter this time around than him.

The lake monster obviously wasn't equipped to come out of the water and it just stood, front flippers up on the shore angrily mouthing its teeth at Rockson. The two creatures—a human and a God-knew-what, stared at each other, the lake creature's huge red eyes bulging at Rock. The thing was obviously quite upset about losing what seemed like a sure meal. It let loose with a roar that made Rock's hair stand on end. Opening its jaws to their widest, the creature snapped up at the pale sky several times as it showed its power and then, as suddenly as it had appeared, it flipped its body around and instantly disappeared back under the midnight black surface of the crater lake.

Rock watched the bubbles float to the surface. "Remind me never to go swimming in there, will you pal," he said to the palomino which snorted in full agreement and perhaps a trace of mockery. They both looked as the ripples hit the sand at their feet and then the 'brid moved out, reaching a full gallop within seconds.

The first few days of their journey went easily enough, but on the fourth evening the drone spy planes grew thicker and thicker, flying overhead every fifteen or twenty minutes. The Reds were sending out everything they had to keep this sector clean, to try and discover more of the freefighter's hidden cities. To avoid detection Rock decided to head a little further south. He would have to take a more roundabout route through an area he had never traveled but there was no choice. If he were detected by the probes a chopper force would be on its way in minutes.

Within several hours they came to more woods, scrawny, diseased, but offering some cover. The land was fairly level except for large ant mounds which Rock had only seen before out West. The ants in these colonies were all long gone. The thirty and forty foot high dirt cones stood as monuments to the ant's history as proudly as any pyramid or Acropolis. Many creatures seemed to seek immortality through their structures—structures that would live long beyond their own quick lives. But only the Russians wanted it all—the whole damned planet as their monument, Rock thought bitterly.

They rested again during the day beneath a grove of thick red-barked trees at the edge of a meadow filled with blue flowers covered with red spots as if they had all contacted measles. Rock half drifted off into daydreams, listening to the buzz of life in the woods and the sharp chirping of the birds as they squabbled over worms and bugs and branches on which to build their nests.

At last the sun headed down again and Rockson set out. The woods quickly grew thicker and thicker and he had to dismount and use his fourteen inch bowie knife to hack through the underbrush. A strange black bush began appearing. About six feet high and wide it was black as coal, shiny and covered with thorns a good five inches long and needle sharp. Rock managed to skirt the bushes at first, but as he hacked on through the dense shrubs they grew more frequent until they became the only vegetation around him. The thorns pricked at him, ripping his skin even through his thick field jacket and pants. The needle thorns left little bloody trails on his flesh and the hybrid, too, was soon covered with a sheen of blood from the constant ripping of the dark brambles. Rockson pushed on, covering his eyes and face, tying bandannas around his hands and neck and around the hybrid's head to protect the two of them as much as possible. They moved through the black thorn patch for a good hour before coming to the end of them. Ahead lay more fields, nearly flat with the nightlife: raccoons and field mice, owls and chipmunks all darting around pursuing their instinctual obligations.

Rock rested at the edge of the first field and wiped himself down with a penicillin-based ointment that Shecter's people had come up with. He did the same to the 'brid and then sprayed plastiseal, a polyurethane shield that dried to a clear plastic to stop germs from entering the wounds. Feeling a little better, Rock remounted Snorter and the two continued on across the flowering fields.

The land seemed fertile here. Large open spaces with dark moist soil. Weeds and flowers of every variety grew wildly with small streams running through the land, bringing life-giving moisture to the flora. Good land, Rock thought. Perhaps it had all been farmland once long ago. They had gone for about an hour when he began feeling strange: in the pit of his stomach a growing nausea and then a numb pain on the spots where the needles had pierced the skin. He noticed that the palomino was slowing by the minute and seemed lethargic, taking deep breaths. Within minutes Rockson felt himself burning with a red-hot fever, his arms and legs tingling madly while other parts of his body became totally numb. The thorns! The Goddamn things must have contained some kind of poison.

Snorter stopped suddenly, and, hobbling for a moment, his legs twitching violently, keeled over like a huge tree felled by lightning. Foam bubbled from the hybrid's wide-opened mouth. Rock fell from the saddle onto the dark wet ground, heavy with night dew. God, he was nearly under already. He could feel the darkness pressing in from all sides, the stars flickering on and off like a malfunctioning light bulb. An intense pain shot up from the lower part of his back through his spine and into his brain cavity, a pain like a razor blade being drawn across his raw nerves. Red hot, ripping, tearing at his neck and skull. Waves of white-hot pain shot up and down his spine. Now the pain was coming from everywhere: from his hands and feet, his ears, even his eyes all hurt with an intensity he had never experienced in his life. The poison was ripping him apart.

The hybrid writhed and made whimpering sounds on the ground next to him. Rock had never seen anything like the thorns before. They must be a new mutation. The radioactive sections of land were always creating new forms of vegetation, many of which died, unable to compete with the already successful species around them. This particular brand of hell looked like it might have some staying power. Anything that messed with it or tried to eat it would very quickly be carrion for the vultures. There was only one chance. Rockson reached for his medical supply pack strapped on the hybrid's back and tried to reach for Shecter's universal antitoxin which had been synthesized from a number of snake poisons. The thorns weren't snakes but perhaps somehow their poison was based on the same chemicals. He had no other chance.

Rockson reached for the pack but nothing happened. His hand felt like it weighed a thousand pounds. The command went from his brain to his arm but the muscles wouldn't respond. It was as if they were dead. He had to get to the bag or he was definitely dead. He reached down inside himself for that power, that extra portion of strength which was his, which had pulled him through before when the odds seemed insurmountable, which meant the difference between life and death in America, 2089 A.D. And somehow, somehow he made his arm reach out. His hand pulled the pouch back. He opened it. Every movement was impossible, painful. His fingers felt like boiling hot lead pipes but he strained and commanded his own flesh to obey his will, not the poison's. Rockson got the anti-venom out: two hypodermics wrapped in plastic filled with the precious liquid.

He swooned as the blackness began hitting him again, sweeping down from the sky like an avalanche of death, the purest black of all, a dark blanket from which he knew he might never return. Rock stabbed one of the hypos into his arm and pushed the plunger home. He turned to the 'brid and did the same, stabbing the needle into the palomino's neck. The hybrid started for a moment and then settled down again. Then he sank down onto the cold ground, pressing against it, incredibly heavy, every cell like iron. The darkness shattered down on him in tidal waves pounding onto the reef of his consciousness with a roar that swamped every sense. Then there was nothing.

Eleven

The Central Processing Hall of Pavlov City was a madhouse. Prisoners or volunteer workers, as the Reds euphemistically called them, were continuing to be brought in from all around the Midwest. Every hour brought more of the workers and lower dredges of society—"garbage" people, thieves, beggars, the lowest of the underclass—into Pavlov City. The entire city was a factory, a factory for turning docile American workers into killing machines for the Reds. Colonel Killov, now in control of the fortress, allowed the processing to continue at full speed as he himself had not yet decided the final outcome of his takeover of the brainwashing center. With KGB guards stationed at strategic spots, the Red Army troops continued to process the new prisoners and funnel them into the mindbreaking building.

The workers were transported in by truck, chopper, and freight jet and fed through Main Processing—a football-field-sized concrete walled building where the workers were photographed, given a set of gray clothes, and tattooed with an electric branding iron on their shoulders. The Red guards continued to tell them they were being trained for working with special machinery which would bring them increased benefits and privileges. Few of the workers really believed this but had little choice as armed troops were everywhere. Besides they had already given their souls over to the Reds years before in their youths when they had learned that obedience meant life, disobedience meant death. So they went willingly into the mindbreaking machines.

Chaplin-47 had been trucked in from the Russian fortress city of Trotskyville where he had been unceremoniously hauled from his cot in the middle of the night and stuffed into a Red diesel truck that joined a convoy carrying thousands of other workers. He was unloaded just inside the gates of Pavlov City and herded into the processing hall. He was frightened and showed it, his squat face, nearly chalk white, his narrow lips pursed tightly as he clamped his teeth together hard. He wasn't a large man, about five feet four inches and not that strong so he wasn't sure just what the Reds wanted with him. Most of the other Americans in the hall were bigger. His life in Trotskyville had not been pleasant but somehow he felt that what lay ahead would make his alleyway cardboard home soon seem like a paradise in comparison.

"You!" a guard said, pointing at him. "Over here!" He pulled the slow moving Chaplip-47 through a checkpoint and onto a line of workers who were standing stark naked. "Take it off!" a second guard said, walking up and down the hundred man line of nude flesh.

"You mean my clothes?" Chaplin-47 asked trembling.

"No, your head if you don't move, idiot," the guard shrieked, walking up to the worker. He pushed him rudely with the butt of his Kalashnikov in the chest. "I said take it off and throw it onto this belt over here." He pointed to a swiftly moving conveyor belt which took all the clothing of the captives and carried it away to two thousand degree furnaces. One thing the military didn't want here was lice and crabs brought in by the filthy Americans. So all their articles of clothing, every possession they brought with them was destroyed.

Chaplin-47 stripped down to his thin knees and knobby elbows. He deposited his prize blue flannel shirt with only three holes in it on the conveyor and watched sadly as it was sucked down a ramp and disappeared through a small door. It had taken him nearly three months to get the shirt—real flannel and now . . . He stood there quivering in the slight chill of the late afternoon, covering his rather small genitals from the view of the other men who stared nervously straight ahead. The line moved slowly with Chaplin at the end and the group entered a large room. The door was slammed shut behind them and shower heads on the walls shot out bursts of hot chlorine-smelling water. The men danced around under the hot streams enjoying the sensation. It was the first time any of them had ever felt hot water. A voice boomed out from a hidden loudspeaker.

"Pick up the brown soap on the floor and the scrub brushes and wash your bodies thoroughly. Any man who is not cleaned will be punished." The cleanest group of men who ever walked the planet emerged five minutes later from the other side of the washroom and were handed sets of drab clothing. They were herded into another room and questioned briefly by Red Army officers about their age, health, place of origin, and job function. After questioning, Chaplin-47 was taken to the mess hall, a huge room filled with tables. Everywhere were workers dressed all in the same gray outfits, slurping away at their thin stews and eating coarse loaves of bread. Chaplin-47 hungrily took a tray, loaded up with food, and moved off to an empty seat to gobble down the meal—more food than he had seen at one time for years.

After the meal the men seemed a little more cheerful and smiles were even seen here and there. After all at least they weren't going to be shot. Who would feed a man and then kill him? Knowing that their lives extended into the near future at any rate, and with full stomachs, the workers faced their unknown fates with a trace less anxiety. Chaplin-47 was led through a series of barracks along with twenty other men. Pavlov City was already huge and growing by the day. A group of barracks laid out in concentric circles, the outer circle growing at the rate of one new hundred-man barrack per day, built by the slave labor under the watchful eyes of the ever present guards. Chaplin was taken to one of the newest of the barracks and shown a small cot.

"Sleep!" the guard commanded the prisoners and left, locking the door behind him. A video camera mounted high on the ceiling swung slowly back and forth, sending the images back to a central video control with nearly five hundred monitors being watched by technicians. Chaplin-47 lay awake for hours, wondering just what the hell was going on and what his fate would be. He prayed to some unknown guard that he not suffer too greatly. At last he fell asleep, dreaming of happier days far back in his childhood.

He was awakened at the crack of dawn by some very burly guards who kicked the sleeping workers as they walked through each barrack. The prisoners were led outside and through hall after hall until they came to Central Processing. This was the tallest structure in Pavlov City—nearly forty stories high and even this building was still growing. President Zhabnov obviously had plans to make this city one of the largest Russian enclaves in America. He was diverting every bit of material he could muster into the construction of the city. The hundred men were taken up in an immense elevator nearly fifty feet wide and led down a long brilliantly lit hall. They could hear screams coming from behind locked doors. Screams of the most intense agony. Suddenly their lack of concern disappeared. Their guts tightened into knots. Something was wrong!

One of the workers made a dash back down the heavily waxed white linoleum floor but got barely fifty feet before streams of Red slugs tore through his chest and stomach. He fell to the floor, a writhing pool of ripped intestine and lung tissue dripping out like badly butchered meat onto the clean shiny linoleum. The guards pushed the prisoners forward with the muzzles of their rifles. Oh sweet Jesus, Chaplin thought to himself, his hands clenched together like little rocks, what are they going to do to me? The workers were led into an immense chamber filled with rows of strange plastic seats with helmets hovering just above them. The rows of seats with what looked like space helmets extended off as far as Chaplin-47 could see. Overhead, burning fluorescent lights hung down, casting the peculiar scene with a merciless brilliance.

"Now sit down in the seats," the guards screamed out, holding their rifles straight out on the Americans. The workers sat one after another, surrounded on all sides by the Russian guards. Once they were seated, guards quickly made their way up and down the rows of seats and threw hand clasps closed on the terrified workers. They were now strapped firmly in place. An officer of some kind with a white smock covering his uniform stood in the aisle between the rows and addressed them.

"Welcome to Pavlov City, American citizens. You are here to be retrained. Retrained in your minds. The way you think and feel. You will not be killed, I assure you. And any pain you feel is only part of the necessary surgery we must perform on you. Just as an operation for a broken arm or leg causes pain but in the long run is good for the organism, so must we perform a sort of operation on your minds. You enter this chamber as workers, but you shall leave here as soldiers for the cause of world communism." As he spoke, guards went up and down the rows of prisoners, lowering the helmets down onto the workers' heads, setting them down so that two long steel prongs, sharp as ice picks, just touched the scalps of the workers.

Chaplin-47 felt the cold steel at his skull. Oh Jesus, no, no—they were going to stick those things in him, into his brain. No, this couldn't be happening. His life hadn't been good but he had built his little cardboard home and had saved a few rubles, perhaps enough to buy a woman for himself. There had been *something*—but now . . . He struggled in his steel containment, his wrists unable to move more than a fraction of an inch in their imprisonment. The officer's words dimly penetrated his panic-stricken mind.

"Go with it," the Red official continued. "I suggest very strongly that you go with the commands you will hear. Do not resist! If you resist you may well die. I have seen those men who have fought back against this mind processing and they made me want to vomit. So, if you care anything about your wretched lives, surrender your will, go with it. You have nothing to lose and everything to gain." He looked at the rows of recruits for the mindbreaker and stepped back toward the control panel at one end of the room. The guards, too, stepped away as they had been splattered before by exploding brains and knew enough to keep their distance.

The officer pulled the activation switch and the helmets above the workers' heads came to life with a dull whirring sound. Ruby red lights came on at the very tips of the prongs which poked down from beneath the helmets. Slowly, ever so slowly, moving at a snail's pace, the laser probes began lowering into the Americans' heads, pushing through the bone, grinding down into the skull cavity. The men heard their own skulls, cracking and melting under the laser beam that shot down into their flesh. The bone beneath the laser's ruby light began melting and went up in puffs of acrid smoke. Then the needles pushed deeper, into the soft gray tissue of the human mind, burning out memories, destroying whole systems of self-regulation and command.

Chaplin-47 smelled his own head burning, the smoke wafting down. He could feel the probes pushing through the bone of his skull and then a sickening slurping sound as the twin laser needles began vaporizing the first layer of brain tissue. He screamed! His shrieks joined the chorus of other human screams. The Russian soldiers stuffed cotton in their ears. Sometimes these Americans could really put up a racket. The pain, the pain was unbearable: razors, knives cutting into his mind, his memories being literally burnt out of him; dreams, hopes, desires exploding in pops of brain sap into nothingness.

Then the rats, the spiders began devouring his flesh. A voice boomed out over the loudspeaker, giving him commands, filling his mind with new thoughts, new orders.

"You are Russian soldiers now. Your obedience is to Mother Russia. Your American self is gone! You are Russian, you are a slave for the Motherland. You will do anything for her. You will kill for her. KILL! KILL! KILL!" The words combined with the pain in his skull and the melting sickening stench of human brain tissue. He was in a new universe, a dimension of pain and torture he had never dreamed existed. He felt himself falling over the edge of his reality like a man in a barrel going over a waterfall. He was falling, dropping, as his thoughts and being, his entire personality dropped away beneath him. There was nothing. NOTHING! He looked down, looked into the face of the purest pain and began the long descent down into the abyss of losing his mind.

Twelve

Where was he? Who was he? He ached all over. He was in the center of a darkness, a spiraling galaxy of black stars. He was falling up, falling into the light. It grew brighter, piercing! He moaned and opened his eyes. The burning sun smashed into his eyes and throbbing flesh. He was lying in a bed of dark brown grass. He was Rockson. Ted Rockson. He heard a noise and startled, swung his head around. A large furry face loomed large. In fear, Rock reached for his shotgun pistol—no, it was Snorter, trying to awaken him.

Suddenly he remembered. The thorns. The poison. So, he was still alive. The anti-venom had worked. And the Goddamned hybrid was stronger than he. It stood firm, looking down at its master who could barely move after the palomino had been revived for hours. Rock tried to stand himself and reached his knees, then collapsed back onto the cool ground. It was early in the morning. The sun was painting a smooth arc of red light above the purplish brown sky.

How long had he been under? Twenty-four, forty-eight hours? It felt like an eternity. Every nerve, every fiber of his being ached and pulsated as if infected. His ears buzzed, his eyes stared straight ahead as he found it hard to focus on anything. But he was alive. He had survived once again.

Rock struggled to his feet and somehow made his way the few yards to the hybrid. He lifted the four quart canteen from the saddle and opened it. His throat was parched, his lips dry as sand. Rock brought it to his mouth and felt a wave of violent trembling sweep over him as the first drops of liquid touched his tongue. No, damn it! He was going under again. He felt himself falling, saw the ground rushing up like a fist and then a strange sensation of smacking face down into the dirt.

When he awoke again it was pitch black. He felt sick and weak, but even as he slowly opened his eyes he knew he was stronger. The hybrid stood several feet away grazing on the knee-high dark grass and wild wheat of the field. Rock again reached for the canteen. Empty! It had poured out when he fell. Shit! He got to his feet still wobbly, dizzy. He felt as weak as he had ever felt in his life. As if his cells had lost their charge, his flesh cold as ice. He needed warmth and food and water. But he knew he wasn't in any condition to hunt. Rock dragged himself over to the 'brid and pulled himself agonizingly up into the saddle. The thick black and white hide of the hybrid felt warm beneath his thighs. He undid the blue blanket from his saddlebag and pulled it around his back and shoulders. Rock leaned forward so his chest and head were resting against the massive steed's furry mane. He commanded it to move.

"Giddyup, pal. You're going to have to take care of things for a little while." Rock slumped forward but stopped himself from slipping back into the darkness. He would fall out of the saddle at this rate. He undid a rope from the saddlebag and tied it around his back, attaching the ends to the saddlepost. The hybrid moved carefully forward. It knew that its master was in danger, that it had to make decisions. The master leaned nearly all the way forward, his head bobbing up and down. The master was sleeping. The 'brid knew that it must go forward in the direction the master had commanded before he slept. The hybrid kept up a slow, even pace, mindful of its unconscious load. From time to time it turned its huge head around and its orange brown eyes took in the master who hung roped down to the creature's back. The master was alive but he was hurt. The 'brid walked and walked, keeping its direction with its strong sense of smell which sensed moisture far ahead. It kept a dead course for the lifesaving liquid.

When Rockson next came to it was late afternoon. He felt himself rocking slowly back and forth in the saddle and opened his eyes. They were moving through fields of bright, madly colored flowers like a rainbow of dayglo paints. Snorter had kept up the journey on his own. Damn smart animal, Rock thought, managing a thin grin even in the midst of his haze. His body felt stronger now, the poison must have nearly worked its way through, though he still felt quite peculiar. He sat up straight in the saddle and rubbed his eyes and face. The skin was coated with a greasy paste, which he wiped off with a bandanna from his pocket. He needed water. Bad. He hadn't drunk for what seemed like days, and his lips and throat felt parched as a desert. But there was no water in sight. Suddenly Rock saw something that would do just as well.

He guided the palomino to the right. The hybrid gave over control of its movements to the master as soon as it felt the tug. It felt a kind of relief that it no longer had to decide things. It was meant for the master to rule. Rock halted the big 'brid near a grove of large plants, red stalks with yellow fruits covering them. Rock slid out of the saddle and landed on the ground, barely keeping his balance. He picked three of the gourd-shaped fruits from the plant and hacked one open with his bowie knife. He had learned many secrets of the land when young. This particular plant had been shown to him by a group of mountain men Rock had hunted bear with for several months when still a teenager. He cut the fruit near the narrower end, making a hole about three inches wide. He looked inside. It was full, filled with a supply of liquid that the plant stored within itself for droughts. Rock took a deep gulp of the sweet nectar. God, it tasted good. His mouth and tongue seemed to expand upon contact with the delicious juice, the cells soaking up the liquid and expanding back to their normal size.

Rock drank three of the fruit's contents down and then fed the hybrid who took to them with great appetite. Then the Doomsday Warrior stripped down to nothing and washed his torn flesh with the cleansing pollen liquid. He looked over his bronze, muscled body, carved from iron. He must have been stabbed over a hundred times by the poison thorns. Little pinpricks still red and swollen blue and purple covered his entire frame. Several wounds were quite infected, puffed up as large as grapes poking grotesquely out from his skin. Rock cut these open with his knife and squeezed the pus and poison out. Then he washed them clean with the plant nectar. The sores burned like the dickens when the liquid touched them but then quickly became cool, soothed. The plant's juices must have medicinal properties that even the mountain men hadn't known about. He'd have to return someday and bring some of these back to Dr. Shecter.

Rock then scrubbed down the hybrid who reveled in his bath, whinnying in appreciation, flapping his long gold and white tail in excitement. When they were both in better shape Rock set up camp for the night and ate a meal of berries and fruits which were plentiful in the area. He fell asleep under the splashing diamond sea of the stars.

When he awoke the next morning he felt almost normal again. Jackdaws and crows were fighting madly in some nearby trees, pecking and cawing at one another with rage. Rockson laughed out loud at the commotion and rose to his feet.

"Come on fellows, we're all fellow Americans. No need to get it on like this." The birds squawked at Rock a few times and then flew off to a safer distance to resume their quarrel in peace. Rock got off to an early start, and Snorter quickly hit a good pace. They were days behind schedule and had a lot of ground to cover. Rockson felt almost totally normal now. Almost. His eyes continued to play tricks as he kept seeing shadows around him, things jumping from behind rocks, leaping down from trees. As they went through a dense pine forest, Rock kept going for his shotgun pistol, sure that things were attacking him from above. Each time, he would quickly realize that nothing was there and return the powerful pistol to its holster, grateful that no one else was along to witness his hallucinations being acted out.

The next few days of travel were uneventful or as uneventful as the world of America, 2089 A.D. ever became. Rock found a large inland lake filled with fish and was able to catch a few catfish-type creatures, rows of needle teeth, and a large coxcomb, red as a rooster's, hanging down from beneath their jaws. But they tasted like heaven. On the evening of the fourth day after his bout with the poison thorns, Rock came to a series of low mountains, very rocky and steep. He found a gully, an ancient dried up stream bed only slightly wider than the hybrid and moving slowly, they started through. He had scarcely gone more than a hundred yards along the primeval stream when he suddenly saw shapes ahead.

A chorus of howls went up as the creatures saw him. Timber wolves, saber-toothed, their fur raised up on their backs, eyes lit up like slot machine windows at the sight of such a big fat dinner that Rockson and the hybrid would make. Rock had had a run-in with these mutant wolves before, but just one or two, never an entire pack. They edged forward, slinking on all fours, until they were about forty feet away. Their huge curved fangs protruded insanely from their jaws, nearly a foot long, glistening with the dripping saliva of their hunger.

Rock slowly eased his shotgun pistol out and unslung his Liberator rapid-fire rifle from beneath the saddle. He set it on automatic and held it cradled in his left arm, the shotgun pistol in his right. There were at least thirty of the large silver and black-haired predators, nearly twice as large as their pre-war ancestors. These stood nearly four feet high at the shoulder and weighed between two hundred and three hundred pounds. But their leader was even larger—a good four-and-a-half feet tall, with eyes as bright as fire, glowing red and orange in the setting sun. Its fur was a brilliant silver, shiny, almost metallic colored. It barred its teeth at the prey and let out a sharp doglike bark, obviously signaling the other members of the pack that this was their next meal. Snorter shifted his legs nervously and Rock patted the hybrid on the neck. "Easy boy, easy." Although its instincts told it to run, its trust of Rockson was even stronger and the hybrid stood its ground.

The wolves came at Rock at a quick gait which changed to a charge at about twenty feet. Rock waited until he could see the saliva covering the leader's immense jaws, the canine teeth shining like pearl-handled daggers in the last rays of the squashed setting sun for off on the radioactive purple horizon. The leader of the pack leaped into the air from nearly fifteen feet away, its powerful back legs propelling it into the air like some kind of immense spring. Rockson let loose with the shotgun pistol which unleashed a spray of .12 gauge shot in an x-shaped pattern. The lead volley flew only eight feet before it made contact with the silver neck of the wolf. It tore through the immense carnivore like a sword, nearly severing the creature's head. The lifeless body of the two hundred and eighty-five pound leader fell to the stream bed like a rock and lay there, its still beating heart pumping out hot blood through myriad holes in its chest and throat. Its lifeless eyes were wide open staring straight up at the darkening sky.

Rockson disliked killing such a magnificent beast. If they hadn't run into each other the wolf probably would have lived another twenty or thirty years, growing even larger. But when he was attacked, Rock had no choice but to survive. In the end that was what life was—the contest of many forces against one another—the strongest lived on.

The pack seemed confused by the death of their powerful leader. They, in their dim consciousnesses, must have thought that it was nearly immortal, having fought off every challenge from the other wolves for years. The next two most powerful members of the pack, nearly as big as the fallen leader, snarled viciously at Rockson, opening their foot long jaws to full extension. Their teeth stood out like tusks in the center of their snapping jaws. Both of the wolves, one a grayish color, the other jet black and shiny as velvet, charged at Rock. Snorter whinnied nervously but stood his ground, backing up slightly as the two killers came forward. The hybrid fought back its animal fears, knowing that its stillness would help the master destroy the predators.

The wolves got within about fifteen feet of their prey and leaped, literally flying up into the air, reaching a height of about eight feet above the ground. Their jaws opened wide; one went for Rockson's throat, the other for the neck of the hybrid. Rock waited until they were a millisecond away and fired pointblank with the shotgun pistol. The gray-pelted wolf took the brunt of the shot, its skull disappearing in a sludge of red spray. It crashed into the hybrid's chest and then fell to the ground nearly on top of the already dead silver-haired leader. But the black wolf only took the shot in the shoulder shielded by its companion. Its murderous leap continued and it slammed into Rockson's chest, knocking him clear off the 'brid.

He fell to the hard rocks of the stream bed, the rifle flying from his grasp, the shotgun pistol clattering loudly several feet away. Without a moment's hesitation Rockson rolled over and over on the stream bed. The second he moved, the black shape, dark as midnight itself, its eyes focused on the fallen man, sprang at the spot where Rock had hit. It spun around as it missed the rolling man and again charged. The guns were out of reach, Rock knew that. He whipped out his Bowie knife and held it straight out in front of him up in the air. The black-pelted wolf flung itself on Rock and felt fifteen inches of cold steel rip into its chest. It continued to slash away with the huge incisors but felt itself weakening. What was wrong? Suddenly it had no strength. It got a grip on the prey's arm but then felt itself falling into a spinning hole from which it could not rise. Rock ripped his arm free from the dead wolf's jaws. The teeth had penetrated the flesh and muscle but hadn't ripped away as the wolves liked to do, shredding their prey into hamburger before they ate.

About five yards away the palomino was rearing and kicking with its powerful hooves. The wolves were trying to circle it, wary of the power of the tremendous legs. One jumped from the ground and landed on the 'brid's back, trying to get its jaws around the big steed's neck for the kill. Rock saw the shotgun pistol half hidden under a rock and dove for it, firing from his stomach up at the wolf atop Snorter. The shot tore into the predator's side, flinging it from the 'brid's back as if it had been hit with a brick wall, its chest bones exposed and poking through the bloody hide. Rockson ran forward and reached the hybrid's side. He took the reins and pulled the animal out of the line of fire as a group of the wolves gathered just ahead of them for another charge. There was no time for finesse. Rock knew that if they all charged it was all over. He had to scare them. He aimed at the lead wolves in the pack and pulled the trigger of the shotgun pistol again and again. He blasted away, firing the remaining four rounds of the 12 gauge pistol into the smoke and the bloody flesh, not even stopping to see what the results were. The moment he ran out of ammo he picked up the Liberator. He aimed into the pack, waiting a second for the smoke and floating fur to settle. But there was no need. The battle was over. The remaining wolves fled, their tails between their legs like a pack of frightened puppies. They had no stomach to fight the killing machine before them. On the stream bed were the bodies of five more of the ferocious carnivores. Four were dead, already stiffening in rigor mortis. A fifth yelped and tried to crawl away, its front two legs blasted to stumps, bloody bones poking through. Rock walked over to the creature and looked down at the terrified animal which stared up at him, its eyes watery and filled with pain. Rock raised the Liberator and pumped two slugs into the wolf's head. It was still.

The Doomsday Warrior killed to survive but never to cause suffering. That was for the Reds. Calming Snorter down and treating his wounds with antiseptic and salve, Rock was soon moving forward again atop the hybrid, wary of every sound, every glowing eye in the immensity of the night. The bodies of the dead wolves lay like monuments to the power of man. The rising moon burned down on the corpses, lighting the red blood with shimmering sheen as nature's second line of predation moved in for their meals. Wild dogs, owls, blood spiders all dug into the warm flesh. Nothing was wasted, nothing was overlooked.

Thirteen

There it lay below him—Pavlov City—stretching off in every direction. Building after building, a maze of barracks in ever larger concentric circles, spreading out across the plains below. And at the outer edge of the largest circle of buildings, trucks, bulldozers, and workers building yet more structures. Rockson looked down from one of a group of low hills surrounding the plains on which Pavlov City stood. He took in the immensity of it. Whoever was building this city of sinister design had plans for it to be truly gargantuan. Sitting atop Snorter, Rock looked down for a long, long time, letting his senses digest it all. He had seen many Red fortress cities before but never one as large as this. Already, it stretched nearly three miles across, absolutely crammed with buildings. Most of the structures were fairly low to the ground, not more than two or three stories high, built in barracks-type design, the favorite of the imaginative Russian designers and architects. In the center of the city, dwarfing everything else, was a concrete windowless building some forty stories high and nearly five hundred feet in diameter. Just from the looks of it, Rockson knew it was where the Reds were performing their tricks. Truckloads of men kept driving up to the front entrance and unloading their cargos of American prisoners, Rock could see through his field glasses.

He unsaddled the hybrid, burying what he didn't need of his traveling supplies. He spoke to the powerful but gentle animal, holding the big brown head in his hands.

"Good luck, boy. I'm going to tether you here. If we're lucky we'll meet again. Make our way back to Century City. If I don't come back, you'll be able to break free from these small branches easily enough." He patted the 'brid on the nose and set off down the steep slopes toward Pavlov City and his destiny. The palomino stared after its master for a long time and then lowered its head, searching for the tastiest clumps of mottled green and brown grass.

Rock took the supplies he had brought with him for his entrance to the Red Fortress out of his small pack—a disguise. He would need it here. His face and name were posted up in every post office and jail in America. TED ROCKSON—WANTED DEAD OR ALIVE—50,000 RUBLE REWARD to the man, Russian or American, who brought him in. Rock put a gray dye in his hair and then a thick gray mustache on. Rath's Special Services' people had given him the stuff along with some other tricks of the trade he might need inside. Satisfied with his masquerade after looking in a small metal mirror, Rock threw the pack over his shoulder and headed down the hill.

He hoped that at least a small American community

had sprung up on the outskirts of the city. The Reds usually paid no attention to the towns that grew around every fort. No more attention to the filthiest lowest levels of society than they would give to a mosquito. Besides, somebody had to carry the garbage out to the dumps and perform menial tasks. He would make his way into the city os one of those "untouchables" that now roamed America like the hobos of old. He got to the bottom of the range of hills and started along some fairly swampy land, the dirt soft and squishy beneath his feet, reeds growing high as corn. He moved cautiously as these kinds of terrain sometimes had quicksand pits which could suck an animal or a man down in minutes.

Rockson had a good five miles to go before reaching the gates of the fortress and that suited him fine as it would be to his advantage to enter at night when the darkness and the shadows and the tiredness of the troops would make detection unlikely. He had gone about a mile when he saw something sticking out of the swampy ground just ahead. It couldn't be! He moved closer. Jesus Christ! A body lay half submerged in the muck, just feet and legs poking out from the ground, the upper half of the corpse buried beneath the sucking black dirt. Must have gotten caught, poor devil, Rock thought. But upside down? Did the guy take a running dive? He moved on slowly, cautiously. Anything out of the ordinary in America 2089 A.D. could mean trouble—death. He pushed his way through a thick clump of high green reeds and emerged into the open.

Ted Rockson had seen just about everything in his life, but even he, as tough as he was, felt himself grow nauseous at the sight before him. Bodies! Bodies everywhere. Strewn around the swamp like so much garbage. Bodies half submerged in the thick foul-smelling mud, buried halfway, heads, hands, feet sticking out like grotesque growths on the soil. He moved his hand down to his pistol instinctively, now hidden beneath an oversized khaki shirt. There were hundreds, perhaps thousands of the rotting corpses—probably all American workers, stripped clean of any bit of clothing. Bodies in every stage of decay from skeletons picked clean as desert bones to foul-smelling, decomposing corpses, ballooned out with the gases of their own rotting bodies. He examined some of the dead bodies more closely, those he could get to close enough to stand the stench of. Strange. None of the bodies had any marks on them except—the skulls had tiny holes at the top of the brain casing. The mindbreaker! These were all rejects of the Red mindbreaking operation. Workers who for one reason or another hadn't taken whatever fiendish conditioning the Russians were trying to instill in them. Men who had gone insane, screaming their guts out as the devilish probes were thrust deeper and deeper into their brain matter.

Rockson walked on, amazed at the extent of the death. A graveyard above ground. And a testament to the nature of the Red beast. He wished every softliner from Century City could see this sight. Their own puking guts would force them to change their tunes of accommodation. It was all too obvious to anyone who would dare to look. The Russian forces of occupation wanted one thing and one thing only: complete domination and control of every American citizen. The sight of so much terrible suffering and wasted life made Rockson realize again with crystal clarity just why he was fighting, devoting his life to the war against the Reds and just how deep his enemy's evil went.

The swamp went on for nearly two miles, every foot of it crammed full of the human garbage. Finally, he came to the end of it, demarcated by a long barbed wire fence. He had to dart suddenly into the surrounding weeds as two Red trucks drove up and unloaded yet another delivery of death. Another hundred corpses, their faces frozen in the most agonizing death masks, lips spread apart, jaws cracked wide open as they must have literally screamed themselves into oblivion. The trucks rolled off again and Rockson found himself on a narrow dirt road that led to the city.

He felt sickened from the sight of so much death. It was one thing for men to die in battle, or from disease, or even to be eaten by the wild creatures that roamed the wastelands of America, but to go like this, for no reason, destroyed like a rodent and then discarded, nothing but garbage. That was something almost too terrible to contemplate. He felt shaken inside and vowed that he would avenge those poor wretched souls whose minds had been torn apart. Someone would pay. He went on about another mile, out of the swampy terrain and onto flat parched fields, one well worn dirt road through the middle which widened slowly as it approached the city. Already the ever present shantytowns that sprang up around Red forts began appearing at the side of the road. Just a few little shacks at first, lean-tos of gnarled branches topped with rusted pieces of tin and cardboard. Then more and more, until the sides of the road and the flat dry ground beyond was filled with the poverty shacks. The dredges of society, who fulfilled the city's lowest tasks and were therefore spared the mindbreaker, stood around outside their hovels talking with one another, clothed in rags. Children scampered through the stinking alleyways formed by the rows of crumbling huts, naked, pursued by starving mongrels barking and snapping at their thin legs.

The dredges stared at Rock, seeming to take too much notice of him. He wondered why with some apprehension. His disguise surely hid his true identity. He looked down at his clothing. What had seemed back in Century City like torn garments, hardly distinguishable from any other untouchable, now appeared to be a rich man's apparel compared with the shredded rags that clothed the hordes along the sides of the road. That was why they stared at this man who looked like he must be rich. But then why was he walking. His disguise already didn't hold together. And if they noticed something wrong, the Red guards at the entrance to Pavlov City would too.

Rockson walked off the road, over to a group of men playing checkers on the ground, having gouged the board into the dirt with twigs and using light and dark pebbles for pieces.

"Anyone want to trade clothes with me?" Rock asked the group. Three men jumped up instantly, surrounding him.

"And who would you be, mister, wanting to trade? Maybe you got some riches in that there satchel of yourn," the largest of the three, a bearded greasy-looking lout with huge blubbery lips said with a sneer. Rockson stared the man hard in the eyes.

"I'm not looking for trouble, mister, and I'd advise

you not to start any. I just want to trade these clothes of mine for one of your sets of duds." The big man reached out with a hand covered with brown warts toward Rock's shoulder bag. Rock grabbed hold of the wrist and twisted it quickly over and down. The man fell to the dirt screaming in pain.

"You broke me hand, broke me Goddamned hand," he moaned. The others stared at Rockson with consternation. He had just taken down the local bully as easily as if he were a child. One of them piped up.

"I'll go for the deal, mister." He eyed Rockson's pants and jacket with greedy eyes. He had never had a set of clothes like that in his life. A little dirty, but not even one hole. He'd be the envy of the shacklands. They went behind a hut and exchanged garments. Rock could feel the bugs crawling around the lining of the man's ripped and filthy shirt but sacrifices had to be made. He looked down at himself with new appearance. Yes, it would do fine. Torn, riddled with holes, stained with years of sweat and filthy toil. Rock thanked the man and headed back down the road toward the fort. The newly clothed untouchable paraded around in front of his neighbors who jealously eyed his new appearance: blue jeans without a hole, a light blue workshirt with just a few threads showing, and an amazingly perfect khaki jacket. The man kept his hand on a long icepick inside the inner pocket of the jacket. He would die to protect his new acquisitions. In the camp of the poorest he was suddenly a man of means.

Rockson headed toward the fort which grew closer and bigger by the minute. The outer walls that formed the defensive perimeter were nearly forty feet high, concrete two feet thick with barbed wire running along the top. He walked up to the main entrance, manned on every side by submachine gun-toting guards. They eyed him without really taking much notice, just one of many untouchables who came and went. Rock passed the first defensive perimeter with a big lump in his throat as he walked into the enemy's camp. If any of these soldiers knew who he was . . . At a second checkpoint a Red Army sergeant stopped him and asked in a weary voice.

"Where you going, scum?"

"Garbage detail, sir," Rock said in as meek and terrified a voice as he could muster. He looked down at the soldier's feet and wrung his hands together in a gesture of submission.

"Oh, get on then," the guard said, turning away and spitting. That had been easy enough, Rockson thought. Almost too easy. He headed down the long open streets of Pavlov City, head bowed down as were the heads of all the imprisoned Americans, for even looking straight into the eyes of a Red soldier could mean death. But he saw everything from the corner of his eyes, saw the work crews marching, the lines of prisoners being taken to the brainwashing center. Rockson blended in easily with the other untouchables who walked around pushing wheelbarrows filled with waste. No one noticed the most wanted man in America. They were too busy building their wretched city.

Rockson walked around for what seemed like miles, taking mental notes on every structure, on the troop quarters and munitions dumps. They must be building the place day and night. Zhabov must have been pouring every ruble he could lay his filthy hands on into the city. Obviously he saw the products of Pavlov City as something that would give him a big edge over Killov in their ongoing power struggle. To confuse matters even more, Rock began noticing what were without question KGB. They wore the feared blackshirt uniform and the death's-head patch on their shoulders. What the hell were KGB doing inside a Red Army fort as important to Zhabnov as this. But if that sight shocked him, Rockson nearly did a double take as he rounded the next corner and saw a squad of about one hundred men wearing a type of Russian uniform he had never seen before, darker than the usual with an American flag patch with a rifle through the center. They marched by in double time and Rock knew instantly they were Americans. Americans in Russian uniforms. A sight that made him want to vomit.

Suddenly the endless low buildings gave way to a large exercise and marching field where thousands of soldiers were going through every kind of battle exercise: obstacle courses, firing ranges, march drills. The trainers were all Russian but the troops were Americans. Every last one of them. Rock walked along the perimeter of the field, picking up little pieces of refuse as if he were one of the eternal garbage pickers who wandered around the Red forts cleaning them as surely as barnacles cling to rocks, sucking every bit of loose waste from them. Totally unnoticed, Rockson took in the bizarre sight of Americans training to be Russians. Then he saw their eyes, when he got close enough—the eyes of the Americans—and it made him shudder. It was the eyes of the dead. Their bodies were still functioning but their eyes stared straight ahead. Rock remembered reading about a creature from the past history of America, South America, if he recalled correctly. They had had a name for men like this—zombies, they had called them.

So the Reds were turning American workers into zombie soldiers to go out and kill their countrymen. His worst fears were confirmed. And by the looks of it they were turning them out by the thousands. The men's heads were all shaven and had those telltale puncture wounds at the very top of the skull. Little bumps that would never completely heal where the mindbreaker probes had burned out their past identity and instilled a command more powerful than love or hate—a command to obey their Red masters.

Rockson felt his entire being tremble. His hatred for the Red beast was at a new peak. He vowed at that moment to destroy the entire city. Somehow, some way he would stop this hideous experiment from being carried to fruition. He made a complete reconnaissance of the city, totally unnoticed by the overconfident Red troops, as he pretended to pick up little bits of paper. As the sun set Rock hid near the large concrete building in the center of the fortress, inside a garbage dumpster filled with construction waste—bits of woods, sawdust, rusting buckets filled with hardened concrete. The dumpster was about two hundred feet from the barbed wire fences surrounding the forty story building. Guards patrolled around it in groups of five, smgs cradled in their arms.

Rock waited nearly three hours until activity in the Red city had died down to virtually nothing. They would all be sleeping now. Even the guards would have their senses at their lowest readiness. It was time to strike. He took out his bowie knife and headed toward the fence. They had set up a defensive perimeter which for the normal man would have seemed impenetrable, but Rock's eyes took in the machine gun emplacements, the guard towers, the bunkers with slits of light and immediately saw the weak spot. To the right, in the space between two towers, the lights of the floodlamps faded to a dark gray. He headed toward the blind zone, crawling along on his arms and legs, his dark filthy clothes hiding him among the shadows. The moon, thank God, was packed between immense jagged brown and purple clouds that filled the skies like radioactive boulders. Rockson got right up to the fence which was electrified. He took out a piece of thick material from his pack and wrapped it around his hands. The fence was nearly ten feet tall. Rock slid right up to the base of the steel mesh and watched the two guard towers. Not a sound, nor a movement. He braced himself for the shock and leaped the height of the electric fence, grabbing the barbed wire at the top. He pulled himself over with every ounce of his mutant strength and soared over the top. The surge of electricity passed through the thick burlap material around his hands, and he gritted his teeth as he soared in a perfect arc over the top, landing on the other side in the dirt. He rolled instantly into a darker shadow created by one of the towers and waited a few seconds to see if he'd been spotted.

Nothing! Rockson made his way, creeping among the dark spots until he reached the base of the ominous brainwashing building. He spotted an entrance of some kind below ground. Some sort of service access, he thought, for taking care of the subterranean machinery of the building. He slid down the steps to a door that was chained shut with a padlock. He fitted the bowie knife between the lock and its chain and pushed with all his strength. It took three minutes but finally the small metal lock had enough and popped off its chain link. Rock pushed the door open and headed into the monolithic structure.

The basement halls were dimly lit by unshielded lightbulbs, and, seeing no one in sight, the Doomsday Warrior moved swiftly through the labyrinth of corridors until he reached the fire stairs. He bounded up them three at a time. He'd start on the second floor and work his way up until he found just what the hell was going on. Rock opened the steel door to the second floor slowly, his knife in his hand, cocked and ready. A guard about thirty feet down the hall sat facing him but his eyes were closed as he dozed, dreaming undoubtedly of vodka flowing down the steppes of Mother Russia. Rock slid into the hall, silent as a cat. He headed straight for the Russian who somehow sensed the motion and opened his eyes. The Red soldier bolted upright in his chair and grabbed wildly for his pistol at his side. Rock's fourteen inch blade spun through the air like a whirling blur of death. It entered the Russian's throat sticking clean through. The man's eyes bulged as big as apples and he dropped to the floor spitting blood and gurgling out death noises. Rock ripped the bowie knife from the corpse's throat and headed down the corridor.

Bells! Everywhere! He heard doors slamming and loudspeakers blasting away in Russian. They were on to him. He rushed back toward the fire door through which he had just entered but heard a click just as he reached it. Locked! Rock tore down the long neon-lit hall toward the far end some two hundred feet away. He reached it and swung through the door just as a squad of Reds rounded the corner to the right. He veered to the left away from them just yards ahead of them. He sprinted with all his strength, and within a few seconds tore ahead of them, coming to another intersection of halls. The place was a Goddamned maze, he muttered mentally, and took a left, down a corridor filled with glass doors announcing Lieutenant this and Major that in gold letters. Ahead of him another squad of Reds suddenly appeared. He was cut off.

The Russians closed in on him from both sides and as they approached, Rock noticed that they weren't regular Red Army at all—every man was dressed in the dark brown fatigues but they all wore the hideous emblem of the death's-head on their shoulders. Elite troops—the officer closest to Rockson smiled and spoke in broken English.

"Ted Rockson, I presume! You may as well surrender. We have been expecting your presence for days. I promise you you cannot escape. The floor is filled with over two hundred of our elite troops. Please—no fuss—yes?"

"Oh no, no fuss," Rockson said, walking down the hall toward the paunchy officer, so handsome in his crisply pressed uniform. When he was about ten feet away Rock rushed the KGB man. It was time to die. For all of them. Rock knew his days of survival were over. He couldn't let them take him alive. But he'd get ten, maybe even twenty before they took him down. He suddenly zigzagged down the corridor like a wild animal, reaching the officer as the man was still trying to find the American in his pistol sights. Rock slammed the long-bladed death dagger through the smart uniform jacket, through the rows of medals on the officer's chest, through the man's heart. The KGB brass fell to the white tile floor, blood spurting from his neatly carved chest.

Rockson turned toward the other troops who fired wildly hitting one another, ricocheting bullets off the walls.

"No! No! Don't shoot! Don't kill that man or you die!" screamed the officer leading the second squad of men from the other end of the hall. Rockson slammed into the cowering elite troops jumping around in confusion behind the body of their dead commanding officer. He slashed away with his blade, a whirlwind of suicide-seeking death. He caught one man in the shoulder, nearly severing it with the heavy razor sharp bowie knife. A Red rushed at him, a bayonet attached to the muzzle of his Kalashnikov. Rockson sidestepped the soldier and brought the knife down on top of his head. The blade pierced the skull, pushing nearly four inches in. Rock withdrew the blade in one even motion as the officer continued walking forward for two more steps, not even realizing he was dead. Then his body fell like a sack of stones to the slippery red floor.

Rockson slashed everywhere around him, kicking backwards when he felt flesh approach. Troops fell around him like blades of grass cut with a scythe—their bodies cut, smashed, bones broken and pushing through their own skin as if seeking daylight. But they hit back, too, slamming at Rockson with the butts of their rifles. The squads closed in from both sides of the hall. He killed and killed but at last the bodies just piled up around him and over him. The KGB elite troops hit at the murderous whirlwind of a man with their guns and fists until he felt himself sinking into a bloody darkness from the combined blows. Goodbye world, he thought with a detached irony for just one second before he slipped beneath the waves of unconsciousness.

Fourteen

Premier Vassily in his sickbed was feeling slightly better. He was thinking, musing about the latest information about America. The rebel attacks were growing more frequent, more daring. In some ways the freefighters, Vassily realized, having read his history well, were like the aboriginal Indians of that continent three hundred years ago. They raided convoys that traveled through their land, were hopelessly outnumbered and outgunned, were scattered and divided, yet fought valiantly on against the conquerers who controlled their land. The analogy was quite complete. The premier had to admit he felt a certain respect for the brave but doomed fighters. He hoped that someday—and it could happen if Tchilichev, the young moderate whom Vassily was grooming to take over—succeeded him instead of Zhabnov or Killov. Perhaps there could be some sort of peace. Some kind of reservations established for the American freefighters in the United Soviet States of America, the way the old Indians, the Apache, the Navajo . . . had made peace treaties with the white man and finally stopped fighting against him, against the inevitable.

Of course, many of the so called treaties had been broken or ignored by the American government. No doubt, he had to admit, being if nothing else realistic in his appraisals, the Russian government would ignore many of the treaties as well. But still, he hated to think of the total destruction of every last American freefighter, even the legendary Ted Rockson. After all they were brave and resourceful much as his own people had been in their struggle against the German Army in the Second World War. Surely land could be set aside for them—wastelands—they were somewhat resistant to radiation anyway. Yes, a good idea, Vassily decided firmly. I will propose it to Tchilichev. Peace— peace . . . He fell asleep thinking of passing on peace to the world. He coughed weakly, his breathing shallow, spasmodic.

Outside the premier's room the three doctors from the Moscow College of Surgeons conferred. They didn't see any chance of the premier's surviving the week. Now that they had regained regular access to Vassily, they had been able to increase the dosage of the slow acting poison.

"Ah," said the bearded Minkin, as they slipped down the staircase of the premier's mansion. "It is a good thing the premier has allowed us to continue the treatments. Killov will surely make his move for power soon. Then we shall be rewarded."

"Shut up you fool," Sverdov snapped. "Even here someone could have a listening device. Spies are everywhere. Keep your mouth shut. It is by no means over yet. Have you seen any more deterioration since we began leaving the injections for his nigger servant to administer?"

"No—" Minkin said nervously, "but—"

"Perhaps the premier only said that he would have Rahallah give the injections in order for us to stop pestering him. Sometimes I wonder if he is really taking it. He still looks too well for a man being given intravenous doses of cancer toxin."

"If so—what will we tell Killov?" Minkin asked as they reached the front door and another black servant handed them their thick overcoats. "That we have failed? That he must rearrange his plans? We must somehow arrange an accident for the black bastard and regain direct access to His Excellency."

"Outside—outside in the park we will talk more," Sverdlov said. "Not here." They reached the bottom of the red-carpeted outer stairs and walked out between the ceremonial guards standing stiffly at attention in the subfreezing temperature, their faces white as the snow that fell constantly from the dark sky. Photographers flashed pictures as the trio of physicians hit the sidewalk.

"How is the premier?" asked the senior correspondent from *Pravda*, holding a microphone in front of them.

"He is progressing quite well due to our treatment," Minkin said flashing a toothy smile. "And of course, His Excellency's strong constitution is helping him along. However, I must be candid, the Grandfather remains critically ill. We should all hope for his speedy recovery for the sake of the empire." Other questions were shunned and the doctors walked to their waiting limousines. They had their chauffeurs drive them to

Gorky Park where the snow was covering the statues of the Soviet Unions' great heros, and the pigeons sat on the heads and arms of the famous Russians, oblivious to their stature. The three physicians walked to the Rocket Pioneers Cosmonauts' Fountain to talk amidst the cooing of the pigeons and the blanketing cover of snow. Here was one of the few places in Moscow they could be sure they weren't being bugged. They sat on a cold wooden bench and discussed further how to kill the most powerful man in the world.

The premier summoned Rahallah when he awoke from his dreams of peace and had him squirt out the hypodermics that the doctors had left and dispose of them. Then the educated servant read some selections from Rilke to the aged premier. Rilke was the Grandfather's favorite poet. Rimbaud, he considered immature however evocative, Blake, too ethereal, Pound and Eliot overly intellectual. But Rilke—Rilke had said it all. The book was inside a cover stating, *Lenin—Glorious Leader* by Menshekov. Just in case someone should glance at his shelves in his library. Rilke was on the proscribed list of forbidden readings. A premier could, of course, have anything. But it was not good for morale or for the underlings, the nurses and housekeepers, to see the premier of all the Russians contaminating himself.

"Read it to me again, Rahallah," the premier said softly. "You know—my favorite. Rahallah opened the book and his clear strong voice recited:

This stood once among mankind

> stood in the midst of fate—the extinguisher
> stood in the midst of not-knowing—as though it existed
> and bowed stars from the established heavens towards it
> Angel I'll show it to you as well—There!
> In your glance it shall stand redeemed at last
> in a final uprightness—Angel gaze for it is we
> o Mightiness, tell them that WE were capable of it.

"Ah yes, beautiful my faithful servant. How beautiful," Vassily said, his eyes remaining closed as they had through the reading. "And you enunciate so clearly, catching every nuance of the poet." He drifted off to sleep once again, a smile on his peaked face.

Rahallah put the book back on the library shelf and went over to the bottle. He had squirted the last doses of the medicine the doctors had left for him to give the Grandfather. He was sure there was something wrong with the stuff—it smelled funny. He sealed the lid on the bottle and put tape on the outside. On it he wrote, TO MKVD CENTRAL LAB—FOR ANALYSIS—TOP PRIORITY—A. VASSILY. TOP SECRET. The chauffeur was handed the container inside a small box and he was off. Now we shall see, Rahallah thought. Now we see. . . .

At six-oh-seven the next morning, five large men plus local MKVD officers, members of the premier's elite private forces, kicked down the door of Dr. Minkin's three story house on Plepalsky Place and entered his bedroom, machine pistols in their hands. The doctor was sitting up in bed, his wife, fat and naked, next to him, having both awakened as the heavy wood door splintered apart.

"What is this intrusion?" Minkin demanded. "I'll have you know I am the chief surgeon of—"

"Shut up, traitor," one of the beefy goons snarled. "Move aside madame. He continued staring down at the terrified wife of one of Moscow's elite. The five officers filled the bedroom, their muddy feet dirtying the white rug around the bed. The wife knew about the poison. She was privy to all of her husband's dealings. So she knew why they came. She had also planned what to do in this case. She would not go with him. She slipped out of bed, wrapping herself in the down comforter, and walked to the other side of the room.

"No!" her husband screamed once before the peaceful domestic scene was shattered by the firing of five machine pistols. The lifeless body of Dr. Minkin slammed into the wall, spurting blood through innumerable holes.

Simultaneously in the Moscow suburbs of Dzernsk and Omsk, similar squads of the premier's private army mowed down the other two conspirators—one making it to his car and getting out of the driveway before high velocity armor piercing bullets smashed through the windows and door, killing him and his chauffeur. In Omsk, the youngest of the trio got down on his hands and knees and begged for his life. The hail of bullets nearly tore his head from his body.

The lab tests had found the poison. The order had been given, signed in the shaky hand of the premier himself when told of the plot by Rahallah. It was over. The conspiracy was over. Now the Grandfather might actually recover. Perhaps he was not nearly as ill as had been thought. Only time would tell. But at least he had bought some extra time for himself, for determining who would rule the world when he was gone. It *was* Killov. The young doctor had blurted it out as his scrotum was crushed before he was liquidated. And Vassily knew that the KGB colonel was already carrying out an operation in America, probably timed with the plot of the doctors to finally finish him off. The last dose of medicine would have done him in within forty-eight hours. There was enough poison in the hypos, the lab tests had said, to kill a horse.

He stared at the aerial reconnaissance photos of the colonel's attack on Pavlov City in the central part of the United States. Not American attackers but Killov's KGB forces had taken over the Soviet science city and taken command away from Zhabnov's Red Army forces. Radio had been cut off but satellite intel was able to eavesdrop on bits of conversation within the fortress city, conveyed over walkie talkie and phone. Indeed, without question, the city had fallen to KGB forces with Killov in direct command.

So, his nephew Zhabnov and Killov were now fighting openly to take control of America, preparing to broaden their power base when the Grandfather died. If it were not for Rahallah's watchful eyes . . . As much as he had tried to avoid it, Vassily could see that he would have to enter the struggle for power. He could not allow Killov to win. No way. The man was a servant of the devil. Even he, though not a religious man, could see that. But how? How to fight an enemy as clever as the colonel, with so much power, so well protected.

Rahallah brought the Grandfather the medicinal tea he had prepared for the premier from his ancestral herbs. Vassily eagerly drank the restorative liquid. At least he had one man around him who was not trying to kill him. No—he, the Grandfather, had been too soft, too pacific. He had thought that the others would struggle but remain at least nominally civilized. But that was not the case. Killov was an animal. He had directly challenged the premier. And now he must die.

Fifteen

Rockson came to with the sound of rifles firing nearby. He opened his eyes. He was in a cell, chained down. His body felt like it had been through a meatgrinder. God, did he ache. He remembered those last few moments—an avalanche of Reds enveloping him. So they had him. For the first time in his life, in his thirty-four years of beating the odds, the Russians had captured him. And worse, he wasn't in the hands of the Red Army from whom he would have a good chance at escape—but the KGB, who would watch him with the eyes of a hawk. They wouldn't allow the man they had spent millions upon to get away now. It didn't look good. In fact things were so bad that Rockson had to grin. He found a kind of detached amusement in such a hopeless situation. But no fear. Death had been his companion for so long that it was more like an old but known adversary than a force that terrified him. Ted Rockson didn't know the emotion of fear—it wasn't in his nature.

One of the guards walked over to the bars of his cell

and peered through with a sneer. "Wouldn't you like to know how close you are to the end? Ted Rockson, the mighty Ultimate American, just a prisoner like all the other idiot bandits who think they can defeat the combined power of the Russian Empire. Do you admit now who is stronger, Rockson? At least will you admit the truth?"

"Why don't you step in here with me for a moment, compadre," Rockson said. "You and I could have a little fun. See, I'm all chained up," he held his manacled hands in the air. "You KGB like to get your kicks." Rock smiled a come-hither grin.

"And get crushed in your mutant arms? No thank you, Rockson. But I think Colonel Killov will be down here shortly and he will get what he wants from you. I've seen our commander work on prisoners. He is a true master of the black arts of getting the information that he wants."

"I'm sure," Rock said cynically. "If there's anything that Killov is an expert in it's torture." The guard walked off to check other prisoners down the hall who began yelling obscenities. Rock sat on the cold concrete floor looking around the small cell for any opening, any weakness. Who was in the next cell? There was a sheet drawn across the bars between the two cells. His imprisonment looked pretty solid and yet . . .

Several minutes later he heard the sounds of approaching footsteps. He knew who it was—his sixth sense told him. At last they would meet face to face after all these years. Colonel Killov walked up to bars of the cell and looked in, his rat-like face twitching from the combination of all the pills he was now popping and the excitement at capturing Ted Rockson.

"So you walked into our trap, Rockson," the colonel said with a lopsided smirk. "I thought you were uncatchable—a legend in your own time."

So it had been a trap. This whole takeover by the KGB of Zhabnov's Red Army forces in Pavlov City. Rock kicked himself mentally for not seeing it ahead of time, although exactly what he could have done instead he wasn't sure.

"I'm flattered," Rock said looking up through the bars. "You make me feel so popular."

"So you have steady nerves and cool eyes, do you?" Killov said sneering, his own body trembling lightly. "Maybe I'll wind up making those eyes decorations on my trophies wall," Killov said, agitated.

"Go to hell with your absurd threats, Killov. You'll get nothing from me. Why don't you come in here and we'll see whose eyes wind up on the cutting room floor."

"So nasty, Rockson. And I heard you were so polite. A defender of maidens and dogs." The KGB colonel said, his personal bodyguards standing on each side of him, their pistols aimed at the prisoner.

"Polite to normal humans, murderer, not barbarian Red savages." His words seemed to enrage Killov who couldn't maintain his cool under the influence of the mood-altering drugs.

"Guards, spray the stun gas in there," the colonel commanded. Two KGB officers advanced to the edge of the cell and sprayed an aerosol spray at Rockson. He gasped and passed out.

When he came to again, he was tied to a post in another room. He glanced around the room quickly and saw its nature: posts, whips, nooses hanging from poles. Rock heard a sound to his right and turned to see Killov heating an already white-hot poker in the flames of a coal-burning stove. The KGB commander had his jacket off and his skinny arms of pale dead flesh held the burning steel up every few seconds to check its heat. Rockson pretended to still be unconscious as he watched the guards around the room and Killov himself, preparing to begin the torture of the Ultimate American.

At last Killov decided that the poker was at the perfect torture temperature. He lifted it from the flames and walked toward Rockson, holding the white steel up toward the captured freefighter's face. With the speed of a panther, Rockson kicked up at the glowing steel, catching it just at the tip. The metal spun up and out of Killov's hand and slammed into the KGB commander's right cheek, searing it instantly with the sound of sizzling human flesh. The colonel screamed and threw his hands over his face.

Two guards rushed at Rock, their pistols out, and prepared to blow the brains out of the man who had dared attack their leader. Rock looked them in the eye. This was what he wanted—death before torture. He had gotten in one last blow for freedom.

"No!" screamed Killov, his hand covering the four inch long bright red slash that ran from his eye to below his ear. "Don't kill him. That's what he wants. We will have our fun later. First psychological torture then the pain. Give him the drug," Killov ordered. A KGB man walked over to Rock and jabbed him with a needle he described mysteriously as an aphrodisiac. For what purpose Rockson couldn't imagine. Though he quickly felt his loins burning with a strange intensity.

The KGB officers took Rock back to his cell and left him there chained up again after slapping him around for a while. Rock sat on the floor again quite satisfied with himself. He was still alive and he had given Killov a scar he would never get rid of—something to remember Rock by long after he was gone. He wondered what they meant by psychological and what the injection had to do with it. He heard the voices of guards outside his cell and then the sound of a female voice in the cell next to his. The guards went into her cell and pulled back the sheet that separated the two prisoners. Then they left. And Rock knew what they meant by psychological torture. For there in the next cell, illuminated in the dim slip of the moonlight from the narrow window overhead, was the most beautiful woman Rockson had ever seen.

The milky rays of the moon bathed her long golden tresses, this lovely ample daughter of America, barely out of her teens. Silky flesh raised on milk and butter and honey, with upturned erect nipples, that lithe turn to her thighs, that flushed rosy-cheeked face. Rock felt his loins swell and throb with desire. Desire that would have been overwhelming anyway, but now with the powerful aphrodisiac injected into his bloodstream, it was unbearable. Desire turned to torture.

The most beautiful girl he had ever seen and she was stark naked, perfectly proportioned with crystal green eyes. He stared at her and she looked shyly back.

"My name is Kim," she said softly. "You're Ted Rockson. I heard the guards talking about you. I—I—'ve heard so much about you. Every American has. I—I—don't know what to say." She looked down at her naked body, hands and feet chained to the wall.

"Well, I must confess, it's not a usual introduction. Please don't feel embarrassed. The Reds want to play with our minds."

"Are you seriously hurt?" she asked with concern, looking at the gash on the side of his head, from which blood dripped slowly. Rock shook his head no. He felt a pain in his left rib cage. The Reds must have really worked him over. He didn't remember it. He was shackled by the hands to a chain about six feet long. He rose and was able to nearly reach the bars separating the two of them, the chains stopping him about six inches away.

"I'm afraid we meet at an inopportune moment," Rock said, looking through the thick steel bars. "How did they get you?"

"I was with my father, Mr. Rockson," the vision of beauty said nervously. "Michael Langford and we—"

"*The* Michael Langford?" Rockson gasped. "Every freefighter knows of his endeavors to politically organize America. Why I met him myself about three years ago. A great man. Is he—" Rock suddenly had the chilling vision of perhaps the most important man in America being tortured by the Reds.

"No, he escaped. We were in the mountains heading from Casperville to Fantown. My father is in the process of organizing a Re-Constitutional Convention to elect a congress and a president so that the Free Cities can evolve politically as well as militarily. We were attacked by a KGB Commando Death Squad. My father and his men managed to shoot their way out but I fell off my damned hybrid and when I came to, I was—here." She began crying softly, obviously ashamed of showing her fear but unable to hold back the tears.

"Don't cry, sweet woman," Rock said, touched by her vulnerability as well as her beauty, though he couldn't offer her a reason not to.

"They plan to use me tomorrow. The officers are going to—" She couldn't finish but the intention was clear. Rockson groaned inwardly. He could feel his anger rising by the second.

"I've heard that you bring luck, Rockson, wherever you go. Maybe my fate is not sealed yet."

"I'm afraid my luck—except meeting you—has fallen off as of late," Rock said, holding up his manacled hands.

She looked at him from the other end of her cell about ten feet away where she stood stretched to her full five foot two inches, her legs spread apart, feet chained. Her expression was strange, curious, fearful, and—something else. "Rockson—I—I am a virgin. They will—I didn't want it to be this way. I may be dead by tomorrow night, but first they will rape me, many of them." She looked down at the cold floor barely able to continue. But her own desires were stronger than her feminine shyness. She raised her head again and this time her eyes were bold, flaming. "I want you!" She said directly. "To make love to me."

"I—I—" Rock stuttered over and over, tongue-tied for perhaps the first time in his life. "It's not that I wouldn't love to. Don't get me wrong, but we're not exactly in the best setup to . . ."

"I have my own secrets," she said. "Watch!" She squirmed in her chains, pulling her feet and hands this way and that, wriggling her extremities like writhing snakes. Slowly, ever so slowly, she began pulling free from the shackles. First her right foot came free, popping out suddenly. She looked across at Rockson who stared in absolute amazement. Kim smiled and continued to move her hands this way and that, first fitting the upper part of the wrist, then the blade of the hand through. Within two minutes she was free. She looked at Rockson and started toward him.

She walked right up to the bars of his cell so her body was about eight inches away from his. He felt the ice-hard erection swelling under his zipper as her fingers traced down his waist to the clasp of his pants. Rockson pulled himself as far forward as he could, holding his manacled hands behind his back and stretching the lower portion of his body as far forward as he could. She opened the zipper with trembling fingers and the engorged member burst forth. She kneeled down in the other cell, her rising nipples pressed tight against the cold steel of the bars. She reached her head through the eight inch wide spaces between the bars, and with her marshmallow soft lips engulfed his manhood. She moaned with innocent erotic delight.

"They never thought of this, Rockson," Kim said, taking the stiff pole from between her moist lips. "The Reds thought only to prevent you from reaching me—their women never want it—they have lost their sex drive generations ago and are mere chattel for the men's pleasure."

"Come to me," Rockson said, his eyes melting at her smooth perfect body. She pressed forward and rubbed her breasts against his waist and then his organ, so large and stiff. She swooned with the power of her desire for this man as she felt her burning hot sex wet and ready for him.

"Do it," she said. "Please Rockson, put it in." She gripped her hands around the bars and put her legs up on the cross bar about three feet above the ground. She pressed the wet lips of her moist furry triangle forward until it met the swollen head of Rockson's manhood. She was wet, very wet, and she pushed her hips forward, spasmodically reaching for him. Tomorrow she would be dead, she thought. And my life, my love, all my body is for this man tonight.

"Do it, get it . . . in!" she pleaded. Rockson guided the probing staff in by moving his hips. She reached down with her hands and put the head between the opened petals of pink flesh. "It's . . . hard . . . it hurts." A single tear fell down each of her alabaster cheeks. He pushed with all his might to penetrate her, and she gasped and rolled her eyes heavenwards as the organ moved suddenly, cleanly into her. She waited a second, getting used to the newness of it all. Then she began moving, slowly at first, up and down on the long shaft, then with increasing vigor and jerking motions, holding onto his hips, her nipples squashed against the firm bars. It slid in and out in stronger and stronger pumps, filling her stomach. She moved on him like a knife cutting into deep velvet, like a girl/woman who has realized her dreams at last.

"Rock—oh—Rock," she groaned again and again. "It's so good . . . it's . . . "

"Don't talk," he said, "they'll hear us. But I know it's the same for me."

They were reaching that peak called orgasm—a series of quivers were the first signs from her; the relentless buildup of a bull-like sperm, of a Hoover Dam about to burst, sent shudders through his tortured body. Then they came. Like a tidal wave, simultaneously gasping out, and heaving in jerks of ecstasy.

At last they both subsided and he slipped out from her as she choked off a groan of loss. "I love you . . . can I say that, Ted Rockson? Can I say it for just this night?" He stood up looking at this beautiful creature before him.

"Always," he said as softly as he had ever spoken in his life. "Always—because I love you too, Kim."

"Tomorrow when they come they'll find a woman. A woman who has already known love. They can do what they want with me now—I don't care."

He looked at her with tears in his eyes. Because he did care. Suddenly he cared terribly what was going to happen. He couldn't let her die. Which meant he had to save himself as well, no matter what the odds. Rockson had seen perfect beauty and it made him feel half crazy.

Sixteen

They were awakened by the sound of guards in the middle of the night. Two KGB men with the skulls smiling hideously on their sleeves. They came for Kim and seemed quite disturbed that she was no longer in her chains. They looked at Rockson, who stared coldly back, then opened her cell.

"Where the hell are you taking her?" he yelled out, struggling against his chains although the motions were absurdly futile.

"You'll have your fun soon enough, Rockson," one of the officers said, grabbing Kim by the breasts and squeezing the nipples hard. "See, this is what we're going to do, scum." Kim closed her eyes in pain but didn't utter a word. She wouldn't give the bastards the pleasure of seeing her squirm.

Rockson felt insane with fury. The veins stood out in his neck like taut ropes. "Let her go, you fucking bastards. Let her go." The guards pulled Kim away, grabbing at her ass and breasts, trying to humiliate her. "We'll have fun with her," one of the officers said to the other. "She's a hot fuck." He looked over his back at Rockson who stared out with the rage of one possessed by demons.

Rock stared after the departing woman he loved and pulled against the chains with every bit of mutant strength he possessed. Nothing! Not even Ted Rockson could snap inch thick steel chains.

He paced back and forth in the six foot area he could move in, furiously trying to figure some way out. Suddenly two more guards appeared at the bars. His break. No matter what, he would escape. The guards opened the door and trained their submachine guns on him. "Out, scum!" one of them said, his black boots shiny as a silver dollar. They led him out and down the corridor. Where was Kim? Every door they passed Rockson tried to sense her, to use his slight ESP powers to feel her presence. He couldn't. As they turned a corner two bodies were stacked against the wall.

"We caught them trying to get away this morning," one of the guards said, turning to Rockson. "Friends of yours?" Rock looked closely as they drew close. The Doomsday Warrior could scarcely believe his eyes. He *did* know them. Lying on the floor were the bloody bodies of Dennis Chapin and Dean Keppel, two of Century City's infiltration experts. Why had they come here to Pavlov City? Poor bastards! Their guts were spilling out from their dissected abdomens. Rock saw something else as well: their F-2 issue boots. He hadn't been able to wear them into the city because of his disguise, but Rock knew that the boots had several special devices built into the heel by Dr. Shecter's Special Weapons Section.

"Please," Rockson said, stopping near the bodies. "They're men from my city, could I just say a brief prayer over them? It's their religion." The guards looked at each other. The taller one said, "Oh let him—he's chained. Besides I want to see if God answers these American's prayers." The guard laughed contemptuously. "Will your fictitious God bring down a bolt of lightning?" He continued, now feeling he was needling Rockson by mocking his dead.

The Reds laughed and pushed Rock to his knees next to the mangled corpses. Rock began chanting and moving his hands over the dead men, and, as he did so, he managed to turn and snag the heel of Chapin's left boot. He pulled it quickly into the palm, shielding it from the view of the sneering KGB guards with his back. He pushed the switch that opened the hidden clasp and the heel revealed two small capsules: a small explosive device and a mini gas shell. He broke the seal on the gas and threw it behind him, holding his breath tightly. He waited, continuing to look at the bodies for about six seconds until he heard the two guards hit the floor behind him. Rock held his breath until the last wisp of gas vanished. He took the keys from the guard's sidepocket and opened his cuffs, rubbing his wrists. It felt good to be free. He lifted the machine pistols from the Red guards and quickly stripped one of them, taking his uniform. Not a bad fit. The black leather garment clung to his body and the dark sun glasses would hide his features. He made a formidable KGB Blackshirt.

He heard a sound coming from down the corridor and hid in the frame of a doorway. An older KGB officer rounded the corner and Rock threw a hand over his mouth and dragged him into the shadows. He slammed the muzzle of the machine pistol into the man's spine.

"Where's the girl?" he said pulling the crook of his arm tightly around the Red's throat.

"The who?" the officer said weakly, trying to breathe through Rockson's grip.

"Don't play games with me, mister. I have nothing to lose. Once more I ask you where's the girl? This time you die." He pushed the gun hard against the man's spine. The officer winced in pain. It felt like his back was about to be snapped in two.

"I'll tell. Don't kill me, Rockson," the chalky-faced major said. "She's in room three seventy-one. Next floor up at the other end."

"Thanks," Rock said sincerely and slammed the man as hard as he could in the side of the head with the butt of the pistol. The man slammed down to the floor, out for hours if not forever.

Rock headed toward the elevator, trying to turn his head down as he passed a guard stationed by the lobby doors of the ten running elevator cars. The guard barely noticed, glancing up mindlessly and then looking down again at a dirty magazine imported from Moscow hidden behind a rule and regulations book of the Red Army. Rock still didn't quite understand the mix of KGB and regular Red Army troops. Apparently Killov had taken over, yet he permitted many Red Army officers and guards to roam and work the fortress. They're all scared, Rockson decided. When the KGB comes knocking they knuckle under. Killov's got them all under his spell of fear. The man was creating his own legend—of death and destruction.

Rock emerged on the third floor and quickly found the direction to the room. There! Three seventy-one. On the other side he could hear gruff male laughter. They were already playing with her. God help every man in there, Rock thought grimly as he opened the door and burst inside, a pistol held forward in each hand.

Kim was in the center of the room, naked and trussed up on a wooden X, her hands and legs tied wide apart. But nothing had happened yet, Rock could see instantly, beyond verbal humiliation. She was fully conscious, unmarked, and defiant. Six men stood around her, two beginning to unbuckle their pants. One, an officer with a black eyepatch over his right eye, turned.

"So, Yuri," he said, thinking he recognized the officer behind the dark sunglasses, "you couldn't stay away, heh." His expression changed suddenly from a sneer to terror. "You! You!" he croaked, backing slowly away.

"Yeah me, fellows. I thought I'd join you, too. Show you how an American does it." He flipped the machine pistols onto automatic and pulled the triggers back on both of them. He sprayed death in front of him and to the left where the six were grouped together, laughing a moment before in the male bravado. The twin hails of slugs ripped across the six like laser beams ripping at their stomachs and leaving a bloody trail of intestine and blood which poured out onto the red-and-black checkered floor. They slid down into their own red blood and lay there unmoving.

Rock ran past the mangled red things that had been men and cut Kim's bonds. She put her hands over her breasts, ashamed and shivering slightly in the cold. Rock stripped off the clothes of one of the dead men and slipped the two large uniform over her slim firm body.

"We've got one chance in hell, Kim. You've got to do everything I say instantly, without question. Maybe, just maybe, we'll get out of here."

"I will, Rock," Kim said, wiping away a few salty tears and standing straight up. "Trust me," she added softly, smiling at the sight of Rock's handsome face and powerful, muscled body right in front of her. She threw her arms around his chest, gripping him with all her strength. "Do you realize we've never even held each other?" She laughed and kissed his neck. He squeezed her tightly, feeling more in love with this young female every second. There was something about her. She was so direct and honest like Rockson himself. And loving . . . and beautiful. He had never felt some of the emotions that were going through him. Rona had always been very special to him and extremely attractive. Their sexual encounters had always been highly pleasurable. And yet . . . There was something between them that was different, something chemical, something electrical, like magnets pulling each other closer.

"I love you," he said, kissing her hair that smelled like the sweetest fruit.

"And I y—" There was a sudden commotion outside in the hallway. He ripped her away from him, throwing her to the floor as a stream of submachine gun bullets neatly scissored their way through the glass partition of the door. Rock waited until he heard voices nervously telling each other in Russian to go in and check. He took out the other pellet he had taken from the dead freefighter's heel—a small explosive charge and set the timer for three seconds. Rock heaved it through the shattered shards of glass still hanging on the door and dove on top of Kim. The explosion rattled the walls deafening the two Americans for a few seconds. Before the roar of death had finished echoing down the halls of the mindbreaking building, Rock was heading through the splintered door dragging Kim behind him. The hallway outside was a butcher shop of blood and splattered guts. Not a man remained alive in the group who had come to get him. Jesus Christ! Shecter's little toys were getting more and more powerful. Kim almost vomited as she slipped on what looked like a spine covered with a slushy red slime.

"There's no time to be sick, baby," Rock said firmly as they moved at a half run down the long hallway. "Nor time to faint, or waver. We must live, Kim! Both of us. I don't care about my life. I'm just another American freefighter doing his best. Death's been on my shoulder for years. But you can't die. I can't let you. There's too much beauty in you. Too much life in this world of death." He looked at her sharply as they rounded a corner. Her pale color brightened slightly and her face took on the flushed pink of anger and the will to survive.

"I'm with you, Rock, all the way. And I can't bear to think of life without you either. We must both survive."

They rounded the end of one of the long mazelike halls. Two officers came running at them with their rifles pushed forward like spears, ready to fire. More bells began ringing all around them. The two stared wide-eyed in surprise at Rockson who reacted with the speed of a lightning bolt. He slammed the butt of his machine pistol up into the nose of the closer man, driving the nasal bone up and into the man's brain. Rock turned without a second look at the falling man and pushed the barrel of the pistol into the second man's stomach as the elite forces' officer raised his rifle. Rock pulled the trigger and let the gun shake for a few seconds before he lowered it. The would-be killer slumped to the floor.

Rockson was enraged now. He barely felt the Reds were human anymore after their treatment of Kim. He wouldn't let the bastards harm her—or any other American in this damned brain destroying building. He didn't want to just kill them—he wanted to destroy them. To obliterate them, the whole stinking lot. Rock lifted one of the dead man's Trakhov 7.2mm service revolvers, wiped the blood from the handle and gave it to Kim.

"Use it, baby, if you have to." She held the big weapon in her small white hands and put her finger on the trigger.

"I'm ready, Rock, and if they catch us again I'll use it on myself before I let them take me prisoner."

"Don't talk like that, Kim," Rock said angrily. "Don't even think like that." He pulled her and ran toward the third floor lobby and the elevators. He had heard some of the guards talking and knew that the mindbreaking equipment was on the twentieth through the thirtieth floors. He pressed the up button on the elevator panel and within seconds the doors of one swung open. So far so good. The automatic shutdown systems hadn't had time to go on yet. He pressed twenty and put his finger on the trigger of the machine pistol. The doors sprang open and Rockson jumped out the moment the shiny stainless doors flew open and sprayed the machine pistol around the floor. Screams and sounds of bodies hitting hard surfaces was the only reply. When he pulled his finger from the trigger, bodies lay strewn haphazardly around like broken dolls covered with red paint. Whoever had been lying in wait, their own guns drawn, had received a murderous surprise, Ted Rockson style. He bent down and stripped the bodies of their weapons, six pistols and three submachine guns and loads of extra ammunition. They'd need every bit of firepower they could muster—Rock knew that a war lay ahead of them.

Alarms began ringing out everywhere, hideous squeals of warning throughout the building. They had minutes at most before this floor, too, would be filled with the KGB and this time they wouldn't be taken so easily. Kim helped Rock to carry the additional weapons and clenched her lips tightly as they stepped across the still twitching bodies. They sped down the main hall, their arms absolutely filled with destruction. They came to a large wooden door with a small glass window at eye level. Rock's sixth sense told him that someone, more than one, probably was just the other side. He stood back and set the submachine gun on full auto and sprayed a line back and forth across the door three times. He dove through the door, hitting the floor in a roll and somersaulting over. He came to a stop again, facing the door, his smg ready to release another volley of death. But there was no need. At least not for these two. He had been right: Two Red Army regulars had been waiting—they waited too long.

Kim ran in and joined Rockson and they moved forward cautiously. They turned the corner and came to one of the holding pens that the Reds stuffed their prisoners in while waiting their turn to be brainwashed. Nearly four hundred American workers cowered behind the bars, sullen, terrified, staring at the half-naked nymph and heavily muscled man.

"What the hell?" they exclaimed as one when they saw Rockson draw up to them on the run. In his uniform and sunglasses he looked like just another of the Red officers.

"Stand back," he yelled over the murmur of the prisoners. "I'm here to help you, not to hurt you." They looked distrustfully at this strange man, his black clothes covered with blood and the blond-haired girl at his side. "Back! Back!" Rock yelled. "There's no time to play games." The workers pulled to the back part of the cell, crunching against one another. Rock held the muzzle of the smg to the lock, and, turning his head away, fired ten rounds into the mechanism. The door flew open and the prisoners filed out of their cell, scared but happy to be free at least for a moment from the fate that they all now knew awaited them in the mindbreaking machines just down the hall.

Rock stepped into the center of the confused prisoners and yelled for them to be quiet. "Listen to me. Listen carefully. We have only minutes. I'm here to help you live. You were all about to be destroyed as men. I know you've grown up in the Russian fortress cities, most of you, and you're used to obeying the authorities. I'm not here to criticize you for that—but now you must fight. They were going to destroy your brains, use your bodies for their filthy work. For the first time in your lives you must fight back. You may all die, everyone of you. *We* may all die but we are Americans and there are things worse than death. The time to strike back, to rebel is here!"

The workers looked at one another nervously. Their whole lives had been spent kowtowing to the Reds. They had been born in slavery, brought up in slavery, sent to work in the Russian factories when they were twelve. They had been nearly crushed, nearly but not completely.

"Are you—the Rockson?" one of the prisoners, a large balding man in prison grays sizes too small for him, asked.

"Yes, I'm Ted Rockson—I'm here to free you."

"*The Rockson*," several of them half screamed. The man who had lived in their most secret dreams their entire lives, the man whose name was scrawled on the crumbling walls of every ghetto in America.

"The Ultimate American," several gasped, their eyes as wide as if they had just seen an angel descending down from the heavens. They had all heard of him. Every single worker in America had. And though they had prayed he existed and would someday come to free them—in their guts they had feared he was not real. No man could fight the Reds with all the strength they had, all their armies and weapons.

But Rockson had. And now he was here! For them! He had come to save *them!*

"We are with you, Rockson," said one of the largest prisoners, an obvious brawler, with a black eye and bruised knuckles. "Give me a gun!" He walked up to Rock, who could see the cold respect in the man's eyes. He had killed already—Russians, Rock knew. He handed the man a submachine gun and five clips.

"Here, you put the—"

"I know how to shoot it," the prisoner cut him off curtly.

"Good," Rockson said. He could count on this one. The other prisoners stepped forward, slowly at first, and then more of them, their eyes and voices growing louder, brighter by the second. For the first time in their lives there was hope. They took the weapons that Rock and Kim handed out, and Rock gave a thirty second course in firing them.

"We must get more weapons—many more. And free *all* the prisoners in this hellhole. Then we can fight our way out. Every Red we kill means another rifle and pistol for us, so let's spread out. Move in groups of ten. If one man falls take his gun and fight on. Many of us will die—but as men. AS MEN!" Rock yelled out. The prisoners cheered him, raising their pistols and rifles in the air. They echoed his words back, rising in ever louder choruses.

"As men! As men! As men!"

"You Americans come with me," Rockson said, picking the strongest and meanest looking of the lot. "You'll work with me. Ours will be the hardest job." The men's faces lit up with pride that the Rockson had chosen them.

The workers tore off in all directions, down the hallways, onto the other floors, killing and grabbing more and more weapons from the Reds who were not prepared for the desperation, the violence, of the prisoners' attack. Rock heard the shots ringing out everywhere and smiled a blade-thin grin. The Reds would be feeling something they weren't used to—

Fear!

"Kim, you stay here," Rock said as he assembled his instant commando team.

"Forget it, Rock," Kim said defiantly. "We're in this together." She held her smg higher in her hands to show him she was as ready as the released men.

"All right then, baby," Rock said softly, looking at her with a mixture of admiration and concern. "But stick close by me. This, as they used to say in the old days, when they had them, isn't going to be a picnic."

With Rock and Kim in the lead and the thirty man force behind them, they headed off down the hall toward the brainwashing operation. Two immense steel doors were tightly shut about two hundred feet down the corridor, clamped tight as a tomb when the first alarms went off. They came to the door and Rock quickly looked it over—no way they could shoot their way in.

"I heard them talking about some sort of weapons cache just before the main mindbreaking chamber," one of the freed prisoners said coming up to Rock.

"Spread out," he commanded the workers. "You—down that way. You men—over there. We're looking for their weapons storage. If you find anything, yell!" They spread out, opening every door. Rock could hear occasional shots ringing out as his men found a cowering Red hidden inside an office. Suddenly there came a noise down one of the smaller hallways.

"Here! We found it." Rock and Kim tore down the white and red checkered tile floor to the almost hysterical voice. They ran into a large room filled with shelves of weapons. Rifles, smgs and—what Rock had been hoping for—small explosives, hand grenades, shells for mortars. It was a regular mini-armory.

"You five men," Rock said, pointing at the first five workers who showed up at the door. "Run down to the other floors with as many weapons as you can carry. Tell the workers you see to come up here to get arms and more ammo." The freed Americans loaded up their arms with as much as they could possibly carry and headed down the hall, hardly able to walk. Rock loaded up with grenades and five heavy mortar shells and went back to the steel doors of the brainwashing center. He set them down right at the crack of the two sliding doors and told everyone to get back about a hundred feet down the hall and behind the corner. He pulled the fuse on a ten second grenade, dropped it in the center of his little altar of death, and tore ass back to cover. He had just rounded the corner when the first of the explosions went off. Even from nearly eighty feet away he could feel the shock waves of the detonation and flung himself onto the floor near the huddled prisoners, sliding nearly ten feet on his stomach.

Behind him the grenade went off, then nothing! Damn, it hadn't det—The thought had barely reached his brain that it had failed when a roaring thunderous blast shook the floor and walls, knocking plaster down from the ceiling. Then another. The shock waves reverberated through the building. Rock and his team of freed workers waited another ten seconds for any secondaries and then ran back through the smoke and rubble that littered the hallway. The doors had been ripped off their hinges and smashed open as if a giant metal-eating creature had taken some big bites right out of the foot thick steel. Rock rushed in, firing at several shadows moving in the smoke on the other side.

Bodies smacked to the floor. The others filed in behind him, grabbing up the fallen weapons of three more dead guards. The lingering wisps of smoke cleared quickly, and Rock nearly gasped as he took in the sight before him.

Men—rows and rows of men, strapped into plastic chairs with the mindbreaker covering the entire top of their skulls. It ate away at them like some hideous parasitic beast, sucking out their brain fluids, burning away at their memory systems with teeth of laser fire. The rows of writhing strapped-down men went on as far as Rockson could see. There must have been thousands on this one floor alone. And they screamed. God how they screamed, their mouths opening as wide as human muscle and bone could stretch. They let out howls of pain—animal screams of the most torturous unbearable sensations of ultimate horror. Their veins stood out on their faces like leather cords. It appeared that their eyes would surely pop out of their sockets, trailing bloody tendrils. And in some cases they had.

Rock and the free prisoners ran down the lines of shrieking prisoners, ripping the helmets up and off their heads. But this only made the confined Americans scream even louder and then fall dead as the laser prongs cut wildly in every direction inside the men's skulls.

"Don't pull them out," Rock yelled above the din of torture. "There has to be a reverse procedure on these devices." He looked around and saw at the far end of the immense brainwashing chamber windowless and filled with the smell of sweat, fear, and fecal matter which exploded out of the tortured bodies, unable to control their own functions any longer, a control room, glassed in behind dark purple polarized glass. Rockson took off, moving with all the speed his mutant body possessed. Like the wind, like a bullet searching out flesh, he reached the door at the far end before the two Red technicians inside could make their escape down a back stairway.

"Hold it!" Rockson yelled out, jumping through the doorway, "Or I'll blast your fucking guts all the way back to Moscow!" The two mindbreaker operators, white-coated and unarmed, stopped in their tracks, raised their arms and turned slowly around. Rock continued. "Now, I don't want any bullshit from you or any stalling. I'm not in the mood to play any games." He let loose with a stream of whistling slugs from his smg that bore into the floor just in front of their feet. The two jumped nearly a foot off the ground and let out with cries of terror.

"Don't kill us, no, no," said the shorter, pudgier one with blood smears nearly covering the front of his laboratory smock. "We can stop them, but we can't undo the process. What's done is done."

"Well, stop the damn thing! Now!" He lifted the gun again and walked up to them, shoving the hot muzzle into the face of the one who had talked.

"I'm moving, I'm moving," the man positively shrieked and started forward. The pale pimple-faced Red ran to a complicated looking set of controls, dials, and buttons and frantically pressed in the code for the mindbreakers to withdraw from their brain drilling. Within a second, the small lights above each helmet went from green to red and the machines began withdrawing their white-hot laser probes from the screaming prisoners.

"Come with me," Rock ordered, leading the two back out to the floor where the victims of the mindbreakers were being released from their living hell. They rose from their blood-soaked chairs, those that still could move. Many were mindless zombies who sat staring straight ahead. Others died on the spot, the shock of the entire experience too much for their weakened nervous systems to take. Out of the thousand being brainwashed two hundred and seventy-three were able to act coherently and speak.

Rockson had the two technicians strapped down to the chairs the American prisoners had been in just minutes before. The two Reds grew white faced and stuttered out pleas, too scared even to yell.

"No, we showed you," the pudgy one begged. "Don't kill us."

"We—we—were only following orders," the older one said, his eyes, usually filled with contempt, now dilated in terror. Rock walked back to the control room and pushed the on button. The computers came to life, lights flashing, meters moving with activity. He walked past the technicians and smiled at them as the helmets lowered and the icepick probes began their descent into Russian skull tissue for a change.

"Have fun boys. You'll have to tell me what it's like sometime." Rockson led the newly released prisoners out into the hall and had his men arm them with as many spare weapons as they had collected. From within he heard the screams of the technicians as the laser teeth began ripping their brains.

"Men!" Rock addressed the new recruits as his own thirty man team stood around him, cradling their pistols and rifles as lovingly as if they were babies.

"You're free now. Free for the first time in your lives. You're no longer slaves to the Reds. But now you will have to fight." The newly freed prisoners listened to this strange man of steel strength who addressed them.

"I am Ted Rockson," Rock continued.

"The Rockson," they gasped, their eyes widening in confusion. The Rockson was real; they could hardly believe it. All these years just a shadowy figure in their thoughts and dreams. But he was real and if he was real, then anything was possible.

"Yes, 'the Rockson,' as you call me," Rock said sarcastically. "But the truth is that I'm just a man like you and you." He pointed at two of the freed workers, still trying to get their bearings, blood oozing from the two swollen holes at the top of their head. "Just a freefighter, like ten thousand, a hundred thousand others around America." They all listened intently, every man around Rock silent with awe. "And what that means is that the Russians are not supermen. They're not immortal. They *can* be killed. You've been raised in fear of them. They've tried to make you think that you were all powerless against them. But that is all lies. You are strong. There are Red bodies lying down below, that these men here have already demonstrated their 'powerlessness' on."

The thirty men of Rock's hastily assembled commando squad raised the weapons proudly with slightly dazed expressions on their faces. Everything was happening so fast.

"Arm them!" Rock said to the workers who carried the loads of weapons stacked high on their arms. The newly freed prisoners crowded around, taking pistols, rifles, smgs from the weapons stack. They held them backwards, tried to find the trigger. Rock held each weapon up one at a time and showed them how to use them, firing down the hall into the wall to demonstrate the use. When they were all as well trained as a two hundred man army of semi-brainwashed, stumbling torture victims could be with three minutes of schooling in weapons, Rockson led them back down the hall to the elevators.

"We're going to split up into groups of forty. Each group will take one of the next four floors above us. We're going to liberate every damn prisoner in this torture chamber a floor at a time. You know where the chambers are—I'm sure they're arranged the same on each level. When you free the other prisoners, arm them and tell them what I told you. You're free men now, fight to save your freedom." Rockson picked leaders for each team and they piled into different elevators heading out to make war on the Reds.

Seventeen

The war between the freed Americans and the Red Army and KGB raged for hours. The workers fought their way up and down the stairs as more and more Red troops, called out from their barracks, poured into the building. But the workers continued to fight their way into each brainwashing sector and freed their brothers after bloody battles that left scores of them dead. About a quarter of all the freed prisoners were able to function enough to join the battle and they were given whatever weapons were available and shown how to point the things and pull the trigger. Below Rockson and his teams of men, pushing down a floor at a time, battled the Reds who tried to come up from the main lobby.

They held them for nearly an hour, laying down a withering fire that the Reds were scared to even attempt to cross, as the first twenty men who had tried lay riddled with bloody holes at the foot of first floor stairs. But then the Reds brought in two men with flamethrowers who started up the stairs, shooting out long streams of thousand degree fire. The workers pulled back screaming. Many or the first two floors burned to death or suffocated from the lack of oxygen. They retreated floor by floor, trying desperately to hold back the Reds. They were free for the first time in their lives and weren't about to give it up so easily. But fighting against bullets was one thing—weapons that sprayed fire were something else. They tried shooting into the walls from above to ricochet slugs down but to no avail. The bullets whizzed back at them just as much.

New reinforcements of freed American prisoners came down from above, bringing some grenades with them. The workers lobbed down two at a time. This time the fire stopped . . . for a minute. The Reds knew they had the rebellion on the run and quickly had other men pick up the equipment and continue on. Again they threw grenades and again struck paydirt. But the flames soon started up. There was no way to fight it. Within an hour they had been pushed all the way back up to the nineteenth floor where they had started.

Rock joined them, running down with Kim and a group of armed workers whom he had already chosen as his special five-man team for extra hazardous and important duty. They had fought their way up to the thirty-sixth floor where they were meeting stiffer resistance. The leader of the force that had been pushed up from below ran over to Rockson, holding his Kalashikov far out ahead of him, as he still had not quite gotten used to the handling of the weapon.

"We've lost nearly two-thirds of our men downstairs, Rockson," he said. "The Reds are using some kind of rifle that shoots fire. They've got the whole lower portion of the building now and, Christ, they must have nearly a thousand troops down there now. They're just blasting through us. I don't know we're ever going to get out of here." He looked panic-stricken. A lot of the workers, after their initial enthusiasm at escaping the mindbreakers, were beginning to show their anxiety and fear. They looked over at The Rockson too in awe to ask whether they were going to escape.

"I don't quite know myself," Rock said, smiling grimly at the leader of the lower forces. "But I'm sure I'll come up with something. Meanwhile, let's do as much damage as possible while we're figuring it all out. If they're using fire let's return the favor. There are bottles of alcohol and other flammable liquids stored in closets along the floors. Get twenty men and bring every one you can find back here." The workers headed off.

Freed workers came running back from all around the building to report to Rockson who had become the general in what was turning into the largest battle between American and Russian forces since the landing of Soviet commando forces a century before. That had been met with violent opposition from small town militia units who had fought back with everything they had. No match of course against Russian armor. But the Reds knew they were in a fight this time, Rock thought to himself, as he surveyed the men under his command running madly up and down the halls, delivering new rifles, pistols, and ammunition to forces under fire from the many pockets of Red counter fire. It made him proud to be part of it. These men who, just an hour before, had been slaves, pawns in the sick Russian designs of total domination. And now . . . now the Red bear had bitten off more than it could chew. A lot more.

The men sent out to get the flammable liquids came back dragging bottle after bottle of the stuff. Rock directed them over to the stairs where they piled it all up. The sounds of gunfire grew ever closer on the floors below and retreating, wounded workers came pouring onto the floor. When the Reds sounded like they were on the floor below and the first spray of fire could be seen rounding the stairs, Rock yelled at the men to fall back away from the door. He kicked out at the stacks of gasoline, ether, alcohol, lubricating oil, and God knew what, sending them tumbling down the metal stairs in a roar of glass. The liquid from the broken bottles poured out and down the steps, an instant waterfall heading toward the Reds. The flamethrowing troops waited a second for the smoke to clear ahead of them, not noticing the pungent stream beneath their feet. They shot the flames forward again, hoping to fry more American flesh. Instead they hit the chemical streams flowing inexorably down.

It ignited with a roar and a flash that shook the floor, nearly knocking Rock and the freed prisoners to the floor. The Reds for three floors below, the flamethrowing team, and about a hundred troops crowded just behind them were burned instantaneously. The river of flaming death sent up a sheet of flame that reached to the ceiling. The Russian soldiers turned into torches of human flesh, their hands, faces, uniforms rippling with beautiful yellow and blue tongues of flame.

"That will hold them below this floor," Rock said to the freed workers gathered around him.

"We'll have to head up now. Most of the top floors are controlled by us. If we could just get hold of some choppers—" The Rock force headed up, leaving a small lake of the flammable liquid covering the floor. When the Reds hit the grenade that Rockson had rigged up by the fire stairs' door they'd get their next big surprise of the day. By the time Rock and his men reached the officers' offices on the top five floors the brass had already fled by helicopter. Colonel Killov had choppered to the ground and reentered the first floor lobby where he directed the Red Army in their attack. The KGB commander knew he had the Americans trapped. Rockson had escaped from one cell but he had just run into another. The rebelling workers were sealed in from below by nearly a thousand men and from above by machine gun mounted helicopters. It was only a matter of time. And this time Killov would make sure that Rockson wouldn't live again to repeat his heroics. He rubbed the painful wound on his cheek. The man had hurt him. No one had dared strike him, ever. How the man had been able to cause all this damage amazed Killov. He had underestimated the freefighter. The muscle-bound, weird-eyed, white hair-streaked mutant was one of the cleverest and toughest adversaries the colonel had ever faced. But all his cleverness would end in a hole in the ground within the next few hours.

"Send in more flamethrower units," Killov commanded over a walkie-talkie. "And have the helicopters start dropping that nausea gas from up top. We're going to squeeze these rebels till they bleed."

Rockson and his army of nearly a thousand freed American prisoners fought on for hours, somehow holding back the overwhelming strength of the Reds. Another three hundred and forty of his men were killed or wounded. Rock knew it was only a matter of minutes before the choppers overhead would land or drop bombs or something unpleasant. He could hear from his momentary command center on the fortieth floor their whirring engines just fifty feet above him, an army of them it sounded like.

It was over. But he couldn't tell them. He hadn't lied to them and said it was going to be easy. Yet somehow he felt guilty. He had led them into the lion's den. And Kim. He turned to look at her across the floor by the window, smashing out the glass with the butt of her submachine gun. She, too, had turned into a warrior over the last few hours. He couldn't bear to think of her hurt or . . . damn! He slammed his massive fist into the palm of his other hand, his twin-colored eyes glowing like beacons in the darkness of the sea of death that threatened to envelop them all.

The men were exhilarated as well as frightened. For the first time in their lives they had fought back—had felt what it was like to be a man among men. They hadn't listened to Russian commands but shot at them. And it felt good. They looked to Rockson, whispering among themselves as to his plan. The Rockson—the one who would free them from this damned building of pain.

Rock heard the choppers drop their loads of bombs and the jarring roar of the explosions above. Plaster fell like oddly shaped snowflakes onto the freed prisoner's heads. They threw their hands above them as if trying to shield whatever was about to descend on them.

"I know you've all fought hard today," Rock screamed out to them. "I told you you would be free—well you are. Free to die as free men. I'm proud to be among men like you. You've proved yourselves Americans as tough as any freefighter out there." The workers seemed to take a pride in Rock's words. The Rockson had come to them and they hadn't failed him. Rock walked over to Kim and put his arms around her.

"Baby, I'm only sorry that you're going to—" he couldn't bring himself to finish the sentence.

"I'm with you," she said. "And believe it or not, Rock, that's all I want." Several more bombs fell and Rock could smell the first acrid odors of gas. The stairs filled with low rolling clouds of smoke and the men began coughing and retching.

Something was happening. Far above, Rock could hear explosions. But they weren't hitting the building. They were going off in the air, as if the choppers were exploding. There were more of them, the force of the detonations rocking the walls of the building. Rock pushed through the crowds of workers and tore up the metal stairs to the roof. He threw the rusting door open and stepped out. Above him was a battle of the skies that had not been witnessed for over a century. About a hundred feet up and spread out over nearly half a square mile were nearly thirty Red helicopters—but half of them were already in flames and falling from the sky. In the distance, nearly a mile away, Rockson saw a single chopper speeding in, in a zigzag pattern firing a beam of pure black energy.

The particle beam! Suddenly the Doomsday Warrior *knew*. The Rock Squad had come from Century City and they had a particle beam—probably against Shecter's orders. Rock smiled broadly, his white teeth and violet and aquamarine eyes sparkling in the light of the flaming Red helicopters. The black beam swept through the skies again and again like a sword cleaving the very heavens in two. Every helicopter the particle beam touched, even briefly, imploded into a ball of white fire and dropped in shards of glowing metal, twisted beyond recognition.

The Red gunners attempted to fire back. The renegade helicopter was still nearly half a mile away. How in hell could it be firing so accurately and what kind of weapon could be causing such destruction? The Russian craft continued to fall like flies and the last remaining five of them fled like bats out of hell as the chopper approached the roof of the mindbreaker building. The stolen Red helicopter soared in at two hundred miles per hour and stopped on a dime over the concrete rooftop. The craft quickly dropped down to a landing and before the blades had stopped spinning the attack force on board came out in a crouch, guns at the ready.

Rock ran to greet his rescuers. Out popped Detroit, followed closely by McCaughlin. Then Chen, knives in hand; Perkins and Archer with his huge crossbow slung over his shoulder, ready for action. The whole damn crew! Rock almost cried tears of joy for the first time in his life as his comrades in arms crowded around him, slapping him on the back and joking dryly.

"Heard you were having a party, Rock," Detroit said, a slight gash over his right eye that he had received while stealing the Red chopper, "so we brought the candles. Shecter's probably screaming up a storm but—"

"Just in time," Rock said. "The Goddamned Reds are nipping at our toes in there." He pointed to the building where freed workers were emerging like ants through the roof door. "I must confess I've never been so glad to see your ugly mugs as right now," Rock said. "But we've got a battle on our hands." Detroit held one of the particle beam weapons, Perkins the other. Perkins walked over to Rockson.

"Want to give it the honors?" the freefighter asked grinning.

"With pleasure," Rock said, hefting the now familiar weapon. The Technicians were about to save his ass once more, Rock thought, remembering the small bald men with fondness. He headed toward the stairwell, making his way through the milling released prisoners.

"We're going back down now, men," Rock yelled out to them. "And this time we're not coming up again." The workers looked at The Rockson in disbelief. Even The Rockson—how could he fight what must be a thousand elite troops below. Rock introduced Kim to his Rock team. They all could see how his eyes glowed when he was near her. So the tough guy had finally fallen. They immediately felt protective toward the vulnerable-appearing blond beauty. Every one of them would instantly have given his life to save hers. She was Rockson's woman and therefore one of their own.

Rock headed down the fortieth floor fire stairs.

Below he could hear the troops firing, preparing for their final assault on the trapped rebels. He set the particle beam rifle on the widest beam—a beam that would instantly knock out any man touched by it for hours. He took a deep breath and with the workers crowding behind him headed down. He waited until the flamethrower team had stopped for a moment to let their troops wipe up any lingering resistance above. Rock met the first wave of assault with the two foot wide beam. The Red troops crumbled to the floor. Taking advantage of confusion and a surprise counterattack which the Reds wouldn't be expecting, Rock tore down the stairs, his finger on the trigger of the three foot long nearly cylindrical plastic rifle. The troops fell like ducks in a shooting gallery. There was no warning, no noise, nothing—just instantaneous unconsciousness. The troops below didn't even know what was happening to their advanced forces. Just a strange quiet which slowly descended down through the building as the freefighter came down. The Reds fell by the hundreds, collapsing onto the stairs, their rifles clattering to the floor. Not a Russian could withstand the power of the futuristic weapon. Slowly, floor by floor, Rockson took out the attack force.

From the roof of the forty story brainwashing building, Detroit set up a line of fire with the particle beam, sighting up the troops barracks, the munitions warehouses, the rows of tanks and armored vehicles parked in an immense concrete square at one end of the city. He put the black beam on maximum power—six inch wide beam. The rifle positively quivered with energy—more powerful than that of an atomic bomb. Whatever was touched by the pure blackness of the ray instantly exploded into its component atoms. Foot thick armored tanks went up like puffs of pine bark, exploding with sharp cracks. The barracks were sliced in half and then the fleeing troops picked off en masse. Detroit waved the black beam of death across the entire city as it erupted into flames everywhere.

Forty stories below, Colonel Killov beat a hasty retreat from the lobby as he saw which way the tide was turning. He fled to his waiting limousine and escort vehicles staffed with the top brass of his four hundred man force. The convoy of KGB bigwigs tore out to the airport, leaving the remainder of their force to face Rockson and his army of workers. Killov shook with fury inside the staff car. Again Rockson and his blasted freefighters had defeated him. Again, they carried those deadly beam weapons, the likes of which Killov had seen just once before when they shot nine of his ten helicopter attack force from the sky. (See Book 1.) He had barely escaped with his life then and now . . . The convoy raced to the airport as Red troops poured from the now flaming mindbreaker building, fleeing for their lives.

Killov grabbed the wireless phone from its wooden box built in place behind the front seat and pressed his priority code. After several seconds of static a voice answered, "Yes sir!"

"Who is this?" Killov snapped.

"Lieutenant Shirovsky and who is—"

"This is Colonel Killov. I am leaving Pavlov City. Get General Manislav on the scrambler and have him ready a bomber jet loaded with two neutron bombs. I want the target to be Pavlov City—dead center. Use the large building as ground zero. When I am airborne I'll call you back and give the order to drop. Is that clear?"

"Absolutely, sir," Shirovsky replied without hesitation. He could hear the rage and fury in Killov's voice and knew this was not the time to make even the slightest mistake. "Order received and carried out." The line clicked off.

"Faster!" Killov screamed through the intercom to his driver. But now his grimace of defeat and fear had turned to a smile of contempt. Let them play back there, Killov thought. Soon they will all be bubbling charcoal. He would loose four hundred men—but he would get Rockson and destroy those damn super weapons. The trade was worth it. He would have sacrificed a million men at that moment to see Rockson burned to cinders. "Faster!" Killov screamed again as the convoy of white-faced KGB men sped, wheels spinning on the dirt road to the waiting private jet. Behind them, the black beams continued to slice apart what little remained of Pavlov City that wasn't yet burning.

Eighteen

Within an hour Rock and his small army of American workers had fought their way to the edge of the city. With the particle beam at his command the Reds fell like flies. Detroit, Chen, and Archer kept up the attack from the roof and arranged to rendezvous with Rockson at a small hill just to the north of the city. Rock led the now seven hundred man force up the steep slope of the first of a series of hills that surrounded the open plain on which Pavlov City had been built. The men stopped at the top and turned to look at the damage that had been wrought. Pavlov City had been reduced to smoking rubble. Everywhere were fires roaring high into the sky, billowing clouds of thick smoke from the burning wooden barracks. From time to time another store of munitions would go up with explosive fury, shaking the ground around them. The men cheered and cheered. Never had they felt such emotions. Emotions of winning, or conquering, of destroying the Reds. They turned to Rockson with worship in their eyes. The Rockson *had* saved them. Everything they had ever dreamed about the mythical freefighter was true. Rock gathered them around him and quieted them down. With Kim at his side and Perkins and McCaughlin standing proudly in back Rock addressed them.

"Fellow Americans, you are now freefighters. You have earned the right to call yourselves such by your courage and heroism under fire. I have been in many battles—this was your first. I remember the fear I felt the first time. You faced death in the eye and have walked out the other side. I bow to you all." Rockson lowered his head in a gesture of respect, one of the few times in his life he had ever lowered his eyes to another.

"What now Rockson? Where will you take us?" one of the leaders of the workers spoke out, his arm wrapped with a bandage made from a shirt, blood seeping through.

"Now I take you nowhere," Rockson said. "You are all free men now. You can no longer return to the fortress cities of the Reds. For better or worse you are criminals in their eyes. You must survive. Make your way to the different Free Cities. Start your own. You are all tough men—you showed that down there." He pointed down to the maelstrom of smoke and fire that burned ever brighter below. "And you have helped strike a vital blow against the Russians—one that they won't soon recover from. This Pavlov City was going to turn you and tens of thousands like you into mindless zombies to do the Reds' dirty work. That city is gone and I feel sure they won't try again. You have struck a blow for America. Now you must survive. You have weapons. Go into the mountains, into the plains.

Build shelters for yourselves. Learn to live in the land that is yours—America—she will help you. Give you the food and water that you need to survive. She will not let you down for you are her children. And you fight to free her."

Every man was silent as they listened to words the likes of which they had never heard before. Words that stirred their hearts, moved their very souls. For they were men. They had proved it in blood.

"Go now," Rock said, pointing to the four corners of the horizon. "It is a harsh world out there but it is your world—our world. We must make of it what we can. Good luck and God be with you."

The workers drew strength from Rockson's words. They broke up into small groups of thirty to fifty men each, divided up their weapons and headed off under the darkening sky, filled to the very clouds with the towering funnels of smoke from the doomed city.

Rock watched them go. Many would die but some would live. And their children would live to see their land free once again. This he knew, deep in his heart. At last he turned to Kim, Perkins, and McCaughlin. "Come on, we've got to hitch a ride with Detroit and the others. They're supposed to meet us over there." He pointed to a steep hill about a mile away. The four of them headed off along the rocky slopes, turning their heads away from the flaming city in an attempt to avoid breathing in the acrid smoke. They had scarcely gone a hundred yards when Rock heard a sound overhead. A sound he had heard before.

"We've got to run—run directly away from the city, as fast as you can," he screamed out to Kim, Perkins, and McCaughlin.

"What's wrong, Rock?" the big Scotsman asked running along side Rockson who took the lead.

"I think our friend Killov has decided to get rid of us by taking out the whole damned city. Atomics—I'm sure of it—the insane bastard is going to kill everyone in the whole area—even his own troops to get us. Run like you've never run before."

They tore over the top of the hill and headed down the opposite slope. Rock stopped for a moment just before heading down to see if he could get a shot with the particle beam which he carried slung over his shoulder. But though he could hear the whine of the jet engine, the smoke and low purple and brown clouds camouflaged the bomber. The three freefighters and Kim ran and slid and rolled down the rock-strewn side of the mountain. If they could just get enough distance and another large hill between them and the detonation—they might—just might survive.

They had just reached the bottom and were heading into a long swampy marshland with ten foot high reeds when the light of an atomic bomb flashed, lighting up the hills and plains for miles with an incandescent glow.

"Hit the dirt," Rock screamed, throwing Kim down and diving on top of her. The roar of a twenty kiloton neutron bomb hit their ears, literally shaking the ground as if it were being grabbed by the hands of hell. Then the winds and heat came soaring over the top of the nine hundred foot hill just behind them. They could feel the energy of the blast but were shielded from the brunt of it as well as the radiation by the solid rock that stood between them and the slowly rising mushroom cloud that dwarfed all the other fires and funnels of smoke. Rock prayed silently that Detroit, Chen, Archer and the freed workers had had enough time to get behind some sort of cover. Any man who was exposed to the direct force of the blast for at least three to four miles would be fried meat.

They waited a minute, allowing the shock waves to totally die out, and began to rise. Another blast filled the sky, this time just below the rise of the hill behind them. Killov wanted to make sure that nothing survived—not a blade of grass let alone a single human. This time the blast knocked them all to the ground, and into unconsciousness. While they lay in merciful darkness in the high reeds, a second mushroom cloud joined the first. Every bit of living matter that the heat and the radiation made contact with melted into dripping black sludge. Whatever had been alive within range of the blast was now dead and returned to the dust from which it had risen.

They awoke hours later, groaning, mouths dry as parched sand. Rock was the first to totally come to. He sat up trying to remember just what the hell had happened. The mushroom clouds still hung high in the sky. The dark tornadolike chimneys of gray and black smoke stared down as if surveying the total destruction they had caused. Rock leaned over quickly to check Kim. She seemed all right, no burns on her skin. The same for Perkins and McCaughlin. God only knew if they'd received lethal doses of radiation. The hill had afforded them protection from the direct force of the neutron radiation but . . . But at least they were alive. The future would determine the extent of their injuries. Still, they were all freefighting Americans who had lived their lives out in the medium and high rad zones of America. If anyone would make it—they would.

Rock helped the others to their feet. Perkins seemed the most out of it from the blast. He kept licking his lips and twitching. His eyes seemed swollen and red. He had glanced at the second explosion without thinking and though his retinas hadn't been burned—if they had he would be blind—he had obviously sustained at least immediate injury. Rock helped him wash out the pupils with water from his canteen and as soon as possible they started off in the orange glow.

"We've got to get away from this area," Rock said. "The radiation will linger for days and fallout from the debris picked up by the blast will start coming down within hours. We'll head straight south away from the city before we start west again."

They headed out through the reeds of the swamp, moving slowly at first, as they all felt somewhat dizzy from the blast, but within a few minutes they seemed to pick up a good pace. They reached the next set of hills at the other end of the mile long swamp and climbed the easy slope. They were just passing the summit, a long flat meadow with the flowers burned to a crisp from the blasts, when Kim screamed out.

"Oh God, Rock, Rock." She stood trembling, unable to move as Rockson ran back about twenty yards to her. She pointed down with one hand, holding the other over her mouth. Five bodies, or what were barely recognizable as bodies, lay on the ground, frozen in time and space. Their flesh had turned to charcoal, black as midnight, their hands and arms held up bent at odd angles. But their faces were the true horror. Eyes burned away so that just black holes stared out, lips thin pieces of dark leather with the teeth still shiny, grinning in their death screams. Five of the freed workers, making their way to a new freedom, caught at the top of the hill when the bombs went off. They hadn't had time to run even a single step. Cut down by the heat of the first bomb, they looked like statues made of black dust, sculpted by death, bound for hell.

Rock put his arms around Kim and pulled her away. She seemed transfixed, her eyes terrified by the vision yet unable to look away. "Don't dwell on it, baby," Rock said. "Death is part of our world, but don't be fascinated by it." She broke down and cried. She had been trying to hold back the tears to show him, the man she loved, that she was strong, tough, worthy of being his woman. But the grotesque black corpses were the last straw. Her heart couldn't take anymore and she burst into tears, her chest heaving spasmodically.

"Cry Kim, cry." Rock said softly. "It's good. Tears heal. Go ahead baby, let it out." The party of four walked on as Rock protectively kept his arms around the shaken young woman who let herself go, tears falling down her cheeks and onto her young breasts; rain—the rain of the body, which lets the spirit release its pain.

Nineteen

They walked for days, barely able to stand at times, hiding in the woods and caves from time to time as Red drones flew overhead. Killov must have been sending them out by the droves, searching for any possible survivors from his atomic massacre of Pavlov City. Well, at least the damned brainwashing city was done for good, Rockson thought grimly to himself. Zhabnov's plans for a zombie army would die in the radioactive ashes along with untold thousands of men, Russian and American. Kim and the two freefighters were holding up well, though Perkins's eyes still seemed to be giving him trouble. They had turned a pinkish color and he constantly had to drip water on them to keep them from drying out. They had to get back to Century City and fast. They all needed medical treatment.

On the third day they began heading west as Rockson figured they had come far enough south to avoid the major search-and-destroy effort of the Reds. He had never been through this stretch of land, and the plant life grew increasingly peculiar with fields of large cactuslike growths, bright yellow and nearly twenty feet high. The largest of them had bright red fruits which Rock carefully tried and found to his surprise that they were delicious. They ate a little of the fruit and waited a few hours to see if any deleterious effects occurred. None! Hungry as dogs they pulled down dozens of the grapefruit-sized fruits and ate until they were stuffed. The first good meal they had had in nearly five days.

Feeling somewhat better they headed off into the gathering sunset, a panorama of rippling green and purple waves as the radioactive layers high in the earth's atmosphere danced under the stars. After several hours a kind of pink fog began rolling in and they moved more carefully as the patches of moisture came up to their knees then their waists. Suddenly in the mist ahead amber lights appeared. Rock stopped with the others just behind him. Was it some sort of optical illusion—fifty or so dancing red lights floating just above the ground, perhaps a mile ahead in the deep blueness of the falling night. They listened. Nothing but the wind whistling softly through the leaves. Then a dim roar—engines—and something else. Human cries, eerie warlike chants in fast singsong rhythms. The dancing, bobbing lights became brighter, closer. The engines' roar grew until it sounded like a swarm of mega-bees angry at having their hive disturbed.

Rock and his three companions got behind a fallen abaoba tree which was downed. Half rotted and shorn of its red bark the thirty foot tree gave them cover. Rock pulled the particle beam rifle from his shoulder and rested it on the tree which stood about shoulder height. Perkins and McCaughlin both unslung their Liberators and took off the safeties. Kim still had the Russian officer's machine pistol that Rock had given her back in Pavlov City and she took it from the jacket pocket of the dead Red's clothing she was wearing. Whatever it was was heading right their way. They could see as the source of the sound came out of the fog that the lights were from some fifty or so motorcycles. Motorcycles—Rock had seen one restored once in the small but growing Century City museum. But here—fifty of them working and ridden by—my God, Indians—feathered, painted Indians screaming war chants, feathers flying in bands around their foreheads. They waved ancient long barreled rifles with one arm while they steered with the other.

"They know we're here," Rock said to the others. "Shoot if they get past that boulder field, but into the dirt in front of them. No use killing unless we have to."

"Ay," McCaughlin whispered nervously, getting a bead on the lead cycle with his Liberator scope. "I've not seen the likes of that ever."

The whoops and war cries continued to grow in volume as the angry unmuffled cycles came forward at about forty miles an hour in a V-formation. At the lead of the pack, riding an immense bike with a Plexiglas visor and coonskins tied to the handle bars, a blue-painted savage-looking man, with a headdress of brilliantly colored feathers and three green stripes of paint down each cheek, raised his right hand in an obvious motion to slow down. Behind him on the other roaring cycles were men dressed in animal skins, feathers, and strips of brightly colored plastic material. All had their faces and exposed flesh on their arms and legs garishly decorated with every color and geometric design imaginable: squares, pyramids, trapezoids . . . The riders carried an assortment of strange weapons over their shoulders, from antique rifles with huge muzzles to bows and quivers of arrows. Their armaments looked as if they had been taken from some museum of past Americana. The lead ten cycles had mounted short-barreled machineguns tied down between the handlebars. Behind the drivers of many of the motorcycles equally strangely dressed women sat on a second seat, laughing and screaming to one another obscenely. This apocalyptic post-war parade headed directly toward the freefighters hidden behind their fallen tree.

"Should we scare 'em a bit?" Perkins asked Rockson, his lips dry, his tongue licking across them every few seconds.

"No, not yet," Rock said, keeping his finger at the ready on the particle beam set at lowest intensity. "They're slowing a bit. Maybe." The band of warrior Indians slowed to a full stop about a hundred feet away. The leader dismounted, swinging his headdress of rainbow feathers over the seat behind him. It fell to his ankles behind him, rippling with subtle shades and movements of nearly two thousand feathers that made up the elaborate symbol of ultimate leadership. The rest of the motorcycle tribe sat on their leather seats, revving their engines with elephantine screams of anger.

The leader walked forward another thirty feet toward Rock and his team. They could see his full regalia now: a bearskin vest to the waist, a necklace of carnivore teeth falling in three rows down around his neck, long loincloth made of some dark hide, and high red plastic boots nearly to the knee. Around his waist the Indian leader wore a long knife on one hip and an old U.S. Army issue .45 automatic pistol on the other. The freefighters watched the approaching apparition with their jaws dropped half open. They had all, in their time, seen some strange sights but this may well have been the strangest. The Indian cupped his hands to his purple-painted lips and yelled out.

"I know you cats are up the ol' tree—hey man—c'mon down—we dig you!"

"What's that mean?" Rock asked Perkins, who was one of Century City's archaeologists and linguists as well as part of the Rock Squad.

"Sounds like he wants to be friends. But Rock, I don't trust him. This peculiarly evolved culture is obviously warlike—raiders, pirates—"

"I'm going out there," Rock said. "Do you think they'll recognize a white flag?"

"It's a pretty universal symbol here in America, even among isolated groups. Rock, let me come with you—I can speak to them—translate."

The Indian leader shouted out again. "Hey man, like cool out. You know we ain't cruising for a bruising. You dig?"

"What the hell is he talking?" Rock asked Perkins. "It sounds like English but—"

"I think it's a mixture of several things, Rock. American slang plus beatnik jive circa 1950s. Quite interesting, really," Perkins said, reaching for small notepad he always carried with him to jot down observations of primitive peoples.

"Beatnik?" Rock asked.

"Yes, Rock. They were . . . It's too complicated. I'll

tell you later." The two freefighters used a handkerchief of McCaughlin's to make a little white flag at the end of a small branch. They stepped from behind the tree, waving the symbol of peace, as a school of fruit bats fluttered out of the branches above them and off into the pink-mooned sky, round as a silver dollar.

"Hey you groovy cats, we dig you, hear?" the Indian said with a broad smile as the two Americans appeared. "Come on over here and slap five, daddy-os. It's cool—you fool—send you back to school." The other riders still perched on their bikes hooted and laughed at their leader's words. Rock and Perkins walked slowly up to the warpaint-streaked leader.

"We're here in peace," Perkins said smiling.

"Groovy, the cat's a hep dude. Peace man," he said, stretching his lips to their widest to reveal a mouth missing half its teeth. The chief held up his right hand, making a V with his fingers.

"Do what he just did," Perkins said to Rockson from the corner of his mouth. "It's *important*." The two freefighters raised their hands and made the ancient hippie gesture of greeting with their fingers.

"Hello," Rockson said. "We're fellow Americans and we come with peaceful intentions."

"Hey man, the cat speaks hip talk," the Indian leader said, slapping his hands together in glee. "Where you at, daddy-o? You hip to the dharma—the road—the oneness?"

"I think he's asking if we're religious and he wants a yes answer," muttered the archaeologist.

"We believe," Rock said. "And believe in the right to believe."

"Man, that's a strange way of grooving to the

smoothness, but you dudes seem okay. At least you ain't Ruskies—you know Redskys."

"We're not Reds, we're freefighters, Americans—and you?" Perkins asked, as he quickly scribbled in his small notebook.

"Hell man—we are the People. The Kerouac Warriors, the beat messengers of ethereal poetry, the chanted-out Tibetan hipster kung-fu fighters from the Outer Galaxies. We, my square peopleitude, are *the Crazy Alligators*." The Indian leader folded his arms across his chest in satisfaction as the tribe mounted on their bikes behind him yelled out in unison.

"The Crazy Alligators!"

"Where your pad, man?" the Chief asked, his smile suddenly turning a trifle icy.

"West of here," Perkins answered, understanding the strange lingo.

"West? Crazy man," the leader laughed. "There is a west—huh? That's strange. First time we heard that." With that he turned to the cyclists and smirked, receiving loud guffaws from the tribe. He turned back to the freefighters. "Now if you all would just drop your boomtubes like nice boys," he said grimly, pulling his pistol and leveling it at Rockson's chest. "I think we can parlay at the Ginsberg's house—that's our top cheese—dig?"

Rockson stepped to the side and the chief pulled the trigger of his .45. But the slug hit empty air. Rock fanned the black beam over the whole assemblage of Crazy Alligators who fell from their bikes instantaneously as did the chief. Within a second every one of them was out. Perkins was groaning slightly and Rockson turned to him. The archeologist had his hand over his upper arm where a second shot from the motorcycles had hit him before the black beam had done its work.

"It's just a nick," Perkins said, gritting his teeth. Rock helped him tie a bandanna around the wound and the two freefighters joined by McCaughlin and Kim from behind the tree walked over and inspected their catch. Perkins, wincing occasionally from the pain of his scratch, had a field day going through the Indian's saddlebags and taking notes on the decorations on their cycles.

"This is fascinating, absolutely fascinating," the archeologist kept exclaiming as he noted the medicine pouches, the beat poetry books, yellow and disintegrating. There appeared to be three Indian societies represented among the motorcyclists: the Bear Claw Clan, all of whom had artificial bear claw scars on their left cheeks; the Coyote People, older men mostly with the mark of a coyote head cut into their left forearms; and the last group, mostly the young men including the chief who wore amulet necklaces containing Buddhist magical symbols and the long-feathered headdresses. Perkins clicked away with a small mini-camera he always carried in his jacket and wrote profuse notes. Rockson refused adamantly when Perkins wanted to take some skin and nail samples.

"But it would tell so much, Rock—"

"Absolutely *not*." Rock shook his head. "These people, friends or enemies, are still people. I don't want anything except a search for security reasons and some photographs for the archives—without their permission—got me?"

Perkins nodded gravely. "It's a mistake, Rock.

Science should—"

"Humanity over science, damn it, man," Rock said a little angrily. "That's how the war started—technology over decent human values. I won't let us act in any way like the Reds."

When the Indians awoke about an hour later they thought it odd that all their cycles had fallen over and they were lying beside them on the cold ground. It had seemed an instant ago that they were drawing their weapons. Now they had none in their hands. Immediately the chief picked himself up and shouted, "Magic! They are magicians." He pulled the black protective amulet into his hands and began chanting *OM MANI PADME HUM* as fast as he could. The others joined in and the chorus of the ancient Buddhist symbology grew in intensity until Rockson yelled out.

"Enough—we are not magicians. We used a weapon we possess on you because you were about to fire on us. You've been unconscious for about an hour—but it isn't magic." The chanting died out and the chief, looking somewhat chastened, stepped forward again.

"You could have killed us cats. We understand man, that you are powerful mean dudes. And we want to be friends. Can you dig it, kemo sabe?"

"I can dig it," Rock said, not without a trace of a smile on his dark rough-hewn face.

"Slip me five, Mr. Rock-around-the-clock. I'm Trickster Diety, and we are the craziest of the Crazy Alligators." He held his palm out and Rock, having learned the ancient American form of greeting from Detroit, slapped him. Trickster and the Alligators let out a whoop of happiness.

"The cat knows the high five, look out," Trickster

laughed and slapped Rock back. Trickster invited the freefighters "No tricks from Trickster, man," to their digs in a nearby mountain. With the Crazy Alligators taking Rock and the others on the back of their cycles, the party of thundering vehicles tore off across the dark fields to the Indians' home. Rock kept his particle beam at the ready but the Alligators weren't trying any funny stuff. At least not right now. The freefighters had never been on this type of vehicle and after a certain amount of nervousness at the speed of the things and the ground flying by so fast just beneath their feet they quickly grew to enjoy the ride. They made good time, with the cycles shooting across the terrain faster than any land vehicle Rock had ever seen. Rock was intrigued by the mobility of the cycles. He'd have to talk to Dr. Shecter about the feasibility of building some of their own back in Century City. Of course gasoline was the basic problem with any sort of combustion engine. The Alligators must have had some secret source of the precious fluid.

Within an hour and a half they were at the foot of a towering red rock mountain that Trickster yelled to Rock was their home.

"See that pile of boulders shaped like a man sitting in meditation to the left?" the chief yelled out above the din of the cycles. Rock, sitting on the rear of a cycle just behind Trickster nodded affirmatively.

"That's the entrance, man. We got guards stationed everywhere. In the rocks. Though you can't see em, they can see you. If the Reds show their head, they're dead." He laughed at the end of his little rhyme and motioned with his hand for the troop to move forward. There was a narrow shaft of darkness among the boulders and they rode into it, barely slowing down. Once inside the bikes moved single file through a narrow canyon. At first they turned on their big lights on the front of the bikes but within a minute or so they clicked them off again. The very walls of the solid rock tunnel glowed with a shimmering blue iridescence bright enough to see by. They rode for about five minutes when the narrow trail suddenly widened before them and they came into a vast stalactite-filled cavern that made the freefighters gasp. The place was gigantic, and absolutely porcupined with the glowing blue spears of rock that made it look like some immense jewel.

"It's so beautiful, Rock," Kim said, on a cycle just behind Rock's, as she sat behind a madly bedecked Indian with an almost Jackson Pollock type pattern of paint covering his bronze body. The cavern sloped slightly and the bikes rode through it as the hanging mounds of pure blue stone dripped luminous fluid that formed streams of glowing water. They came after several minutes to a tranquil black lake that disappeared in the distance. There was some sight of light far off at the other end.

"Heavy place, cats, right?" Trickster asked, as the Alligators brought their cycles to a stop on the banks of the lake.

"Heavy, man," Rock said, dismounting from the steed of steel.

There were twenty outrigger canoes on the white sands of the shore of the lake which stood quiet and shiny as a mirror. The canoes had bizarre names painted on their bows like *Disneyland One* and *Roadrunner Three*. Perkins ran around frantically jotting the names down, muttering it had something to do with the lost legendary city of Hollywood. The cyclists split up into groups ten to a boat. Rock and his team were in the lead canoe with Trickster and several Indians who grabbed oars from the floor of the craft. The canoes were long, nearly thirty feet, but very slender with a balancing outrig to the right of the boats. The glow of the rocks faded as they paddled out across the black water. Soon it was utterly black except for the glowing compass dial that Trickster held in his hand at the front of the canoe. He muttered to Rock, "Compass doesn't tell north—it just points to the Great Hall. There's so much spiritual energy around the Ginsberg—the leader of our underground Pueblo—that the compass always leads us home. And good thing, too, man, because there's a huge waterfall off this lake about a mile to the right. Bottomless, the legends say."

"How big is this lake?" Perkins asked.

"No one knows. We are content, man, to groove on the area we have and be happy. There are stories that these glowing people roam the unexplored edges of the caves down here. Have you dug on these glowing cats?" Trickster asked as he paddled slowly and smoothly with a long wooden paddle.

"Yes—the Glowers—many of our freefighters have seen things in the distance," Rock said, his arm protectively around Kim who seemed a little cold and scared in the immensity of the lake's darkness. "But never face to face. If they are real and not just some apparition created by radioactive conditions, they seem to not want to be too social."

"Well, they aren't human," Trickster said a trifle nervously. "They sail their huge boats out there on the lake, glowing in the dark. I saw one as a kid—gives me the willies to even think about it. But they don't bother us thanks to the power of the Ginsberg." When Trickster stopped talking, all that could be heard in the impenetrable darkness were the grunts of the men and the oars lapping away at the flat water.

They arrived, after about twenty minutes of rowing at the opposite bank where the glowing blue rock again permitted them to see. As they hit the sand and jumped out, the freefighters could suddenly see that what had at first looked like a sheer black face of a mountain was in fact the cliffside city composed of hundreds of adobe buildings piled atop one another in an immense hodgepodge of sand and stone.

"How many people live here," Rock asked Trickster as they walked along the sandy shore toward the city.

"Four—five thousand. I don't know, man. We don't keep track of that sort of stuff. We found this place seventy years ago—that is—my grandfather was wandering in the wilderness when he found the hole in Red Mountain and came inside. The Chumec Indians built this whole thing for protection some ten thousand years ago and we moved in like cockroaches into a tenement—dig?"

The cliff dwellings of the Chumecs, now occupied by the Crazy Alligators, had been hand hewn into the mountainside. Rock looked up, taking in the impressive living sculpture. The rock had a brownish almost rusty appearance, he noted, probably containing a high iron content. That explained the magnetic pull—hence the compass that Trickster used to guide them in. So it was the iron, not the supernatural powers of the Ginsberg, that made the needle always swing toward the mountain city. But superstitions were best not challenged, as Perkins was always telling him, so Rock would keep that fact to himself. But it made him feel a little more at ease since he had been beginning to wonder whether there might actually be a psychically powerful monk at the head of these beatnik Indians.

With Trickster in the lead the freefighters walked up the steep steps that laddered the slopes of the rock mountain. Hundreds of faces appeared in the square stone windows and doors, taking in the strangers with curiosity. Children ran down the steps, their eyes huge, pupils as big as grapes. Many of them had never seen real daylight, living their lives under the artificial light of the glowing blue stones that seemed to hang from the huge underground cavern's every square inch. They giggled and touched the party of Americans. Kim delighted in the beautiful young Indian children who gawked at her long blond hair. Both boys and girls wore pigtails, and the girls, most not more than ten, were extremely well developed. Rock suddenly realized he hadn't seen any old people or crippled or sick people.

"Where are your old people, Trickster?" Rock asked as the party continued to make their way higher and higher up the mountain city.

"The old are sent to the waterfall on the lake, on flaming rafts to join the spirits at the bottom of the bottomless cavern into which the waters fall."

"They're killed?" Kim asked horrified.

"They are sent to their creator," Trickster said simply. Kim squeezed Rock's hand.

"Oh how awful," she whispered. Rock was about to say something about cruelty and lack of compassion when Perkins whispered in his ear.

"Don't criticize, Rock. We don't know enough about their situation. Besides we're on their land. We'd better be careful about anything we say for now." They proceeded up the steps until the top which leveled off to a wide plateau covered with more of the adobe mud and brick buildings—these the largest of all, some nearly a hundred feet high. They entered what was obviously the main building, brightly festooned with Indian markings and totems, through a door nearly three times human height.

"Behold the Temple of the Ginsberg," Trickster said. "But first let us arrange for your accommodations, man and some chow-chow for some hungry squares."

Twenty

They entered a large ceremonial hall filled with long oak tables and candelabras hanging from the vaulted ceilings.

"Is this where we meet the Ginsberg?" Perkins asked, excited.

"No fool, be cool," Trickster snapped back. "We engage in dining, you know, ceasing the gurglings. The Ginsberg holds court tomorrow. Hey man, let's bring on the eats," Trickster yelled out, jumping up on top of the table. Within minutes a small parade of maidens in short leather rawhide miniskirts and raccoon skin halters brought out trays of steaming food. Rockson speared a slice off the tray of meat in front of him and sniffed it, then tasted it carefully.

"It's buffalo, man," Trickster said, grabbing a whole side of beef with a bone handle and began chewing on it furiously. Flagons of foaming beer were brought out, cold, sparkingly tasty. "To our groovy, crazy new friendcats," Trickster said, raising his glass. "May we always have far-out times together."

"Groovy crazy," Rock said with a broad smile and he, Kim, Perkins, and McCaughlin happily swigged down the delicious brew. They ate and drank with the Indians whooping it up and dancing on the tables from time to time. It was hardly the way they had dinner back in Century City, Rock thought, but it sure as hell was fun. After about an hour, the heads of the freefighters began to spin. Things in the room, the spears on the wall, the large dayglo-painted shields that dotted the walls seemed to tilt at off angles. The singing of the Crazy Alligators and their mad slang seemed more and more hilarious to the freefighters. Kim looked like an angel to Rock and the touch of her hand across the table sent chills up his spine.

"Hey, what's in this brew?" he asked Trickster, whose face seemed to be melted into rainbow trails. The smile on the chief's face looked wide as an atomic chasm as he answered.

"Why it's just good ol' Mexiquatyl Beer. Hallucinogenic mushroom brew, like we always chug." Rock looked over at Perkins inquisitively.

"Probably from the peyote family, Rock. Moderate hallucinations. Nontoxic unless you're stricken with beri-beri. Anybody here got beri-beri?" he asked, falling back in his seat in an explosion of laughter. Two young nubile maidens sat on his lap crushing their firm breasts against him. Rock sighed. He always prided himself on staying off things like this—but at least it wasn't dangerous. In fact, everyone seemed to be having a good time. He shrugged and decided to go with it.

"What the hell, you only live once, right Kim?" He leaned over and kissed Kim on her bare ivory neck. She beamed and kissed him. The touch of her lips were like ice-fire, so passionate. Rock nearly swooned before he pulled himself away, his manhood suddenly bulging in his fatigues.

"Perhaps we should go somewhere more private," Kim said, looking shyly down at the floor. Indeed, many of the braves were slipping away with female friends, and McCaughlin and Perkins seemed quite content with the bubbly creatures who nipped at their cheeks and slid their hands down to firmer targets.

"Your guest of honor suite is two flights up those spiral stairs over there," Trickster piped up. "There's a Chumec-sized bed. Don't do anything I wouldn't do." He laughed uproariously. Rock and Kim rose and made their way unsteadily through the raucous throng and to the stairs which were illuminated by the ever present glowing blue rocks. They were slightly dizzy from the ascent as they pushed open a large wooden door. Holding his angel in his arms, Rock whisked her over the threshold to a nicely furnished chamber with a hearth in the center burning merrily up through a raised circular chimney. The bed was at the far end of the room—an impossible walk that seemed like miles under the influence of the drug.

Kim unloosened her dress that the Indian women had given her and was out of it in a whisk. Her nubile, full, alabaster-skinned, angelic body was cast in the cherry orange glow of the fire. She pulled Rock to the bed and fiddled with the zipper encasing his enormous organ. It felt like a steel girder to her fingers. Rock helped her pull down his pants and felt her warm lips engulf his engorged erection. She traveled, it seemed, thousands of miles down around the steel girder to its base. He groaned and they toppled together onto the bed. She released her prize and sidled up his strong muscled body, which seemed like climbing a mountain of flesh. Her long platinum tresses slipped across his lips and then her marshmallow pale softness pressed against his mouth. Their mouths opened and miles of wet tongue rolled out like carpets and entangled in one another. Kim's moans broke into an angel's chorus as she pushed Rock over on his back and mounted him the way she had when he took her virginity in the cell at Pavlov City.

HE WAS LOVE SHE WAS LOVE HE WAS LOVE SHE WAS LOVE HE WAS LOVE . . . She was a pulsar of radiant diamonds, a quasar sending its bursts of high energy galaxy-collapsing flashes out to him. He was an approaching universe of ten billion stars swirling around a central mass of pure black gravity, a hyperspace warp of intense sub-neutrono particles coalescing inside her. They collided out there in infinite space and he entered her. She slid down his nether universe pole to the anti-matter center of his being and they were like deity and consort—the Supreme Essence of all matter and thought. The mandala that lies at the center of the oneness of negative and positive, of being and nothing, of man and woman.

Meeting the Ginsberg was a male-only ritual. The Indian beatnicks had never heard of equality of the sexes, and Kim was disappointed that she could not get to see the ruler of the Crazy Alligators. Rock however would don a black robe and get to partake of the Question Session—the most sacred of the Alligator's many religious practices. Rock was curious about this man and his powers—but he kept thinking about the previous night of lovemaking between himself and Kim, his mind returning to the erotic paradise like a fish to water. He was, he had to admit it—in love. It was a strange emotion, in a way. For Ted Rockson had felt many things in his tough life and had cared for many people. But never had he felt the energy of passionate love course through his veins like a Mack truck out of control. Every time he thought of her his stomach turned to jello. He loved her more than life itself; her face was everywhere he looked. And for the first time in his life Rock felt worried. For her. There were so many things that would gladly kill her, eat her, rape her, destroy her—in the world of America 2089 A.D. He wanted to protect her, to keep her safe from all harm, yet . . . it was impossible, even for him.

"Hey man, check you out," Trickster said, approaching Rock who had donned the ceremonial black robes that covered him head to foot. "Look pretty cool Mr. Rock-Around-the-Clock. So you ready for the Ginsberg rap. Everybody's going to be there. It's what's happening." Trickster himself had put on the black robes, though he still wore his two yard long headdress of feathers and the blue streaks of war paint on his face.

"What makes the man so powerful?" Rock asked as the two men walked to the roof of the main temple up flight after flight of carved stone stairs.

"He *knows* man! That's what gives him the power," Trickster answered. "We are allowed to come to him twice a year and ask him about the Truth. Once, years ago when I was a little j.d., one of the monks asked him a question so profound, so brilliant. A question that so expressed the ineffable essencelessness of suchness that the Ginsberg gave a signal and the gongs were rung and the monk who gave the question was accoladed and given the title, Meritorious Thinker."

"And what did that entitle him to?" Rock asked skeptically.

"It isn't that, man," Trickster said as they continued up the stairs, passing a square window every ten feet or so. "Oh, Rocky boy, I'm disappointed in you. It's the *Recognition!*—plus of course, the favors of all the temple dancers, raised in the art of erotic reality, trained in the esoteric arts of lovemaking; but of course pure as the driven snow. They train only on phalluses of the golden statues. They were sent to the Meritorious Monk for seven days. He reveled so much that he died. Can you dig it, man?"

They came to the roof and walked outside. Crowds of Crazy Alligators were everywhere, hanging on the edges of wide stone outcrops from the side of the mountain into which the pueblo city was built. All those who dared asked the unaskable along with the several hundred monks who lived austere spiritual lives hidden in small holes in the mountainside were gathered in even rows around the roof. They seated themselves in the back row and watched as the first monks rose to question the Ginsberg. Some hundred and fifty feet away from them, in the mist of incense bowls that always burned around him, sat the Living Master with his purple robes hanging down over the long armrests of his glistening golden throne. On the marble platform around him were sprinkled rose petals—one hundred and eight of them—which was the number of statues along the Great Hall Of Wisdom which ran through the subterranean chambers of the temple.

The first monk prostrated himself before the Ginsberg and asked his question. The echoing acoustics made it possible for everyone present to hear the question and the master's sacred answer.

"Oh Master, what is the original face before one is born?"

The Ginsberg whisked a flybroom and said bored, "The face of noface."

"Thank you, Master," the monk stammered and ran. Another made his way down the red rug that dissected the gathering, shooting out from the bottom of the Ginsberg's throne all the way across the roof.

"Master, how do you know that you don't know?"

"Oh, I don't know," the Ginsberg snapped back. The next came, a thin pale-faced man who trembled as he spoke.

"W-what is the reason to be a monk?" he asked. The Ginsberg's eyes were like slits as he replied.

"To become less stupid than you are." The monk bowed quickly and left. The next monk took his turn and the next. Each time in a bored, exasperated voice the Ginsberg answered.

"Why is he so impatient?" Rock asked Trickster.

"It is very hard to ask the right question. Only if the Ginsberg hears a good question does it amuse him. He has listened to dumb questions all his life. He grants none of his time to teaching anymore unless someone asks him a profound question. No one has for years."

Finally the line was exhausted and it was Rock's turn. He slowly walked through the rows of seated men, feeling quite foolish in his long black robe. The Master looked up, one eyebrow raised at the American freefighter, approaching respectfully with palms together but body unbowed. The Ginsberg had heard of these visitors, now was the time to size them up. Their leader came closer—a strongly built man with different colored eyes and a shock of star-white hair down the middle of his scalp. Odd—a mutant perhaps—with psi ability.

"Sooo," said the Ginsberg, stroking his wispy white beard. "You newcomer, Ted Rock-son. Have you a question?"

"Yes."

Rock looked him straight in the eyes and asked, "And what pray is that question?"

"What is the question?" The Ginsberg's face lit up like a strobe light. He jumped up and forward, landing a fist across Rockson's face that was too swift even for the Doomsday Warrior to block. Rock leaped to his feet from the floor, ready to do battle when he heard the gongs go off. People were cheering him and he was hustled away on the shoulders of the Indians. Flowers were thrown on him as he passed.

"Hey man, how'd you get so hip?" Trickster screamed out, running alongside Rock. "That was far out."

"It's easy," Rock answered. "No tricks, that's all."

With Rockson being treated like a royal god for the afternoon, and given the honor of having a private audience with the Ginsberg that evening, Perkins decided to scout around the area and see what other archaeological wonders he could dig up. He walked around the edge of the lake, looking for shards of pottery, artifacts in the sand. No luck at first until after about twenty minutes of searching when his eyes suddenly saw some color in the white sand. There! He reached down and picked up a plastic ashtray, totally eroded on one side by the lapping water. "Alameda Drive Liquor Store" it read on one side. Perkins was elated and stuffed it in his rucksack on his back. He pushed on until he came to a cave which had a trail going into it as if in recent use. He entered and once in about thirty feet was amazed at the change. The rough cave walls suddenly gave way to an absolutely smooth surface. Gold statues lined the walls—divinities set in specially carved niches. He came to a large open chamber filled with rugs and boxes overflowing with jewels, pearled daggers. The archaeologist's eyes were positively bulging. Never had he seen such a wealth of artifacts in one place. He ran over to one of the treasure troves and began looking through it.

"Can I help you?" a voice asked seductively at his shoulder. Perkins turned with a start, nearly falling over. Before him was one of the most beautiful women he had ever seen, stark naked. All that covered her flesh was a stripe of purple that ran from beneath her throat down between her ample breasts just to the top of her triangular patch of fine blond hair. The archaeologist swallowed hard three times and then spoke.

"Who are you?"

"The dweller of this cave, of course. I'm called the Contrary."

"Why Contrary?" Perkins asked, rising to his feet, his face widening into a broad smile as he saw just how beautiful the woman before him was.

"Because contrary to whatever people expect, I do

what I want."

"And what do you want?" Perkins asked, growing more aroused by the moment as he looked at her firm red nipples perched like fruits on the ends of perfect fleshy melons.

"I want a strong man like you to make love to me," she moaned softly, slipping to the floor of the cavern onto a thick white rug. She held her hands up toward him with a desperate sexual urgency. When in Rome . . . the archaeologist thought to himself. He dropped to his knees and then on top of this luscious vision of paradise. She took him in her silky arms and kissed him hard. They embraced passionately for several minutes as the Contrary helped him off with his clothing and took his stiff member in her warm hands, cradling it like a sacred sword. At last, the archaeologist went to enter her but she stopped him.

"I'm contrary, remember—we do it my way." She pushed him on his back and, getting on top of him, facing away, she pressed the aroused organ into her spread lips. She slid up and down him for several minutes, moaning with delight and then came to a furious orgasm, collapsing in a heap on top of him. After several seconds she rose and lay on top of him, this time face to face. She kissed him deeply and thanked him.

"So good, so good," she said with a big smile. "Now for your pleasure. I want you to close your eyes," she said coyly, "for my sexual surprise." She pushed him down onto a pillow, and Perkins closed his eyes, waiting in ecstatic anticipation. He felt her take hold of his enlarged member and kiss it and then . . . Oh my God, something was happening down there. So painful, so painful! He opened his eyes and tried to reach forward but the exquisite sensations of what she was doing knocked him back. He could feel the blood pouring from down there, as a silver fire ripped through his center. Then he passed out.

The Contrary stood up, looking at the dying man on the white rug below her now mottled with streams of bright red blood. She smiled a smile of inscrutable mystery and looked at her prize. In her left hand she held a foot long curved dagger as sharp as a razor still streaked with red. In her right she held the archaeologist's manhood: stem, roots, and testicles high in the air. Hers! All hers! She would add it to her collection. She walked away from the freefighter who was already dead from shock. The rug was ruined but there were more, so many more.

That evening Rock prepared himself for his interview with the Ginsberg—the special fifteen minutes of teaching that all the monks had been vying for for years. He was concerned about Perkins who had been out nearly the entire day and usually returned for meals. He shouldn't worry—the archaeologist was probably digging up some dinosaur bone or something in one of the pueblos to bring back to the Century City museum. Trickster came with five maidens of honor, their hair braided with flowers and they accompanied him to the sacred temple.

He entered through the large bronze doors of the Ginsberg's private chamber and walked up to the Master. The Ginsberg stared at him for a long time as if looking at an extremely odd species of life. Finally he shrugged his shoulder and said, "Sit over there." He joined Rockson on an adjoining chair and poured them both a cup of jasmine tea. As they drank he began speaking.

"You know how the world tried to ward off the great atomic doomsday?" the Ginsberg asked, taking a sip of the golden brew.

"Yes—the Mad policy," Rock replied.

"Correct—you are well read, Rockson. The Mutually Assured Destruction Plan—whereby there was roughly a balance of power between the Russians and the Americans. Only when it became lopsided—with the killer satellite network of the Soviets did the war occur. So is the human body and mind like this—in balance, without which it will explode into annhilation. But in the body there are five elements to be balanced: earth, air, fire, water, and space. And the five colors red, blue, black, white, and gold as well; they must be in balance—in a single harmony of one of them will take over and destroy the others. Such is the way of all things."

"I see," Rock said, trying to understand the Ginsberg's words.

"This limitless war against the Reds that you're engaged in. Are you attached to it? Do you truly hate the Russians?"

"In a sense. At least as long as they are here. Once they leave, then I don't know. I'd have to see," Rock responded.

"Ah, so, you are not blinded by hate. Good. You are familiar to me, Rock-son. We have met in another time, another life."

"Perhaps, but I have no such memory."

"Ah yes, Rock-son—always straightforward. Good,

very good. Life is a straight whiskey—without chaser. You Rock-son are a son of rock—hard and solidly founded upon the ground." Rockson said nothing. "Ask more," demanded the Ginsberg.

"What is the truth?" Rockson asked.

"Ah, Rockson. The truth is that there is not any relative truth. All things which arise depend on the five elements. All phenomena is the mere display of secret-in-itself unobstructed mind. True mind. When we do not recognize that all things are the wisdom-display, we fall into the hell of clinging to this and that. With our mistaken concepts having arisen we then divide things into good and bad. Thus the wheel of greater-time spins on infinitely pushed on by misconception. Through unenlightened mind, ignorance through the eons has accumulated much karma. This is because people and animals in previous lives failed to recognize the essential truth. They commit wrong acts, furthering their misunderstandings and leading to even lower births on the wheel of life with even less chance of understanding. Rock-son, accumulate merit, work for peace, for the time when freedom is more possible for the human mind. Heed well brave Doomsday Warrior, for doomsday is everyday and all around us."

"That's a mouthful," Rockson replied.

"Yes, it fills my mouth," the Ginsberg replied smiling. "Now come on, you won the contest, you get to ask some more relative-truth questions."

"Why did you hit me?"

"I felt like it," the Ginsberg replied.

"Where is Perkins?"

"He is dead. Or rather he is not among the living."

"What?" Rock jumped to his feet, his face chalk

white. "What the hell are talking about?"

"He ran afoul of the Law of the Contraries."

"What's that?" Rockson asked, hardly believing that Perkins, whom he had known for over ten years, could be dead.

"A maiden he had carnal knowledge of was a Contrary—a sacred dancer of the temple. This is blasphemy."

"But Perkins wouldn't rape anyone."

"He didn't—you see—she asked for it. The Contraries, as penance for their actions, take a pledge to say and do everything backwards. Your friend, by the laws of the Crazy Alligators, could not have sex with her, but he did."

"Why didn't she say no?"

"She did, by saying the opposite. And once he had slept with her, she carried out the law—castration."

"Oh God," Rockson said, putting his hand to his mouth. "I've had enough of all this insanity. Why can't anyone speak or do anything straight around here? We're leaving this Goddamn place tonight." With that he tore out of the sacred temple, sending guards at the bronze doors flying in all directions.

"Wait, Rock-son, don't leave yet. You must ask me more. We were just getting going. It's been years. Goddamn it come back. I'm so bored." The Ginsberg yelled out after the departing freefighter, who didn't look back.

Twenty-One

Rockson found McCaughlin and Kim back in their rooms and told them to pack immediately, that they were leaving right away.

"What the hell's wrong, Rock?" McCaughlin asked. "I've never seen you like this?" The Doomsday Warrior looked down at the stone floor, his eyes misting over.

"Ah, damn it, they killed Perkins." Rockson explained the story as the Ginsberg had told him.

"But we've got to do something, Rockson," the big man said. "We can't just let them get away with this."

"There's nothing to do," Rock said bitterly. "It's just their ways—their stupid crazy ways. We can't take on a whole culture. I just wish we'd never stumbled onto these people, let them live out their lives and we, ours. But now Perkins is gone. A victim of cultural miscommunication."

They got their few things together and headed out of the lodging temple and down the stone stairs that descended for an eternity. But they had hardly gone more than a hundred paces when they were surrounded by hordes of Crazy Alligators and by the fierce war paint on their faces they weren't in the mood for any more peyote parties.

"Come with us," Trickster said, his eyes as cold as the dark side of the moon. They were rudely dragged along in what seemed like some sort of torchlight lynching committee and taken before about twenty Indians wearing black hooded cloaks that covered every bit of their faces and bodies. With their lynch party holding spears and guns on the three freefighters, the leader of the judges addressed them.

"One of you has screwed a Contrary. That means that you are all guilty by the laws of contrariness and must suffer the same fate as the sadly recently deceased." The other judges echoed in a shrill chorus, "the recently deceased, the recently deceased." The Ginsberg, Rock noticed, sat off to one side, looking quite perturbed about the whole affair.

"So get ready to dig a whole heap of death," the leader of the judges said, his face totally hidden beneath the hood. The warriors pressed forward, their spears digging into soft flesh.

"Is there any way out?" Rock yelled out to the Ginsberg.

"Yes," he answered. "You may challenge the gods."

"May challenge, but not win," the lead hooded judge said angrily.

"Then I challenge!" Rockson said, standing tall, thrusting his chest at the proffered spears. The Doomsday Warrior was taken away by six Indians while Kim and McCaughlin were kept prisoner. The judges followed closely behind. They walked for about half a mile through glowing cave walls as albino bats, white as flour, cheeped high-pitched screams as they flew overhead. At last they came to a second underground lake, this one lit with a green-shaded phosphorescence from beneath the waters.

"Mean Motherfucker," one of the Indian guards yelled out at the edge of the lake. On a small island some two hundred feet away a huge man stepped out— one of the Crazy Alligators or one of their gods, Rock thought when he saw it. The thing stood nearly nine feet tall with legs like trees and arms as thick as Rockson's chest. He had never seen a man that big in all his travels across America.

One of the guards looked at Rock and pointed to the giant standing on the island. "Kill *him*," he said with a smirk, "and you go free."

"Do I get a weapon?" he asked, looking around at the judges who remained hidden beneath their robes, except for the Ginsberg who looked at Rockson with sadness in his eyes.

"No, Rock. The challenge of the gods means one fights with only that which one possesses. It is the pure spirit that wins or loses." The giant started forward. It had been a long time since there had been a challenger. A long time since he had killed. It would feel good. He walked slowly toward Rock, stepping with his long legs from rock to rock which poked up through the green water every three or four feet. The creature looked at the challenger. The man was bigger than usual, but still a mere mite compared to him. They both hopped from rock to rock and within thirty seconds the two men stood facing each other only yards apart.

"Why do you challenge me?" the giant roared.

"To live," Rockson said softly

"Then die," the creature laughed. He leaped at Rockson with pantherlike speed. Rock spun out of the way but still received part of the blow on his shoulder. He knew the Indian giant was strong but he could hardly believe the man could move so fast. With two long slashes of red on his face it looked as if the Mean Mother had jagged scars running ear to chin. He opened his mouth when he charged, revealing elephant-sized, cavity-mottled teeth.

The creature charged again and again and it was all that Rock could do to just keep retreating, ducking, leaping out of the way of the giant's attacks. Somehow he had to figure out the weakness in the tough man of the tribe. He waited on a wide flat rock for the Mother to charge again. Just as the nine foot thing jumped toward him from a nearby stone foothold, Rock also flew into the air, swinging his foot around into the Indian's stomach. The Mother landed on his stomach on the rock ahead, half in, half out of the water. He rose to his feet and laughed, turning around to Rockson who waited about ten feet away.

"You smart boy, huh?" the giant said smiling. "Good, more fun this time. They all die so quick, it's a shame." Rock's kick hadn't even fazed him. A kick that most men wouldn't have risen from had been a stomach massage to this overgrown hunk of flesh. The giant started at him again and Rock retreated, looking for an opening. The immense killer didn't seem to have any particular style of fighting. His strength was so overwhelming he had never had to rely on skill. He just came at you until you were dead. He charged Rockson reaching, grabbing, punching, smashing. Rock kept jumping backwards, glancing behind him every few seconds to see where the next stepping stone was. As he glanced around once again the Mean Mother charged. Rock heard the heavy breath of the giant at the last second. He threw himself down and forward, landing in the lake between two rocks. The Mother flew over him and slammed into the boulder Rockson had just been standing on. The Doomsday Warrior swam three feet to the next foothold and crawled on as the giant stood up.

"You hurt me, Rockson!" the creature said almost gleefully. "That good. Me not be hurt before." The Mother wiped his wrist along his face which was smeared with blood where he had crashed onto the jagged rock. "You fun!" It laughed and jumped across at Rockson who barely had time to leap out of the way. He couldn't go on like this forever. The big killer wasn't tiring at all, but Rock was, from the constant jumping every second. He skipped ahead four or five of the stone steps that seemed to dot the entire lake, trying to gain a bit of breathing space, time to make some sort of plan. If only he had a weapon.

Suddenly the water just ahead of him broke into ripples, then waves, then a boiling foam. A dark shape cruising beneath the green water suddenly broke the surface. Good God. Rockson cringed back as the snapping dragon's head on a neck nearly twenty feet long appeared in the air just feet away from his head. Some sort of mutation, he thought. Much like the thing he had seen on his journey to Pavlov City. That one had wanted him for dinner as well. Its huge jaws snapped at Rock's head, red eyes cold and hungry.

"That my friend," the giant yelled out some forty feet away. "It hear you in water. Now it want to play too. Which get you first challenger?" the Mother laughed. The immense amphibious monster swam at Rockson on large green flippers, trying to push itself onto the stones around him. Rock headed back toward the giant. As big as he was he suddenly seemed like more welcome company than this green lizard thing from the depths of hell itself. His only chance was to get by the giant, race out of the cavern and somehow free the others. He approached the Mother and faked as if he were going to jump to the right. The Mother turned quickly in that direction. Rockson leaped from the wet boulder, his feet extended straight out like a rapier as he slammed into the giant's testicles. The Mother let out a roar of pain and Rockson jumped over him as the creature fell to the stepping stone. Rock started to run but had gone just one step when the Indian's long arm shot out and a hand as big as a shovel slammed around Rockson's ankle.

"You hurt me bad," the giant screamed, pulling the struggling Rockson back toward him. "You hurt enough. Me kill *now*," the Mother said with a gleam in his black eyes. It stood up, lifting Rock with a flip up into the air. It lifted him in a bear hug and began squeezing. The giant turned to the subterranean lake creature and called to it. "Here, Ferlinghetti, I kill now—you eat." The monster headed swiftly toward the Mean Mother's voice, opening its jaws wide to receive its meal. Rock pushed with all his mutant strength at the Indian's neck. He could feel the giant's arms tightening, pulling at his backbone. Rock was strong as steel but he could feel his spine bending, almost ready to crack. The giant's strength was immense. There were only seconds left. Rock stiffened his index fingers, pulled the top of his body back with a superhuman effort and jabbed forward into the Mother's eyes. The fingers, like little spears, sliced right through the eyes which gushed out like bloody broken eggs from the slimly eye sockets. The giant screamed in mortal agony and released its arms from around Rockson as it slammed its hands to its face.

"Eyes! Eyes," it moaned incomprehensibly. The lake monster was almost upon them. Rock spun the giant around so he faced the water's edge. The dinosaur, or whatever the hell it was, closed its eyes as it slammed its jaws down on its prey, not realizing it had taken its keeper. It gobbled down the body, chewing the huge bulk into bloody food in seconds and disappeared back beneath the green glowing surface, leaving little ripples of blood that floated back toward shore.

Rock lay still on the boulder for a minute. He could not really believe that he was alive. That he had won. Death had been so near just seconds before. But he *had* won. He rose and walked toward the gathered judges and chiefs who watched him in awe.

"You are free, Rockson," said the Ginsberg. "You have won." Rock looked at the Living Master with disgust and walked past the Indian warriors who parted at his coming.

Twenty-Two

Three motorcycles pulled up to a fork in the hundred-and-fifty-year-old road which was strewn with pebbles and debris but still flat enough to travel on. Three roads came out of the intersection, each going off at a ninety degree angle. At the side of the crossroads lay rusting pieces of metal that had once been roadsigns indicating exits and towns ahead. Now they were barely distinguishable from the reddish yellow dirt that lined the sides. The cycles came to a stop. Then one moved ahead about a hundred feet and waited.

Rock looked at Kim atop her Harley 600 that they had received from the Crazy Alligators after Rock had vanquished the Mean Mother. He had taken a 750, McCaughlin, a monstrous 1000. The sun was just setting, almost beautiful tonight in its purple haze. The pink and brown electric clouds of a brewing megastorm were writhing far off in the distance like stampeding beasts of pure energy. Rock eyed them nervously.

"You mustn't go off by yourself, Kim," Rock said. "Come with us."

"I've told you already, Rock, I must find my father and see if he's safe. When I was captured by the Reds my father was trapped. I don't know for sure what happened. I must find out."

Rock looked down at the ground. He didn't know the right words. He had never been called on to say them before. He felt a strange feeling in his gut. Something new. Not even love or desire. But something he had never experienced in his life. He felt fear. Not for himself but for her. For the woman he loved. Would always love.

"I must go, Rock. I must," Kim said, a single tear glistening at the edge of her green eyes. "I love you and we shall be together again. I know it." Rock's eyes were like razor blades. He knew what the world was like out there. Knew better than any man. The dangers were everywhere, every second. Only the strongest survived. She was tough but . . .

"Do you know what it's like out—"

"Rock, I've traveled around. You know my father is organizing a convention. A Re-constitutional Convention. He is a powerful man, Rockson, as powerful as you. Can you imagine what a new United States would mean? A new government? A new constitution? A . . . a president?"

Rock heard her words. It would be incredible. It would change the spirits of all downtrodden Americans. It would create the way for a new unity among the Free Cities . . . and with the particle beam weapons they must really win now.

"I want the same," Rock answered slowly. "But I can't bear the thought of losing you. I've never cared for anyone, anything in this way before. I've hardly known you but—" She leaned over from her motorcycle and put her finger on his lips.

"Shhh," she said soothingly and then stepped off her bike and replaced her finger with her lips. She held him against her, a one hundred and ten pound woman cradling a two hundred and twenty-five pound man of the purest iron in her arms, like a baby. Rockson let himself feel her love, let it penetrate into his cells and he sent out his own. Love. How strange. Somehow he had thought he would never feel it. Had certainly not searched for it. And now, in the midst of the purest violence and horror she had appeared. They kissed and touched each other for many minutes as McCaughlin kept glancing back from his cycle some one hundred and fifty feet ahead.

Damn Rockson, can't keep his hands off the girl, the big man thought with some irritation. He snorted and looked up at the gathering storm clouds. Oh, come on Rock, he thought, trying to send the mental signals to the Doomsday Warrior that it was time to get the hell out of there.

At last the lovers parted, looking at each other. Then Kim started her cycle and with a submachine gun tied around the handlebars pointing straight ahead, and other weapons and supplies mounted on the back, she clicked the big bike into gear and tore off in the direction of the storm. Rock stared after her, watching the cycle quickly disappear over the rolling hills to the north. He watched until he couldn't even see a dot on the horizon or hear the slightest trace of engine roar.

Then he started his Harley and joined McCaughlin ahead. The two freefighters turned their accelerators up to max and screamed off into the gathering darkness as the first bolts of lightning began cracking behind them.

More Adventure in
THEY CALL ME THE MERCENARY
by Axel Kilgore

#14: THE SIBERIAN ALTERNATIVE (1194, $2.50)
When Frost wakes up straitjacketed in a ward deep inside the Soviet Union, he doesn't need two eyes to see they are going to plant electrodes in his brain and turn him into a weapon for the KGB!

#15: THE AFGHANISTAN PENETRATION (1223, $2.50)
Penetrating a tightly secured Soviet base in Afghanistan to rescue an old Army buddy, Frost uncovers a Soviet weapon of frightening potential being readied for "testing" against Afghan freedom fighters!

#16: CHINA BLOODHUNT (1288, $2.50)
Frost doesn't know whom to trust as he works his way across mainland China—with a Chicom secret agent. With China and Russia moving closer to a shooting war, Hank has to keep America out of it!

#17: BUCKINGHAM BLOWOUT (1346, $2.50)
Left broken and bloody in a London alley, Frost doesn't remember his own name, or that he's discovered a brutal terrorist plot. But the terrorists haven't forgotten and are getting ready to write his name for him—on a gravestone!

#18: EYE FOR EYE (1429, $2.50)
After being buried alive under the rubble of a blown-up building, Frost takes a well-deserved rest. But the KGB would rather he rest in peace—and they kidnap his girlfriend to lure him out!

Available wherever paperbacks are sold, or order direct from the Publisher. Send cover price plus 50¢ per copy for mailing and handling to Zebra Books, 475 Park Avenue South, New York, N.Y. 10016. DO NOT SEND CASH.

NEW ADVENTURES FROM ZEBRA!

THE BLACK EAGLES:
HANOI HELLGROUND (1249, $2.95)
by John Lansing
They're the best jungle fighters the United States has to offer, and no matter where Charlie is hiding, they'll find him. They're the greatest unsung heroes of the dirtiest, most challenging war of all time. They're THE BLACK EAGLES.

THE BLACK EAGLES #2:
MEKONG MASSACRE (1294, $2.50)
by John Lansing
Falconi and his Black Eagle combat team are about to stake a claim on Colonel Nguyen Chi Roi—and give the Commie his due. But American intelligence wants the colonel alive, making this the Black Eagles' toughest assignment ever!

THE BLACK EAGLES #3:
NIGHTMARE IN LAOS (1341, $2.50)
by John Lansing
There's a hot rumor that Russians in Laos are secretly building a nuclear reactor. And the American command isn't overreacting when they order it knocked out—quietly—and fast!

MCLEANE'S RANGER #2:
TARGET RABAUL (1271, $2.50)
by John Darby
Rabaul—it was one of the keys to the control of the Pacific and the Japanese had a lock on it. When nothing else worked, the Allies called on their most formidable weapon—McLeane's Rangers, the jungle fighters who don't know the meaning of the word quit!

SWEET VIETNAM (1423, $3.50)
by Richard Parque
Every American flier hoped to blast "The Dragonman," the ace North Vietnamese pilot, to pieces. Major Vic Benedetti was no different. Sending "The Dragonman" down in a spiral of smoke and flames was what he lived for, worked for, prayed for—and might die for . . .

Available wherever paperbacks are sold, or order direct from the Publisher. Send cover price plus 50¢ per copy for mailing and handling to Zebra Books, 475 Park Avenue South, New York, N.Y. 10016. DO NOT SEND CASH.

ZEBRA BRINGS YOU EXCITING BESTSELLERS
by Lewis Orde

MUNICH 10 (1300, $3.95)
They've killed her lover, and they've kidnapped her son. Now the world-famous actress is swept into a maelstrom of international intrigue and bone-chilling suspense—and the only man who can help her pursue her enemies is a complete stranger . . .

HERITAGE (1100, $3.75)
Beautiful innocent Leah and her two brothers were forced by the holocaust to flee their parents' home. A courageous immigrant family, each battled for love, power and their very lifeline—their HERITAGE.

THE LION'S WAY (900, $3.75)
An all-consuming saga that spans four generations in the life of troubled and talented David, who struggles to rise above his immigrant heritage and rise to a world of glamour, fame and success!

DEADFALL (1400, $3.95)
by Lewis Orde and Bill Michaels
The two men Linda cares about most, her father and her lover, entangle her in a plot to hold Manhattan Island hostage for a billion dollars ransom. When the bridges and tunnels to Manhattan are blown, Linda is suddenly a terrorist—except *she's* the one who's terrified!

Available wherever paperbacks are sold, or order direct from the Publisher. Send cover price plus 50¢ per copy for mailing and handling to Zebra Books, 475 Park Avenue South, New York, N.Y. 10016. DO NOT SEND CASH.

TRIVIA MANIA
by Xavier Einstein

TRIVIA MANIA has arrived! With enough questions to answer every trivia buff's dreams, TRIVIA MANIA covers it all—from the delightfully obscure to the <u>seemingly obvious</u>. Tickle your fancy, and test your memory!

MOVIES	(1449, $2.50)
TELEVISION	(1450, $2.50)
LITERATURE	(1451, $2.50)
HISTORY AND GEOGRAPHY	(1452, $2.50)
SCIENCE AND NATURE	(1453, $2.50)
SPORTS	(1454, $2.50)

Available wherever paperbacks are sold, or order direct from the Publisher. Send cover price plus 50¢ per copy for mailing and handling to Zebra Books, 475 Park Avenue South, New York. N.Y. 10016. DO NOT SEND CASH!

DYNAMIC NEW LEADERS IN MEN'S ADVENTURE!

THE MAGIC MAN #2:
THE GAMOV FACTOR (1252, $2.50)
by David Bannerman

With Brezhnev terminally ill, the West needs an agent in place to control the outcome of the race to replace him. And there's no one better suited for the job than THE MAGIC MAN!

THE MAGIC MAN #3:
PIPELINE FROM HELL (1327, $2.50)
by David Bannerman

THE MAGIC MAN discovers Moscow building a pipeline from a Siberian hell—with innocent men and women as slave labor. Only he can stop it . . . but only if he survives!

THE WARLORD (1189, $3.50)
by Jason Frost

The world's gone mad with disruption. Isolated from help, the survivors face a state in which law is a memory and violence is the rule. Only one man is fit to lead the people, a man raised among the Indians and trained by the Marines. He is Erik Ravensmith, THE WARLORD—a deadly adversary and a hero of our times.

THE WARLORD #2: THE CUTTHROAT (1308, $2.50)
by Jason Frost

Though death sails the Sea of Los Angeles, there is only one man who will fight to save what is left of California's ravaged paradise. His name is THE WARLORD—and he won't stop until the job is done!

THE WARLORD #3: BADLAND (1437, $2.50)
by Jason Frost

His son has been kidnapped by his worst enemy and THE WARLORD must fight a pack of killers to free him. Getting close enough to grab the boy will be nearly impossible—but then so is living in this tortured world!

Available wherever paperbacks are sold, or order direct from the Publisher. Send cover price plus 50¢ per copy for mailing and handling to Zebra Books, 475 Park Avenue South, New York, N.Y. 10016. DO NOT SEND CASH.